Fables From the Fountain

Fables From the Fountain

Edited by Ian Whates

NewCon Press
England

First edition, published in the UK May 2011
by NewCon Press

NCP 037 (hardback)
NCP 038 (softback)

10 9 8 7 6 5 4 3 2 1

ISBN: 978-1-907069-23-9 (hardback)
978-1-907069-24-6 (softback)

Cover art by Dean Harkness
Cover layout by Andy Bigwood

Invaluable editorial assistance from Ian Watson
Text layout by Storm Constantine

Printed in the UK by MPG Biddles of Kings Lynn

For many reasons,
this book is dedicated to the memory of
Arthur C Clarke

Contents

Fables from the Fountain
An Introduction

Peter Weston

As you might guess there's a back-story to this volume, and for me it goes right back to 1957 to a slim paperback with an outrageous cover; a sozzled little alien being booted out of a pub with a big smile on his face and clutching a foaming tankard in his tentacles. That's the Ballantine first-edition of Arthur C. Clarke's *Tales from the White Hart* I'm talking about. It appeared at a time when you simply couldn't buy 'foreign' books because of currency regulations, but I managed to order it anyway (with a few others) direct from the publisher in New York, a long-winded process that involved applying to Whitehall bureaucrats for permission to send a £1.50 postal order overseas – yes, really – and my precious copy might have been the only one in the country!

I thought it was marvellous. Arthur was already a Big Name over here and not just in science fiction circles. He'd shot to success with a book titled *The Exploration of Space,* which sounds pretty matter-of-fact now but was quite revolutionary in 1951. He took obscure concepts understood only by rocketry experts (and SF fans) and made them intelligible to the general public; the edition I have proclaims proudly on the cover, 'Over 375,000 copies sold'.

Arthur was famous, but only recently so. Just a short time earlier he'd been one of those fans himself, an aspiring writer as many of them were (in fact he 'aspired' for something like ten years before making his first professional sale) and for a few glorious years in the late forties and early fifties they met weekly in a London pub – the 'White Hart' of the title – and Arthur wrote down the stories they told each other.

Well, not quite, but the fable is easy to believe. The pub was actually the White *Horse*, characters like Harry Purvis are invented or are heavily fictionalised versions of Clarke's contemporaries, and the 'tales' came almost entirely from his fertile imagination, written in locations as far apart as Miami and Sydney. But the fifteen stories in the book drag you in with their wonderful feeling of intimacy and familiarity; you can almost imagine yourself to be one of the in-crowd of boffins and admirers, noisily meeting every Thursday in that legendary bar.

Other SF writers have used the form and people often mention *Tales from Gavagan's Bar* by Fletcher Pratt & Sprague DeCamp (though I find this contrived and almost 'twee' by comparison), and Larry Niven has brought things up-to-date with his *Draco Tavern* stories. But none have the charm, the grounding in reality or the sheer quality of 'Britishness' which underpins Arthur's construct.

That could have been a problem. I didn't realise it then but Ballantine was the new kid on the publishing block and their operation had been launched with the untested belief that good science fiction would sell to a mass audience. They signed-up Clarke when he was still relatively unknown in the United States and brought out two original collections of his SF short stories, in itself a somewhat risky strategy. But their third volume, *Tales from the White Hart*, might have been a publishing disaster!

You can almost hear Bob Newhart playing it for laughs; "You wanna bring out this book by some British egghead no-one's heard of, telling stories about some other British eggheads with crazy ideas that don't work, in some bar that doesn't exist? Don't call me, I'll call you!"

But Ian Ballantine's faith in Arthur Clarke was well-founded and *Tales* went on to become a minor classic, always in print somewhere in the world and fondly remembered by everyone who encountered it in their youth. Clarke himself wrote an additional story in the series, 'Let There Be Light', and he collaborated with Stephen Baxter for one final story, 'Time Gentlemen Please' in a special 50th anniversary edition from PS Publishing in 2007.

All of which brings us (by the long way round) to the book you are holding in your hand, conceived by ringleader Ian Whates while sitting in a London pub in Knightsbridge in April 2008, a few weeks after Sir Arthur's death and the day after that year's Clarke Award ceremony (which gives a prize annually for the best new science fiction novel released in the UK).

Ian, like me, cut his SF-teeth on Clarke's short-stories. Like me I'm sure he would love to zip back sixty years to the real White Horse; to see the young Arthur, bubbling with enthusiasm and proudly opening his briefcase on his latest press cuttings only to be shot down with a few acerbic words from Bill Temple. To meet those other fans trembling on the brink of success – John Beynon with *The Triffids*, Eric Maine with his radio plays and novels, John Christopher with *The Death of Grass*. Science fiction was young and everything seemed possible, but without a time-machine, alas, we can never go back.

However, Ian thought, we *can* go forwards; not to the White Hart (especially since the real building was demolished by vandals in the eighties) but to 'The Fountain', a magical London pub that exists, perhaps, in one of Harry Turtledove's parallel universes where a similar bunch of Mad Scientists and their friends have a weekly rendezvous.

Fables from the Fountain has in this way been conceived in homage to Arthur Clarke, with stories from other British writers who have grown up, not exactly in his shadow but, rather, inspired by his boundless imagination. There's Steve Baxter, who was privileged to win Arthur's confidence in several collaborations; Peter Crowther, publisher of the 50th anniversary volume; Adam Roberts and Charles Stross, both of whom have wilder ideas than Harry Purvis ever did; David Langford, who in his time really has *been* a Mad Scientist, and thirteen others – you can read more about them inside.

And now it's time to step through the doorway of the cosy little pub you've just found down one of those side streets off Chancery Lane, don't ask me exactly where...

Peter Weston
March 2011

No Smoke Without Fire

Ian Whates

I have to admit, there was a time when I feared for the traditional London pub. So many favourite watering holes had disappeared, to be lamented with a raised glass and sorrowful shake of the head. The spread of the wine bar had faltered, true, but the baton had been taken up by the tapas bar and the brand-name chains. Dark beams, uneven floors, tables whose legs were never quite stable no matter what combination of folded drinks mats you slipped beneath their feet and whose surfaces had been seasoned by generations of beer stains, cigarette ash and tall tales, all swept away as if they had never been. One day a familiar, much-loved boozer, the next a restricted zone, guarded by the dreaded sign, 'Closed for Renovation'.

We all knew what that meant: transformation; high ceilings, bright open spaces, rows of light-wood tables with identical matching chairs, gleaming chrome swan-necked beer pumps serving continental lagers with suspicious names, each new re-opening indistinguishable from the last, the whole staffed by fresh-faced trendies in starch-white shirts and blouses. Another character-infused London landmark sacrificed on the altar of homogeneity.

Of course, I need not have worried. Like wine bars before them, the poured-from-a-mould pubs made inroads but then faltered, as if hitting some impassable line drawn in the sand with arcane purpose: 'Thou Shalt Come No Further!' The London pub survives, as it always has, and, I suspect, as it always will.

In truth, my *real* concern in the matter focused on just one pub in particular; the Fountain. No, not the *Old* Fountain in Baldwin Street, close to Old Street Station, redoubtable establishment though that may be. Ours is simply *the* Fountain, and it's timeless.

At first glance the Fountain is not perhaps the most spectacular of buildings. It is homely, welcoming, with a hint of mock Tudor in its bold facade... and somehow *right*. Nor is it the easiest place to find, I'll grant you, and all the better for that. The Fountain is in Holborn, within a short walk of Chancery Lane tube and Lincoln's Inn Fields. It nestles on one of the network of little lanes that leads eventually to the far broader Chancery Lane, though I've never yet managed to arrive there by the same route twice. It's the sort of hidden gem you come upon unexpectedly when cutting down towards the Strand and Fleet Street without any clear idea of the way. You might stumble upon the Fountain and slow down, perhaps make a mental note to come back here sometime, only to never find the place again. You see, there's little point in my explaining *how* to get there; either you will, or you won't.

There are, of course, several reasons why we meet at the Fountain rather than any of the City's other hostelries. It's the perfect size, for one. On a good night, we can all but fill out the back room, the Paradise bar – which is really just a partitioned extension of the lounge with its own small door to the outside world. I say 'we', but that small word encompasses a flexible roster of dynamic components. There are regulars such as Brian Dalton, who is a chemist, Professor Mackintosh – our geo-metrodynamics theoretician – Dr Steve, whose voice I'd heard even before we met, since he frequently guests on radio programmes offering listeners advice on back pain and other ailments, and Ray Arnold, a man around whom it's never advisable to quip 'it's not rocket science', since where Ray's concerned it often is. He worked for the European Space Agency in the Netherlands before returning to these shores a while back.

There are also the irregulars, such as Eric, a Yorkshireman

living in exile in Cambridgeshire, a professional author who can't join us every week due to family commitments, though he travels in whenever he can; and then there's the Raven. A somewhat dramatic moniker, admittedly, but that's what we took to calling the dark brooding presence with his long hair, beard, and painful-looking piercings, before we actually met him. Every now and then he'd be there on a Tuesday – our night – always at the same table in the corner, alone; sitting at the fringes, listening, watching; an enigmatic, swashbuckling figure. Until we came to know him a little better that is, and discovered that he goes by the decidedly mundane name of Paul and is a librarian.

Tuesday; I'm not quite sure *why* we settled on that night in particular, except that Tuesdays aren't Fridays, when *everyone* descends on the nearest pub after work, and nor are they Thursdays, when those seeking to avoid Fridays tend to do the same. So Tuesdays it is.

When I refer to the Fountain as a 'traditional' London pub, I don't mean to imply that it's a complete anachronism, far from it. Michael, the landlord, is quite happy to see the place move with the times, he's merely selective about *which* times he moves with. So while bottles of Mexican beer lurk in the chill cabinet and you might on occasion be served by Eastern European bar staff – Bogna from Poland was particularly popular, as I recall – no jukebox or fruit machine stands sentry by the wall, and no plasma screen TV churns out live coverage of the latest big game; not at the Fountain. Such things would be out of place among the beams and framed pictures of Victorian London that adorn ceiling and walls respectively. I've a mind to suggest they might even sour the fine selection of ales that are invariably on offer at the many hand pumps. One recent concession to progress that Michael *has* made is to affix a bench to the outside wall of the pub, where a narrow passageway runs between one lane and another. This for the convenience of smokers – there's no 'beer garden' of course, not in central London where space is at such a premium.

I confess to viewing the smoking ban as a sort of guilty pleasure. I'm not a smoker, never have been, but when the ban was first mooted I felt far from comfortable with the idea of central government dictating to the individual in such a way, and by the time the reality of the legislation loomed large, I found myself objecting strongly. Yet, now that the ban is actually here, I'm secretly delighted that it is – pubs and restaurants are so much more pleasant for those of us who don't partake of the old baccy. Hence the guilt.

Others were less ambiguous in their objection. Take Professor Mackintosh, for example. When the ban was first enforced he took to sporting a pipe, either chewing on its stem or holding it by the bowl and gesturing dramatically when making a point. Oh, don't get me wrong, the pipe was neither lit nor indeed filled and I can't recall him toting such a thing with any regularity prior to the ban. No, I believe this was simply the Professor's way of making silent protest.

I remember one particular Tuesday. There was a good crowd in that evening; I was sharing a table with Crown Baker and Eric – both science fiction writers so always entertaining – while Professor Mackintosh was beside me, at the next table.

"Smoking once saved my life, you know," he declared as he reached across to tap his pipe against the side of the hearth, as if to free non-existent embers from the bowl.

"Really?" I felt obliged to ask.

"Oh, yes."

Such a pronouncement did not go unnoticed, needless to say, and within moments a group had gathered around us, the professor waiting patiently while feet shuffled and chairs scraped, as people manoeuvred into hearing range.

"All down to an acquaintance of mine, Edward Blaycock," he then continued. "Interesting fellow, old Blaycock. He had a passion for collecting religious books; not merely those *about* religion, either. As well as various rare editions of the bible, the Koran, the Tao Te Ching etcetera, he had a truly impressive collection of prayer books, hymn books and missals..."

"Missals?" I asked.

"Yes, liturgical volumes containing the texts and formulae for use in various church services."

"So I suppose a scathing attack on the content of a church service would be a *dis*-missal?"

There were a few appreciative groans from the assembled throng, while the prof stared at me blankly for a second, as if I'd spoken in an unfamiliar language, and then chuckled. "Ah yes, very good." Though his tone implied the contrary.

"By day," he went on, "Blaycock was a scientist. He worked at the Yarlsbury Research Centre in Lincolnshire, not far from Market Rasen, usually on matters that were extremely hush-hush. I was there for a year or so in an advisory capacity and worked with Blaycock on a project relating to Electromagnetic Pulse weaponry. We were tasked with developing a defence against the triple component EMP effect of a high-altitude nuclear explosion. This meant designing countermeasures to all three stages – the three are designated in accordance with the speed of their respective effects. E2, the middle one, isn't such a threat on its own. Its impact is similar to that of a localised lightning strike and can be countered with standard measures... unless those standard defences have already been knocked out by the higher amplitude E1. This is the fastest of the three components – a field generated when gamma rays from the explosion collide with electrons in the air molecules of the upper atmosphere. These electrons are punched out from their parent molecules at close to the speed of light, colliding with others and causing a cascade effect that's analogous to a sonic boom. The interaction of all these electrons with the Earth's magnetic field produces a very brief but intense electromagnetic pulse; very difficult to defend against. The E3 component causes problems all its own. Much slower than the first two, the impact of E3 is similar to that of a really big solar flare, which can cause havoc with the Earth's magnetosphere – the sort of thing that disrupted power supplies throughout Quebec in 1989.

"So E1 and E3 were our real targets, and buggers to deal with they were too. Brilliant chap, though, Blaycock, and he'd already come up with a way of dampening the processes involved in E1. I can't go into details, obviously – national security and all that – but our only real problem was finding a way to trigger the countermeasure quickly enough."

I wasn't sure whether to curse 'national security' or feel relieved; at least this meant avoiding a complicated and doubtless lengthy aside, and I'd already had my fill of E1s and E2s thank you very much.

"Anyway," the professor continued, "those of us involved were summoned to a demonstration one Sunday. Very unusual. Blaycock was clearly excited about something, and we assumed he'd solved the triggering issue. We were the only people at the centre apart from the security guards on the gate. First thing we did was divest ourselves of anything electrical – laptops, phones, watches – no point in risking them in range of anything relating to EMP – and then we went into 'the bunker'. The bunker is a fair sized room, underground as the name suggests, lead-lined and airtight. The perfect place to test all manner of things."

I could see knowing looks pass amongst my fellow listeners. It would have been rude to interrupt now that the professor was in full flow but you could read people's thoughts clearly enough in those glances: *an experiment goes wrong; something terrible happens.*

"So there we all were, eight of us, sealed away from the rest of the world and anxious to hear Blaycock's big announcement, when it happened.

"Without any warning, the place was hit by...." He paused to cough.

"Lightning," Brian Dalton cut in, politeness evidently forgotten in the heat of the moment.

"A tornado," Eric said.

"A bomb," Crown Baker suggested.

"A terrorist attack," Dr Steve added, as if to give credence to

Crown's suggestion.

"A flock of crazed birds," someone else – probably Graham O'Donnell – said, clearly getting carried away.

"No, no, nothing like that," the professor assured us. "It was hit by an earthquake."

"An *earthquake?* In Britain?"

The professor smiled. "Certainly. We suffer around 200 every year believe it or not, though only twenty or so are ever actually felt by anyone."

"And this was one of those," I prompted, concerned that the good prof was about to meander down one of his beloved sidetracks strewn with tangential information.

"Oh yes," he confirmed. "5.8 on the Richter scale – hardly earth-shattering in global terms, if you'll forgive the pun, but certainly significant for the UK. We get hit by a quake at that sort of magnitude just once every thirty years or so.

"As it turned out, the epicentre of this one wasn't far from Yarlsbury, so we felt the full force of it; the whole place shook something terrible. Quite an alarming experience when you're stuck underground in a sealed space, I can tell you. However, as things calmed down we were all greatly relieved to realise that the room remained intact.

"We were just beginning to relax… when the lights went out."

A few murmurs greeted this part of the story and I noticed Crown Baker shudder. Not that I blamed him. The fear of being confined underground in the dark, of being buried alive, is about as primordial and instinctive as it comes.

"Not just the lights were affected, as we soon discovered," the professor continued. "All the power was down, which meant no air conditioning, no external communication system, and – most concerning of all – no means of opening the doors."

"A bit like the effects of an EMP," somebody noted.

"Quite," the prof agreed. "We were well and truly trapped, with no phones or indeed any means of communication, and the only people who even knew we were at the centre were the guards at the gate, who doubtless had their own concerns, what with the facility they were charged to safeguard having just lost its entire security system. Besides, we hadn't told them we were going into the bunker, so there was no reason for them to appreciate the seriousness of our predicament."

"What about back-up generators?" Ray Arnold asked.

"Damaged by the quake," the prof explained, "We were on our own, in the dark, with only a limited amount of air and no immediate prospect of rescue. Realisation began to sink in that somehow, on what had started out as a perfectly unremarkable Sunday, we were facing the very real prospect of dying. You never really know how you're going to react in a situation like that until it actually happens. One or two panicked. It was difficult to tell precisely who was sobbing in the dark, but I could have sworn they included old Blaycock himself. I, on the other hand, kept a remarkably cool head, which was just as well for all concerned."

"So... what did you do?" Eric asked, perhaps realising that the professor wasn't about to continue until *somebody* asked.

"Why, I did what any civilised soul would do... I lit my pipe."

"You did *what*? In a confined room like that?"

"Of course," and the professor grinned. "How else was I going to trigger the smoke alarm?"

"Ah!" Nods and knowing smiles spread throughout the cordon of listeners.

"It was the only thing in the room that possessed its own heavily protected power source and was connected directly to the guard station. I reasoned that security couldn't fail to investigate a potential fire, and, sure enough, they were there within minutes and had us out in no time.

"So don't you go telling *me* that smoking's bad for my health!"

Appreciative chuckles were the prof's principle reward, that and Ray Arnold's offer of another pint. My attention was dragged rudely away from the ensuing discussion courtesy of a strident voice.

"No, no, it's called *the Fountain*."

I turned to scowl at the lad in the wrinkled suit leaning back against the bar; City-type, buttons of his striped shirt undone, no tie in evidence, one ear glued to a sliver of plastic which presumably constituted a phone. His voice was raised to a level suggesting that he didn't entirely trust the flimsy gadget to do the job either.

"It's… ehhm…" He looked around, his gaze meeting mine beseechingly.

"Near Holborn," I supplied, taking pity.

"Yeah, it's near Holborn," he repeated. "Turn right out of Chancery Lane station, take the first right, and then, ehhm… No, no, it's not far. You can't miss it… The Fountain. All right, babe, see you in ten minutes."

I looked at Eric. He looked at me. We shared a smile, and, I feel certain, the same thought: *you'll be lucky*.

Transients

Stephen Baxter

Our Fountain regulars boast a plenitude of talents: scientists of various stripes, of course, like Prof Mackintosh, who bemoan the science fiction writers among us who steal their ideas without credit; and the science fiction writers, like Crown Baker – the natural heir to E.G. O'Brien, according to Crown Baker – who bemoan the scientists who won't take their work seriously, and besides secretly want to be science fiction writers themselves; and the super-fans, like 'Tweet' Peston – who continually denies he has a grandson on the telly – with their intense enthusiasms, encyclopaedic knowledge, and such habits as speaking to each other in archaic computer languages which never fail to reinforce the Way Others See Us; and of course there are crossbreeds between these groups – we all have a little Neanderthal in us – such as Ray Arnold, a bona fide scientist who also writes bona fide SF; and, I suppose, you could call us all fans at heart.

But then there are those in the interstices of the group, as I think of them, those who fit no category, those of no discernible talent whatsoever, and yet with a certain knack, a trick, if you will, that can be brought out on occasions to enliven the ongoing intellectual party that is the Tuesday gathering in the Fountain's parlour.

One such man of no-fixed-talent was Brian Dalton, whose peculiar social, if not sociopathic, ability was regularly to inject transients into the bloodstream of our host of regulars. What is a transient? A transient is to a regular as a one-hit wonder pop starlet is to Abba, though generally, but not always, without the legs; it is as an antiproton is to a proton, though generally, but not always, without the mutual annihilation. A transient is a guest, you might say, who will show up once or twice, who if we are lucky will have something interesting to say, and if even luckier will have a fecund credit card to be lodged behind the bar, before passing on into that good night that awaits all those without a bar tab.

One such transient, diffidently introduced by Brian on an otherwise unremarkable night, was called Barry Noakes. Or it may have been Norrie Boakes. He was tall, slim, elegant, dressed in a nondescript way, and his accent was either transatlantic, as Ray Arnold remembers, or pan-European, as Prof Mackintosh maintains. In the course of Brian's clumsy introduction we learned he was a full professor with a list of citations as long as his own slim arm, and, even more valuable, tenure – though afterwards none of us could quite remember in what field, at what institution.

He was more of an impression than a personality. The hallmark of a true transient.

With a brimming pint of Old Downsizer in his hand, Noakes made the schoolboy error of asking if any food was available.

In the Fountain!

Well, of course, there was. Soon, over our heads, without any fuss, the ploughman's lunches were coming out.

Noakes peered at the plate, and through the dusty film that covered it. "My God, it's full of chutney."

"What you have to understand about Michael's ploughman's lunches," Crown Baker earnestly advised Noakes, "is that nobody has ever seen one consumed. And nor has anybody ever seen a fresh one made and installed on the plate. As far as any of us can tell these are the *same three ploughmans* that are mentioned in the autobiography of one of the London Group who happened on this place in 1946. That was E.G. O'Brien, actually, to whom some say I am the natural –"

"Unlike you, my friend," I said hastily to Noakes, "these ploughmans are not passing through. They are enduring phenomena – not transients. They are as much regulars as we all are. But don't let me keep you from your snack."

"Cheese, pickle, or cheese and pickle," Bogna said, getting bored. "Make mind up."

"I'll pass, thank you," Noakes said politely.

"Transience!" Prof Mackintosh said now. "The bane of science! For repeatability, as you know, is at the very core of the scientific method. I'm not inclined to take your claim of turning lead into gold seriously, sir, if I can't repeat it myself. And yet the world is full of phenomena which by their nature are transient in character."

"Meteorites," said Brian. "Stones from the sky? Pooh-poohed for generations."

"Ball lightning!" cried Ray Arnold.

"UFOs," said the Raven, his voice a quiet rustle, and we all turned with something of a shiver, for none of us had quite realised he was even there.

Of course there was a loud explosion of protest at this contribution, from the scientists who felt that the mere mention of UFOs brought their profession into ridicule, and from the science fiction writers who had failed to see *The X-Files* coming. "The Royalties Were Out There," protested Norm Desmond Ploom.

Barry Noakes spoke now, and his voice either carried a quiet authority, as some remember, or was pitched so low you could never be sure what he was saying, according to others. "But what you might term the respectable branch of UFOlogy, that is SETI, the Search for Extraterrestrial Intelligence – the search with radio telescopes for signals from the sky – is likewise plagued by the curse of the transients."

"Quite true," said Doctor Steve, a notorious name-dropper who now lived down to his reputation. "As you know, Ben Gregford, physicist and science fiction writer, is –"

"'An old friend of mine,'" we all chorused.

"Ben was telling me of his suggestion that a smart culture, trying to signal to the whole Galaxy on the cheap, might set up, not an omnidirectional blast of electromagnetic noise –"

"Like the Raven's mobile phone," Brian remarked pointedly.

"But rather a beacon – a tight-angle beam sweeping across the plane of the Galaxy like a lighthouse. You could reach much of the disc, but only once a year, perhaps, or even less frequently."

"Exactly," Noakes said. "It's not enough to go listening for a bit to some corner of the sky or other. What we really need is a full-sky survey of continuous listening at all plausible frequencies over a period of years, or decades. Without that, even a respectably repeating signal like a Gregford beacon would come across as a transient.

"And of course the SETI searches *have* turned up transient signals. I myself was involved in the detection and decoding of what has become known as the Gosh Signal –"

"You said decoding?" I asked immediately.

"You said Gosh?" asked Brian.

But Prof Mackintosh barged in, "Ah, I know about that. 15 August 1977. Picked up by a telescope operated by Ohio State University – an instrument unfortunately called 'The Big Ear', as I recall, a typically colonial lapse of taste. Lasted for seventy-two seconds, never picked up again."

The Raven glanced around. "This is well known. 15 August '77, ET phones from the sky. And on 16 August '77 – *the very next day* – the King is dead. And you still believe in *coincidence*, people...?"

Mackintosh ignored him. "The signal was so-called because the researcher wrote 'Wow'" in the margin of the printout."

"But Barry didn't say 'Wow'," said Brian. "He said 'Gosh'."

"And," I added, "Norrie said, 'decoded'."

Like the world's radio telescopes swivelling to pick up a signal from Vega, all our eyes turned on Barry Noakes.

He inspected his glass, which was mysteriously drained of Old Downsizer. And, just as mysteriously, before he spoke again it was brimful once more. For a first-timer at the Fountain he had acculturated quickly.

"This was back in the year —" he began, and later we couldn't agree *what* year he'd said it was back in. "And it wasn't even my project. I was a consultant, working on the neutrino communications monitoring facility being developed by the CIA beneath a training compound in Virginia."

"There's no such thing as a neutrino communications monitoring facility," scoffed the Prof.

"Of course there isn't," Noakes said, unperturbed.

"And if there were," Ray said, "the CIA hasn't got one."

"Of course it hasn't," Noakes said. "Any more than a neutrino-based communication system is the latest weapon in the arsenal of the Folks Who Don't Love Freedom. Any particle that can pass through light years of lead is just what you need for a wifi connection if you're holed up in a cave in Afghanistan. What a shame you can't create neutrinos short of detonating a supernova, or shutting a nuclear reactor on and off, and what a shame it's an impossibility to detect one without thousands of gallons of cleaning fluid. But I digress.

"There I *wasn't*, if you prefer, in this *non-existent* location *not* running routine tests on this *non-existent* piece of equipment – its cover story, incidentally, being that it was a relic Cold War stash of post-apocalyptic wetwipe impregnator, or rather it was *not* – when I *didn't* notice a signal."

"Enough sarcasm," Brian protested. "What signal?"

"Very brief, but clearly very complex. I immediately passed it through the computer suite to look for structure, and simultaneously began a sweep to detect where it was coming from. My first thought being that it was from an earthly location, of course."

By now we were all drawn into this strange chap's strange story. I said, "It wasn't from Earth."

25

"No. I established that by tapping into records from other neutrino detectors around the globe. Triangulation and dispersion studies quickly proved that it came from much further away than a cave in Afghanistan. Many thousands of light years away, in fact. Which made it all the more surprising when the computer suite — a standard signal-processing cum linguistic-analysis bucket-chain system — started producing output. *In English*."

"What did it say?" I asked.

Prof Mackintosh blustered, "But hang on. How could a signal from such a remote source, too far for our own signals to have reached yet —"

"What did it say?" Brian asked.

"To translate an extraterrestrial message into human languages would be a cultural achievement on a par with the assimilation of texts from antiquity during the European Renaissance. And that took generations. I mean I could understand some form of entropy level analysis to establish signal complexity, but no conceivable suite could deliver an English translation *in seconds* —"

"Oh, no, not seconds, Professor," Noakes said smoothly. "Minutes at least."

"*What did it say?*" the rest of us chorused.

"It was what you might call a goodbye — or perhaps an au revoir." He closed his blue eyes, or they may have been brown. "Let me try to recall... *We are the People of the 16. And our destiny is at hand. For many generations we have looked up to the solemn calm of the People of the 12. And we have looked down on those swarming scum of the People of the 28. Following the advice of the 12 we have done nothing to intervene in the repulsive habits of the 28. Yet now it has come to our attention that these degenerates have themselves started to spawn a new breed, the People of the 56, whose behaviour defies descriptio...*"

Ray was frantically writing down the numbers. I think we all were.

Michael murmured to us all, "Beer mats don't grow on trees, you know."

"Funny you should say that," said Tweet Peston. "...But that's another story."

Noakes continued the message: "*Our only option is a campaign of total war. Some might call it extermination. Others genocide. To us, to end their existence of pointless squalor will be an act of mercy. To arms! To arms! You'll miss us when we're gone.* I paraphrase loosely, of course."

We were all staring at him.

"And that's the message," I said.

"That's the first *part* of the message," he replied. "Call it Chapter One."

"The first of three," murmured the Raven. "Mysterious messages always have three parts."

"As a matter of fact, you're right –"

Prof Mackintosh protested, "But look here, the sheer implausibility of the whole scenario –"

"Lottery numbers," Brian Dalton suggested. "All those numbers. Maybe they're lottery numbers."

"28's a perfect number," said Ray.

"Spooky," I said. "Shame the others aren't."

"That's true." He frowned. "Maybe there's some scientific basis behind it. Carl Sagan always believed we'd receive science-based number puzzles from the stars..."

"16 – the date Elvis died," the Raven put in. "I'll say no more. Of course Hitler's birthday's probably in there too. It usually is."

Noakes said, "The second chapter of the message emerged a few moments later –"

"No, it didn't," shouted Prof Mackintosh, "any more than the first. *Because it's impossible* for some remote source to send a message which is translatable into a human language –"

"Viruses," Noakes said to him, unperturbed as ever.

"What? What?"

"The second chapter," Brian said. "Go on, Barry."

"Norrie." Or it may have been *Norrie* and *Barry*. "You have to understand this is all fragmentary. I had the impression I was like a man outside a burning library, snatching charred scraps of text out of the air... The computer-synthesised voice was impersonal, of course. Yet I thought I detected a different tone. Elegiac. As if this came from a different source – a different age, perhaps."

Mackintosh said, "*Viruses...?*"

"*The end days are coming. As prophesied in the Book of the Living and the Dead, as written by the Prophet <untranslatable>. The Great Goddess beneath us, She Who Gives us Heat and Light and Life, is dying. Her ages-long Collapse Upon Herself is almost over. We Who Remain, in the dark and cold ages to come, will carve her Name in the – oh. Hang on. I wasn't expecting that –*

"And there it ends. I hope you get the gist. Once again, a loose translation, and I apologise for my imperfect remembering."

Mackintosh wouldn't be put off. "I really must insist you come clean about the basic implausibility of all this, Professor Boakes."

"Noakes."

Or it may have been Noakes and Boakes.

"Viruses, you say? What have viruses to do with it?"

"Computer viruses. Or at least, that's the nearest terrestrial analogy to the technology used to send this signal set. Except it wasn't so much a signal as an artificial intelligence *encoded in* the signal. And once it was loose in the environment of our computer suite, it began to appropriate resources, self-replicate, organise, study the outside world, listen –"

"Listen?" Brian asked sceptically.

"This *was* the CIA," the Raven put in. "Ears everywhere, chief." And he glanced around at the fixtures and fittings, almost apologetically. "Didn't mean to call attention, guys."

And I thought I heard a whispered, *No problem*. I was, presumably, mistaken.

Noakes said, "You can see that by downloading an intelligence into my machine the remote senders were able to overcome the barriers of interstellar distance. This local agent was able to monitor English, and other aspects of human culture, and so translate its content into a language I could understand. We could even have had a dialogue..." He sighed. "But it was not to be. As for the third chapter –"

"What did it say?" I asked.

"That's all utterly implausible," Mackintosh blustered.

"What did it say?" Brian asked.

"It's also 'utterly' nicked," said Tweet Peston gloomily. "You pinched this virus thing from *A for Andromeda*, didn't you?"

Noakes turned to Tweet, as if noticing him for the first time. "You look like that chap off the telly –"

"No relation."

"*What did it say?*" we all chorused.

Noakes sighed. "Once again – to the best of my imperfect recollection – there was a change of tone. First, you'll remember, I'd had a declaration of war. Then an envoi. And now – a burst of joy." He cleared his throat, and closed his brown eyes, or they may have been blue. "*We fly, we fly! We of the 207 fly through the burning sky, and our young coalesce and cluster and swarm! We flock with our cousins of the 197! We propel our faeces towards our enemies of the 238!*"

"More bloody numbers," muttered Ray, scribbling furiously on his beer mat.

"*We look forward to an age of peace and harmony and synchronised flying, when all will join as one, and gang up on those worthless flutterers of the 238!...*" Noakes sighed heavily. "There was little else. Some static. A surge of energetic neutrinos that blew some of the circuits. Make of it what you will..."

From a glint in Crown Baker's eye, I could see what he was thinking of making of it – royalties.

"And there's no record of all this," Mackintosh said heavily.

"Sadly not."

"Nor of the original neutrino pulses."

"Sadly not. As I said, the circuits were blown."

29

"Or of the translations – any of the stages of information-theoretic and linguistic processing this stuff must have gone through."

"Sadly not. As I said, the signal was essentially viral in nature – and much too powerful for human technology of the year – the system crashed beyond recovery..."

Ray muttered, "197... 207... 238..." He asked me, "What date did he say this time?"

"I missed it again."

"20... 238..."

"So it was all trashed," Mackintosh said heavily. "All the equipment and any records conveniently destroyed from end to end, by the very signal in whose existence you expect us to believe."

"This *is* a story about transients," Noakes protested. "That's the whole point, isn't it? If you'd wanted an anecdote about some dully repeatable phenomenon or other I'd have happily supplied it."

"Be fair, Professor Mac," said Brian Dalton, who'd introduced Noakes in the first place. "He's earned his pint, you've got to admit that."

"Speaking of which..." Noakes drained the dregs of his Old Downsizer, a practice which isn't generally recommended. "My round, is it? Anyone for another?"

He was pursued to the bar by a chorus of somewhat distracted cries of "Mine's a pint." For we were all exercised by the puzzles of the story we'd heard.

As Prof Mackintosh put it, "But what's it all supposed to mean? Even if one can bring oneself to believe a single word of it..."

"Look to the numbers," said the Raven. "The answer's always in the numbers. Wouldn't be surprised if the masons haven't got something to do with it. They usually have."

"No," Ray Arnold said excitedly, peering at his beer mat. "You're right about the numbers. But it's nothing to do with masons. *These are atomic weights.* Crown —"

"Yeah?"

"We both write hard SF."

"True."

"It follows that you know your science."

"Umm."

"Check these with me."

"Ah."

"12 – carbon. 16 – oxygen. 28 – silicon. 56 – iron. 197, 207, 238 – gold, lead, uranium. Have I remembered that right?"

Crown Baker was shamelessly googling on his mobile phone. Mackintosh said, "What are you getting at, Ray?"

"Supernovas," Ray said, somewhat breathless. "Giant exploding stars. Noakes actually mentioned supernovas, didn't he? I think these numbers reflect stages in the evolution of a supernova detonation."

That's the sort of sentence that hangs in the air, while we all try not to demonstrate our ignorance by making the first response. Fortunately, Ray is an expositor by nature, and needs no prompting.

"Look – consider a massive star. Ten or more times the sun's mass. You see, every star is a balance between radiation pressure blowing it up, and gravity collapsing it. So when you start losing your inner heat source, which is hydrogen fusion in the core, you're in trouble. A massive star runs through its hydrogen fuel quickly, in a few million years. The helium ash starts to fuse too – but when that's used up, the core starts to collapse. And you have a flood of neutrinos which carries heat energy right out of the star, and the central collapse worsens.

"The star tries to prop itself up. It begins ever more complex fusion processes, producing ever heavier nuclei. You end up with the centre of the star like an onion, with layers of nuclear types." He showed us his beer-mat sketch. "Nickel-iron at the very centre, then silicon, oxygen, carbon, helium, and the hydrogen mass. Each layer is produced from the fusion ash of the next layer out."

"My God," I said. "What were those numbers again, from the first message? The People of the 16, looking up at the 12, and down at the 28..."

"The 16 is oxygen," Ray said. "Its atomic weight. With carbon – 12 – above, and 28 – silicon – below."

Mackintosh snorted. "Oh, this is all –! Are you seriously suggesting *life* in the core of a massive star?" He looked around for Noakes to attack, but the chap had yet to return from the bar.

"You need an open mind about these things," Crown said. "Anywhere there's structure and energy flow, life is possible. That's one idea I've pinched, er, learned from the biologists."

"But that's only the first chapter of the Gosh Signal," I said. "What about the rest?"

"Okay," said Ray. He jabbed his little diagram. "So when the core gets clogged with iron, fusion is no longer any use. The trouble is, the fusion of iron into even heavier nuclei *absorbs* heat energy, rather than releases it. There comes a point where the iron core, used up and useless, bloated and too hot, can no longer support itself against the pull of gravity, and it just collapses."

"Like Brian Dalton after a few too many Downsizers!" cried Tweet Peston, to general hilarity.

"Ha ha," said Brian.

"The core collapse is rapid. The iron breaks up into nucleons, a process which absorbs still more heat – and there's another flood of neutrinos which takes away still more energy – and the collapse becomes catastrophic."

I thought back. "And all this is going on underneath, so to speak, your onion layers."

"The second chapter," whispered Brian Dalton. "The Great Goddess below. An energy source in the centre of the world..."

"Oh," Prof Mackintosh protested, "this is all so, so –"

"So useful," said Crown Baker, furtively making notes.

Ray went on, "But the core collapse can only go so far. You finish up with a massive blob of neutronium, all the neutrons jammed up against each other. That's the state of maximum density – and then you get a bounce back. That produces a shock wave, which can be strong enough to blow apart the outer layers of the star altogether. But as it passes through the star's substance the shock triggers a further nucleosynthesis pulse."

I could see Crown longing to ask how he spelled that.

"More heavy elements created," Ray translated for the rest of us.

"Ah," I said. "Gold, lead, uranium –"

"That's it," said Brian. "The third chapter. Creatures of fusing gold and uranium, created in a flash, flying through the detonation of a supernova. What a vision! Wow!"

"You mean, Gosh!" Tweet Peston pointed out.

I shook my head. "It's a fantastic vision. It sounds like you're talking about, not just life, but three whole domains of life: the onion-shell world, the ages of the core collapse, the uranium birds. As distinct from each other as the great ages of life on Earth – the ancient anaerobes, say, the dreaming oxygen-producing stromatolites, the multicellular domain that we humans belong to. And each of them somehow left a trace, each managed to signal out –"

Prof Mackintosh said, "Each of them learned how to modulate the neutrino flow from the core, I suppose... No! I'm contributing plausibility! I won't be drawn into this nonsense!"

Tweet said, "I'm no biologist, but what about the timescales? Life on Earth has had billions of years to evolve. I thought you said a supernova star collapses in a few million years."

I said, "That's not necessarily a problem. We're talking about realms of nuclear fusion processes, remember. Very short timescales, compared to our wet chemistry. If a form of life was able to operate on such scales, a million years could seem forever."

"But these creatures didn't have a million years," Ray said sombrely. "Remember, we're talking about stages in the *final detonation* of the supernova. The onion-shell stage – the final layers might have taken only days to form."

Brian frowned. "You're talking about a whole civilisation – no, a *whole domain of life* – rising and falling in a matter of days?"

Tweet said, "Why, that's barely time enough for Crown Baker to write another hard-SF trilogy."

"Ha ha."

Ray said, "It gets worse. The final shock wave travels out at perhaps a tenth the speed of light. A massive star can be pretty big – many times the diameter of the sun – but even so the shock would take only minutes to pass through the body of the star, and blow it to pieces."

"And the uranium birds with it," I said sadly. "So *they* only had minutes. And the Great Goddess of the core? How long would she take to collapse?"

Ray shrugged. "Less than a second."

"*A second!*"

"But as you said, these were creatures of a different physics. To them that might have felt like a billion years. Plenty of time to live and love, to die in peace."

"They were transients," said Tweet, a bit grandly. "But then so are we all, before God."

"Or," said Crown Baker, "before the ploughman's lunches."

"Amen to that," we all murmured gravely.

And that's pretty much the end of the story. Save that as we came out of that moment of solemn contemplation, we realised we each had two things: an awful lot of follow-up questions for Barry Noakes, and an empty glass.

But he never did return from the bar. He never did answer our follow-ups. He never did buy another round.

A runner had been done.

He didn't even leave enough detail to check out his story independently. We couldn't agree on the year he had quoted, and so couldn't check out which supernova event he might have been talking about. Ray Arnold did once try to find out if the CIA really does have a neutrino communications monitoring facility in

Virginia, USA, but he was met with nothing but a series of denials of the existence of the neutrino facility, of the CIA, of Virginia, of the USA, of the phone call taking place, and in the end of Ray himself, and he gave up.

We couldn't even agree on the man's name. Barry Noakes, or possibly Norrie Boakes, simply vanished from our lives, leaving nothing but a lingering memory in our minds and our hearts – a textbook transient, as ephemeral as the creatures of his supernova biosphere.

But at least *they* don't owe us a drink.

Forever Blowing Bubbles

Ian Watson

Professor Mackintosh admired his pint of newly pulled Old Bodger, with an excellent head on it, and sang happily:

"I'm for-ever blow-ing bubbles,
"Pret-ty bubbles in the air!
"They fly so high,
"Nearly reach the sky —"

Mischievously, Brian Dalton continued:

"Then like your *dreams,*

"They fade and die. West Ham," Dalton pointed out, "lost two-one away in extra time."

"Whatever are you talking about?" asked Mackintosh, and took a swig of the dark ale.

"Footie! What do you suppose?"

"I fail to see any connection."

"For God's sake, *Bubbles* is the anthem of West Ham United. I thought you were a supporter."

Mackintosh said loftily, "The only interesting thing about a football is that it is spherical. As opposed to a rugby ball, which is a prolate spheroid."

Indeed our pale geometrodynamics boffin was lofty as well as quite skeletal, and needed to avoid bashing his balding head on low beams such as graced the ceiling of our historic watering hole. At least I think Mackintosh's field was called geometrodynamics, a rather airy-fairy discipline if you ask me. Spacetime curvature, physics reduced to geometry, wormholes, quantum foam and stuff. Fortunately for our camaraderie,

Mackintosh's taste in beer ran to the robust.

Dalton, our inorganic chemist, on the other hand, whose freckles almost joined up, was chunky and had no problem at all passing his ginger curls under low beams. He could be a bit pugnacious, but never offensively so.

At this point Jocelyn joined in by saying, "Harpo Marx used to play *I'm Forever* on a clarinet that would blow bubbles. I suppose he put some soapy water in it."

"*Really?*" asked Mackintosh with apparently considerable interest.

Buxom blonde Jocelyn, our forensic chemist, was into folk music and played big Irish whistles, which required going to pubs at least once a week. She certainly liked a pint, and had infiltrated herself into our predominantly male group some months earlier. Her full name was Jocelyn Elizabeth Sparrow, Dr Sparrow indeed. Not entirely appropriate, perhaps, since she was a big girl, necessarily as regards coping with the pints, and to some extent because of those. Her presence in our midst demonstrated that we weren't a bunch of confirmed bachelors. In fact Dalton himself was married – to a woman called Alice, I think – and had kids.

"*Really?* I hadn't thought about wind instruments blowing bubbles..." Mackintosh mused. "And lo, God blew his trumpet and the cosmos issued forth and inflated harmonically..."

It was Dalton's turn to exclaim, "What in the world are you talking about?"

"Not exactly *in* the world, as such," said Mackintosh.

"The world is the totality of all that is, according to Wittgenstein," piped up young Tuttle-Derby, whose schoolboyish face was pink and chubby, his oily brown hair slicked to one side, giving him the look of a Hitler cherub. "Anything you say that is not of the world has no meaning."

For some reason – tradition, probably – we often stood around the bar, though not like muskoxen so as to exclude other customers, and several more pints of Old Bodger had already been pulled when I called for a refill of my glass. A *re*fill, in vain as usual, since for some reason connected with hygiene or health and safety regulations Michael insisted on fresh glasses for each order. Personally I preferred my own bacteria to infest my glass rather than a previous customer's with added traces of detergent.

"The Greek for world is *kosmos*," added Tuttle-Derby. "Cosmos. So this applies to the entire universe."

"Mathematically," said Mackintosh, "that is bollocks. Since our cosmos is simply an inflated bubble within a higher matrix."

I received a fresh beer whose head flattened suspiciously fast. The brew smelled dodgy and the merest sip hinted at sour.

"I think the Bodger's off," I told the actual barmaid, who was Polish.

"I pour another?"

"No no, end of barrel, kaput."

"Sorry, no other barrel of Bogna."

"Bodger."

"Oh yes. In Polish bog means God. Bogna is godly."

"So is Bodger. Drinking Old Bodger was a communion."

"*I* am Bogna," said the big-eyed barmaid, who wore her dyed blonde hair in a pigtail rope.

"I thought you were called Brenda."

"Bog not so good a word in English."

No, exactly. Bogna-Brenda must have been brooding about herself, or her homeland, or maybe about God.

Alas, no more Bodger tonight. A tragedy. God was dead, for tonight anyway. I scanned the other real ales on offer. "Make it a MacPherson's Mild." At least that should taste strongish even if it wasn't. Besides, I ought to support Mild. Relegated over the years to a shrinking clientele of cloth-cap-wearing codgers in the Black Country around Birmingham, Mild was now bouncing back like an almost extinct species re-invigorated.

As if to safeguard his own Bodger by putting the holy and now rare liquid out of reach, Mackintosh took a large gulp, then he wiped his mouth.

"Hmm," he said, "I'm supervising a postgraduate at the moment, name of Jones-Jones, who's doing his doctorate on bubble universes."

"Is he so good," asked Jocelyn, "that they named him twice, like New York New York?"

"His mother and father were both called Jones. It's a Welsh thing. The valleys, you know. When they married, they decided to double-barrel their names to add a bit of class."

Tuttle-Derby was obviously protective of hyphenated surnames. "Makes sense. A bride changing her name from Jones to Jones, how can people be sure she's actually married?"

"Aside from attending the wedding? Being Welsh, Jones-Jones plays rugby –"

"With a prolate spheroid," added Jocelyn, to show she'd been paying attention.

"No less. I do wish he wouldn't. He might break his ruddy neck, thus depriving the world of great insights. Though come to think of it, if he survived as a quadriplegic he might seem quite Stephen Hawking. Or rather, I *did* wish Jones-Jones wouldn't break his neck, although now I'm not so sure in view of what happened earlier this week." And Mackintosh paused significantly, until we egged him on with a chorus of *So what happened?*

"Hmm, I'll need some lubrication for the throat." Mackintosh drained his glass. "Brenda, I'll have the Bishop's Best."

A bit too appley for my taste. With a lurking demon of rotten appley. If I get an ale that's gone off, this can taint all future experiences of the same brew. Forever after a particular ale, even if excellent today, will remind me of cobwebs, another of vinegar, another of rancid butter. There's the potential for evil in the background. A bit like the supposed homeopathic memory possessed by water that was once in contact with a single molecule of arsenic or whatever. I'd lost access to several famous ales this way. That's why I'd been very careful to take the merest sip, not a swig, of the dodgy Old Bodger. Of course not everyone has my sensitivity and fine discrimination.

Mackintosh was duly supplied by Bogna.

"Now I don't know how much you know about bubble universes," began Mackintosh, doubtless knowing the answer full well from his tally of those of us present in the Paradise Bar on this particular evening. Come to think of it, that may have emboldened him to burst into song in the first place. None of us was remotely a geometrodynamicist.

He proceeded to hold forth about how our universe is like a soap bubble, although it lasts for billions of years. Our cosmos inflated itself dramatically just over thirteen (unlucky for some, I remember thinking, though not for us!) thirteen thousand million years ago. So dramatically did it inflate that nowadays we can only see a little bit of our own bubble because light hasn't time to reach us from the walls of the bubble, and never will. Setting down his glass, Mackintosh held his hands wide apart, rattling some horse brasses on the blackened oak beam. *That big a bubble!*

"What's more," he continued, "space and light might bend around inside the bubble, such being the nature of a universe. Well now, that bubble originated from *foam*, namely quantum foam."

"Quantum Foam!" squeaked Jocelyn enthusiastically, causing Mackintosh to raise an eyebrow.

"It's an, um, music group," she said.

Quite! The general public might buy any old cobblers featuring the word quantum – quantum power crystals, quantum bath salts no doubt – but we were all scientists, and weren't going to be sold any quantum snake oil, though of course Mackintosh was a ranking authority on the subject of universes, at least from the theory point of view.

"An infinite multiverse," said Mackintosh, "should contain an infinite number of Hubble-bubbles – "

"I thought Hubble-bubbles are those Arab things you smoke from," interrupted Dalton.

"Not in this case. I perceive I'm losing you – think of gas pockets in a loaf that's rising."

"I detest big holes in my toast," said Jocelyn. "The butter escapes."

Evidently Mackintosh would need to contend with a spot of badinage; so maybe at this point he decided to abbreviate his explanations.

"Or maybe you should think of the background spacetime foam as resembling the head on a beer…"

"That's more like it," said Dalton.

"Anyway, foam is the foundation of the fabric of the universe…"

"I'll raise a glass to that," I agreed. Didn't somebody once say that having a beer without a head is like kissing a girl without lips! Not that I'd actually kissed a girl *with lips* all that recently, come to think of it… I glanced at blonde Bogna, who was at that moment coincidentally putting on some lipstick, or maybe it was lip-salve. Which was naughty of her – traces of grease could ruin the head on a beer. Jocelyn's sumptuous lips which accommodated large whistles were rather intimidating; a chap could get swallowed.

"So Jones-Jones came up with the notion of a buildable bubble that might cause a mini-cosmos to evolve – call it a cosm for short. According to the maths the vast majority of the spacetime of the resulting cosm would evolve *internally* – rather than externally from our point of view, so we wouldn't suddenly be pushed aside by the bubble expanding exponentially. Yet with ingenuity we might still inspect what went on inside the bubble-cosm. Are you with me? Hmm, the Bishop isn't half-bad tonight."

"Wouldn't an optimist say *half-good*?" I asked.

"No no," Tuttle-Derby told me. "Not half-good would mean that more than half is bad."

I shrugged. Maybe he was right. I was worried about the effect of the lip-salve on subsequent pints. Admittedly Bogna wasn't going to taste what she pulled, but a trace of grease might remain on her finger.

Due to brooding about lips, or lack of lips, I may have missed a connection in Mackintosh's discourse, for the next thing I heard him say was, "I'm not opposed to experimentation, so Jones-Jones rigged up a holder for a hoop which he would first of all dip – in the same way children do – to produce a soapy membrane across it. And beyond the hoop, what we might call a bubble-chamber to contain the resulting mini-cosm. Now what gas should he introduce into the bubble by, well, not to put too fine a point on it and begging your pardon, Jocelyn, *belching* into the membrane? Jones-Jones reckoned that carbon dioxide and organic traces should give the mini-cosm a good start in life. So with all the gusto of a rugby player he drank deeply from slightly shaken cans –"

"*Cans?*" I protested.

"Yes, this is the indelicate part, and I blush to relate it: green cans, indeed, of Heineken."

"*Heineken!*" I expostulated, clutching my diminished pint of Mild. "But that's blasphemy!"

"I know, I know. Experimentation can be a dirty business. That's why I'm a theoretician."

I struggled to cope with the concept of someone voluntarily drinking lager. Had the Campaign for Real Ale fought in vain? A scientific fact came to my mind.

"If Jones-Jones had drunk Guinness, the bubbles are nitrogen... I suppose that might have caused toxic blooms in the mini-cosm."

Mackintosh nodded grimly. "It gets worse." He paused, and we all knew that he was readying himself for the climax of this amazing account.

"So Jones-Jones poured all of that lager into himself. And presently he faced the membrane on the hoop, poised quite like a rugby player about to join in a scrum. Jocelyn, perhaps you should cover your ears."

"Certainly not," said Jocelyn indignantly.

"Very well. I abdicate responsibility. How shall I best put it with a lady present? The experiment succeeded. But *not* until Jones-Jones turned around... Because..."

"Because the gases that Jones-Jones let loose to inflate the bubbles, the baby cosms, were all coming out of the *other end*, if you take my meaning. They were coming from *the dark side*."

"Professor!" I exclaimed. "I never knew you were a fan of *Star Wars*."

Mackintosh beamed benignly and said in a mock Alec Guinness voice, "There is much you do not know about me, Luke."

"Ha ha," said Jocelyn to me. "That'll be your name from now on."

"It will not be!"

At the time we were much taken by the notion of malign, almost demonic mini-cosms, if such were to be how the products of Jones-Jones's experiment should evolve. I imagined those floating in that bubble-chamber, evolving internally at high speed. Dark cosms, in a manner of speaking.

Yet when I thought about all this in retrospect the next day, I spotted a flaw in what Mackintosh had related.

I don't mean a scientific flaw. Foam, bubble cosms, bubble chambers: those made as perfect sense to me as morphological pattern formation in the budding of sponges – a subject I felt I had a reasonable grasp of after watching a nature programme on the TV.

Nor was I thrown by Mackintosh invoking the sacrilegious word Heineken in the Paradise bar of the Fountain.

No, it's just this: if Jones-Jones generated those bubbles by flatulating whatever mixture of carbon dioxide, nitrogen, oxygen, hydrogen sulfide, and methane through the soapy membrane, he would *not only* need to have turned round but also *necessarily* pulled down his trousers and whatever underpants he might have been wearing. Or not, as the case may be.

The conjunction of our good Professor Mackintosh and a student, all be it a postgraduate, bending over baring his buttocks in private before him isn't one that I care to contemplate! Nor the potential implications! Avowedly Mackintosh wasn't an experimenter but a theoretician. Otherwise he might have taken this into account.

On the Messdecks of Madness

Paul Graham Raven

I can still recall clearly the occasion when the Raven ceased to be a lurker at the fringes of the group and became accepted as one of us. It was a particularly slow evening on the story front. Crown Baker had entertained briefly with an anecdote about a strange, alluring woman he encountered at a convention who might or might not have been an alien, and Dr Steve had spun an unlikely but amusing yarn involving the accidental creation of a laughing gas far more potent than nitrous oxide. After that, however, came a distinct lull, until the Raven stepped forward to fill the breach.

"Ehm, would anyone be interested in hearing how I came to stop working for the Navy?" he asked. "It's a story that involves mystery, skulduggery and gold."

Does a sailor like rum?

We gathered around to listen and invited him to proceed. He began a little nervously, but soon found his voice as the tale unfurled.

One bright spring afternoon I emerged from the archive stacks of the Royal Naval Museum Library to find my boss waiting for me in the office. Not that unusual, but the armed escort was.

"What's the matter?" I asked. "Someone steal Lord Nelson's hankie?"

"Come with us, Mister Raven," said Lefthand Navy Goon, who had a vacant look about his eyes to match the deadpan voice; I figured he got a lot of guard duty.

"I don't know what they want, but they're to take you over

to the Admiralty Branch." Alison said, stammering slightly. "You've not done anything... *stupid*, have you?"

No more than usual, I thought to myself; certainly nothing that rated guns, anyway. Still, I figured men with guns are best placated and obeyed, especially when you know you've nothing to hide. "Nope," I replied. "They've probably just got some bigwig in who wants to quiz me on the Bounty Mutiny conspiracy theories again. I'll be back in a bit."

I turned to Lefthand Goon with more confidence than I felt. "Lead on, gents."

Without another word, they ushered me through the reading room, out of Number Twelve Store and into the brine and oil tang of the afternoon air, which was turning cooler as heavy clouds rolled in from over the Solent.

Three things must ye know of the Admiralty Library.

First of all, it's not at the Admiralty in Whitehall any more. Well, *most* of it isn't, and what *is* still there is the stuff whose existence they make a point of denying. But that's a whole other story.

Secondly, the main branch of the Admiralty Library is situated in Her Majesty's Dockyard, Portsmouth, facing the main building of the Royal Naval Museum (my erstwhile employers) from the other side of the dry-docked HMS Victory.

Thirdly, well over half of what is technically the Admiralty Library collection is, in fact, housed in the Royal Naval Museum Library, so as to facilitate the foisting off of the more common-or-garden crank enthusiasts and conspiracy theorists (of whom there are many) onto the RNM's civilian staff, such as – until recently – yours truly.

The Admiralty Branch is staffed by a curious and select breed of professionals: chartered librarians with commissioned rank equivalence in the Naval hierarchy. They divide their time between babysitting visiting dignitaries with historical obsessions, devising names and crests for newly-commissioned ships of the fleet, and poking through their extensive archives in order to produce answers to obscure and pedantic questions in Parliament, as well as requests from history buffs of a more academic (if equally eccentric) type.

The Admiralty archives contain not only Naval documents of great antiquity or rarity – logbooks from lost ships, inquest reports conveniently limited to a single printed copy, that sort of thing – but also items with a more peripheral connection to the Royal Navy's past. Hand-drawn maps and notebooks from the golden ages of exploration and colonial ambition; technical drawings and treatises by the nigh-legendary inventors and engineers of the Victorian age; leather-bound vanity-pressed novels by obscure Naval notables. It'd take a mind utterly uninterested in anything beyond their immediate experience not to be awed by the stuff in the Admiralty library catalogue.

And the catalogue doesn't even list the *really* weird stuff.

Thanks to the dubious glory of my own partial security clearance, yours truly would occasionally be summoned across to the Admiralty Branch for some sort of fetch-and-carry gig, so the journey was familiar enough, but for the spasms of my lower back flinching from the glare of two submachine gun barrels. The Goons hustled me up the side exit (staff only, y'know), carded us in, and delivered me to a genial-looking scrambled-eggs officer of indeterminate middle age sitting behind a suspiciously clear desk. (Tip from inside the industry: you should mistrust a library with tidy offices in the same way you'd mistrust a mechanic's workshop without smudges of oil all over it.) His dockyard pass proclaimed him to be Commander Waytes.

"Is this, ah... is this about that blog post?" I enquired.

"No, Mister Raven, it's not about your... *blog* post. Sit down."

I sat down. Waytes made a church-and-steeple with his fingers and leaned forward. "This is strictly a formality, Mister Raven, but nonetheless I need to ask: where are the Pepys ledgers?"

The Pepys ledgers in question were really Pepys apocrypha, of little interest to anyone who didn't study the history of Naval accounting; small sub-ledgers from years of Admiralty book-balancing, stashed away with Pepys' meticulous – some might even say anal – care. They were on the Admiralty Branch catalogue, but I'd never seen 'em, or even been in the climate-controlled room where they were kept. They were precious enough that anyone who wanted to see them would have had to do so here, in the rather more secure Admiralty Branch reading room.

"Given that you'd not be asking me otherwise, I'm going to assume they're not on a shelf somewhere in Archive F where they should be." Waytes nodded, slowly. "Then I have no idea where they are. Er, sir." Bit of toadying couldn't hurt, could it?

"I'm very sure you don't, Raven. But as you surmise, they're not where they should be."

"Then why ask me, sir? Unless that's, uh, classified?"

"Because the only lead we have on their disappearance points straight at you, I'm afraid." Waytes slid a few sheets of hardcopy across the desk. "No one has so much as queried their shelf location in three years. Until last Friday." He tapped a finger at a line of logfile which contained a very familiar username.

"I never looked up the location of these. Not last Friday, not ever. As far as I can remember, anyway."

"I'm sure *you* didn't, Mister Raven," said Waytes. "But as you can see, your user account on the Branch catalogue system clearly did. Which triggered an automatic stockcheck this morning – standard procedure, yes? – which revealed a handful of folios missing from the last year of the Pepys ledgers. No other catalogue queries, and no one here has been into Archive F in weeks. Which leaves you rather in the frame, doesn't it?" He sounded apologetic, as if the whole business seemed a little ridiculous to him. Perhaps this wouldn't turn out to be too big a deal after all.

"This is my first visit to the Branch in at least a month, sir; card records will show that. And I'm not cleared for Archives F through K, either."

"I understand, Raven," said Waytes. "Us fans should stick up for each other, after all, don't you think?"

"You're in fandom?" I started thinking back over the day so far, trying to work out whether there was any point at which I could have been spiked with something strongly hallucinogenic.

"Oh, yes – more horror than SF, but we're all just genre to the literati, aren't we?" A brief smile. "Nonetheless, there are formalities to be followed in this situation, as I'm sure you know."

There'd been pages of boilerplate on the security check paperwork. I nodded.

"Good. Then I hope you'll forgive me for sending you home."

Forgive him? Even if the clouds broke, an afternoon off was an afternoon off...

"I've spoken to Julie over at the Museum offices; you're to be suspended indefinitely. Without pay, I'm afraid."

What the...? "Without pay, sir?"

"Due to the nature of the crime, I have no choice. By the power vested in me by her Majesty's Government, I hereby charge you with theft of government property, damage or circumvention of government security and conspiracy to sell stolen goods." The corner of his mouth jerked tight momentarily; was he finding this as weird as I was? Funny, even?

Waytes cleared his throat. "And of espionage in or near Her Majesty's Dockyards. Which is the tricky one, you see, as it's one of the few remaining statutes that counts as high treason."

I thought, fleetingly, of the yard-arm of HMS Victory, glinting in sunlight high above the concrete outside.

"No need to worry. We'll find the ledgers and the culprit, and it'll all get cleared up, I'm sure. But in the meantime, well, we need to get you out of the way." His brow furrowed. "And quietly... no need for any public embarrassment, eh?"

Back in my flat an hour later, I paced figure-eights while waiting for my ageing PC to boot. The public's embarrassment may have been spared, but being shoved at gunpoint out of a quiet side entrance to the Dockyard hadn't really done much for *my* self-esteem. Nor had Waytes' reassurances; given his status as an officer, he was probably obliged to think well of the RN's ability to solve what seemed to be little more than a classic (if expensive) example of military bureaucratic SNAFU. After a year or so in the auxiliary trenches, so to speak, I had a rather more jaundiced outlook on that particular battlefield.

And in the meantime, an indefinite pay-less holiday; that'd be fun to explain to my landlord. Though not as fun as explaining the lingering stain of a treason charge on my otherwise spotless criminal record as regards any future prospective employers. I hauled out my phone, poked at speed-dial. At least I wasn't under house arrest.

"Just don't leave the country, eh?" Waytes had said, cheerily. "We're more than capable of knowing exactly where you are. When we need you, we'll find you."

Don't call us, we'll call you: quite possibly the least reassuring sentence in the English language. Well, if I was free to roam, I might as well start working toward clearing my name. It'd kill the time, if nothing else.

Daryl picked up after two rings. "Afternoon off, is it?"

"Sort of, yeah. I could do with a hand, Daryl."

Daryl's an old buddy from university; he completed the course I dropped out of, and makes a very healthy living out of sporadic paid gigs in grey-hat computer engineering and other elite code-monkey work. I explained my eventful afternoon, supplied him with a few URLs and my login details for the catalogue servers, and settled down to do some googling. Assuming this wasn't just the bureaucratic foul-up it appeared to be, there had to be a reason why someone would steal —

seemingly by magical means – a bunch of old Naval accounts books.

Of course, there were many motives suggested online, ranging from the unlikely to the unhinged. However, searching for needles of truth in the internet's infinite haystack of woo is exactly what us librarians are trained for; when Daryl rang back half an hour later, I had narrowed the possibilities down to a handful of browser tabs mentioning the ledgers which I thought were worth following up.

"You weren't joking about the RN's attitude to system security, were you?" asked Daryl.

"Easy job, was it?"

"Well, not *easy*..." Daryl's a modest type. "I've just emailed you a dump of the catalogue server logs. This Waytes bloke is quite right; no search for those items for years, then your user account checks their shelf location last Friday. However, it does so from an IP address outside the Dockyard. Outside of Portsmouth, in fact."

I clicked open a not-too-crankish-looking website from my shortlist, where terse academic phrases extolled the dry virtues of a paper entitled "Pepys & Newton – alchemist co-conspirators?" *Click here to download PDF.* Well, why not?

"Can you tell me where that IP address is located, Daz?" I asked.

"Just a mo..." A clattering of keys on the other end of the line. I clicked open the PDF. It seemed to have been corrupted; weird characters from no alphabet I'd ever seen before covered a few dozen pages. A gentle chuntering started up somewhere in the dusty heart of my old desktop.

"There you go: WC2, London. MOD owns the nameservers. Best guess for location is along Whitehall somewhere. What's that noise? Sounds like a hard drive writing zeros to every bit on the platter."

"Shit!"

Half past ten the next morning saw me sitting on the first off-peak train up the line to London, blinking my sore eyes over a small sheaf of printouts and some scribblings in my notebook. Having turned up shortly after that phone call to do an autopsy on my PC – which was, as he guessed, completely defunct, thanks to the boot sector of the hard drive being scrubbed over with random bits – Daryl did his best to assuage my rising sense of panic by plying me with alcohol. Sleep remained elusive, but the hangover was successfully distracting me from devoting my full attention to the mystery of the missing ledgers.

A 4 a.m. plan to scour the British Library for clues and connections – and maybe a copy of the PC-killing treatise, if it actually existed – had seemed no less fruitless or foolish come sunrise. After an hour and a half spent huddled over my notebook in the carriage (and one unedifying instance of rushing to the toilet cubicle to talk with unspecified deities on the big porcelain – or in this case chrome-plated – telephone) I shambled across central London and into the figurative temple of my profession.

Two hours and three cans of energy drink later, and I'd worked my way through maybe five percent of the titles in the British Library catalogue that mentioned both Pepys and Newton. The hangover had receded, leaving me with a lingering sense of panic accompanied by the feeling of being watched. *When we need you, we'll find you*, Waytes had said; perhaps they had another goon on my tail? Seemed like a waste of resources... and the only person who'd shown even a passing interest in me all day was a bookish-looking girl I noticed peering at my borrowings in the reading room as I returned from a quick smoke, who scurried off as I approached. *You're just being paranoid, Raven*, I told myself.

Of course, librarian is as librarian does, and geekdom is not easily displaced, even in moments of great adversity. As such, I'd become very wrapped up in reading the machinations of Restoration London, not to mention the madcap doings of the nascent Royal Society. I was headed for the gents, absently considering angles for a paper on Stephenson's *Baroque Cycle* reconsidered as a work of gonzo historical revisionism, when I heard a faint rustle of fabric. A steely something pinched at the nape of my neck, and my left ear slammed into the unforgiving wall of the corridor.

So much for losing the headache.

My assailant maintained a vice-like pressure on my neck from behind me, grinding my cheek into the wall. Was this Waytes' watcher-goon? Was I 'needed' already? My stomach sank, mirroring its earlier hungover queasiness; *what if this the person who'd stolen the bloody ledgers?* I felt my assailant's cool breath on my neck as their grip and stance shifted slightly. A voice spoke quietly but firmly in my ear.

"Struggling isn't going to get you anything but broken. All we need you to do is talk, which leaves plenty of scope for... persuasion." The film-villain brutality of that last word was skewed by the educated Home Counties accent that delivered it, as did the fact that the voice was clearly that of a young woman. This week was getting weirder by the minute.

"But you can make it easy on yourself, can't you? So," and the voice drew nearer to my unobstructed ear, "why don't you tell me where the gold is located?"

Unable to respond rationally to such an unexpected question, my instincts took over. I began to shake with a shrill and breathless laughter.

"I thought you were someone else. Well, no — I thought you were you, but that you'd done something very bad." My assailant, who introduced herself as Caroline, wrung her hands together while I tried to stretch out the knot she'd embedded in my shoulder.

"Like stealing some gold?"

"Planning to, yes. And stealing something else in the process."

"That wouldn't be a sheaf of Restoration-era accounts ledgers, would it?"

Her eyes narrowed, and her stance loosened, her hands hanging ready at her sides. "If you think you can get out of here before I catch you again —"

"I think I'd better tell you about my week so far," I interrupted. "I don't make a habit of asking this of girls I've only just met, especially not ones who've just given me the Vulcan death-grip in a library corridor, but would you like to go and get a drink?"

"It's not even five o'clock!"

"Fine. Would you like to watch me have a drink?"

In a quiet corner of the Euston Tap, Caroline frowned into an untouched half of fizzy cider as I told my story between gulps of a boutique ale with a silly name. When I had finished, she downed her drink, got two refills from the bar and told me her own.

Caroline was an archivist for the Royal Society, and her story was very familiar. A few weeks earlier she'd discovered some items from the Society's early papers had gone walkabout without being checked out on the catalogue system. No sign of forced entry, no damage. The only clue was a shelf-check for the documents in question that had been run using her own user account on a day when she'd been at a conference across town. Not so weird, really — library staff often use each other's accounts for quick searches all the time — but the IP address from the server logs seemed to belong to...

"The Admiralty buildings in Whitehall, right?"

She nodded. "So I thought maybe someone over there had borrowed something; the Navy and the Society are pretty chummy like that. So I rang up and made a few enquiries, with little success. Until a visit later that afternoon from your Commander Waytes, that is; he's something of a regular at the Society, as it happens."

"And he told you that I was trying to steal some gold?"

"Not just any gold."

"Does it make a difference?"

"Yes, if what Waytes was saying had any basis in truth."

"So what was stolen from your archives, then?

She looked up. "The last known alchemical notebook of Sir Isaac Newton, covering the period up to 1696 when he became Warden of the Mint. According to Waytes, there are those in the Admiralty who believe that Newton succeeded in creating the fabled Philosopher's Stone, transforming base metal into gold and triggering his obsession with pure coinage and currency reform. Horrified at creating a transgression of natural laws in his attempt to follow a path of spiritual self-perfection, he gave the gold to someone who could be trusted to stash it away, someone who was used to cleaning up behind the early members of the Society when their experiments went awry."

Sam Pepys, of course – who, despite the legendary diary, knew how to keep his mouth shut when it was politically or financially expedient to do so. Waytes had told Caroline that the thief who'd taken the notebook and the ledgers would probably return to London in order to use the British Library collection to stitch clues from the manuscripts together and reveal the hiding place known only to Newton and Pepys themselves. He also told her that the thief would be around six foot in height, have dreadlocks and facial piercings, and wear an ugly shirt.

"Waytes told me yesterday that he didn't think I'd stolen anything, and that it was all a big misunderstanding!" I sounded petulant; the shirt dig had riled me.

"He gave me your description a week ago," she replied.

"A week ago? But the ledgers only went missing the night before last!"

"Right. Which would suggest that Commander Waytes is playing us both for idiots, and already has both pieces of the puzzle."

I threw up my hands. "The guy's searching for a myth made of mumbo-jumbo. Alchemical gold from the hand of Sir Isaac Newton himself? Even if it did exist, that sticky-fingered bastard

Pepys would have got rid of it as soon as he was sure Newton didn't want it anymore." Times became hard for old Sam in his twilight years. "In the meantime I'm wandering around with a charge of treason hanging over my head, while you managed to let an officer of the Royal Navy convince you to capture an alleged enemy of the state by force in the biggest public library in the country."

Remorse locked onto her face like a wheel clamp. "He said we had to keep this a secret. The bad publicity, you know."

"Sure, bad publicity. Best avoided by deploying karate-trained archivists, every time."

"Wing Tsun, actually," muttered Caroline.

"Whatever. I'm pretty sure the law doesn't allow Waytes to delegate violence to civilians, which puts you down for at least a conspiracy to kidnap and aggravated assault, as well as being at the end of a thin chain of evidence concerning the theft of another incredibly valuable manuscript. Furthermore, the only man whose evidence can clear our names is sitting somewhere poring over said missing manuscripts in order to make off with some nonexistent magical gold, which was supposedly buried three hundred years ago by a serial cuckold in a flea ridden wig. From where I'm sitting, Miss Caroline, we're pretty much screwed."

"Maybe," she said. "Unless we get a bargaining chip from somewhere."

"Such as...?"

"The location of the gold."

"You don't believe it actually exists, do you?"

"I doubt it. I mean, there might be some gold, but it's more likely ordinary stuff Newton had acquired through one channel or another. But what matters is that Waytes clearly thinks the gold exists; if we can find where it's supposed to be, we can bribe him with that information. Or, better still, frame him for the theft by tipping off the authorities and letting them catch him red-handed. He's not as practiced at finding minor anomalies in old manuscripts as we are."

"Perhaps, but he actually has the manuscripts, and we don't."

"Then you've forgotten the same thing that Waytes forgot, or simply didn't know." She grinned. "Digital scans."

Caroline's Brixton basement flat was more spacious than I'd expected, and unsurprisingly meticulous. It also contained an enviable collection of Kim Stanley Robinson signed first editions. "So you're a fan too, huh?" I asked her as she returned from the kitchen with coffee and an ashtray.

"I suppose so, though I don't do conventions. Why?"

"Just wondering if that's how Waytes targeted us, knew where we worked and what sort of people we were. He told me *he* was a fan."

"Oh God, yes, he's a Lovecraft nut." Caroline shuddered. "Dirty icthyophobic old racist; can't stand the stuff myself. But that's what Waytes came to the Society for. Told me one afternoon he was working on a paper that posited Ascension Island as the actual site of R'lyeh. But with that creepy smile of his, I could never tell whether he was joking or not."

"His smile seemed quite genuine to me," I said. So much for my people-reading skills.

"You know," said Caroline, brow furrowed, "he seemed more charming than usual when he was telling me about you and the theft. And when he wanted something in a hurry, of course."

"That's borrowers for you, eh?" I replied. Librarian humour. Hey, it works for us.

Caroline's flat had also yielded two battered but functional laptops. With their batteries refreshed (as ours were with glutinous black coffee), we got to work downloading digital versions of our respective missing manuscripts. High-res scans are huge, but museum archive servers are slow, so I decided to do a little more poking about with respect to Commander Waytes. He was surprisingly hard to Google; very little about him or by him other than a few reviews and papers in obscure online horror journals.

"Well, you of all people should be able to find out plenty about him," said Caroline.

I probably puffed up a little at that. "Perhaps you rate my search skills a little too generously."

"I wouldn't count on it. But I know where you work." She rolled her eyes at my incomprehension. "He's a bloody Naval officer, isn't he? What was it you told me earlier you spend most of your working day doing?"

Caroline didn't wait for me to reply before turning her attention back to her own screen. In my defence, I'd had a rough and sleepless couple of days. Still chagrined, I logged back into a few databases and started scanning for our friend Waytes in old paybooks and digitised editions of the Navy List. After the drought, the flood: *lots* of results. Though never more than one at a time.

"What do you mean?" Caroline peered over my shoulder.

"Many mentions, but only one Waytes. The Navy List only goes back to around the time of Trafalgar, but every year that's been scanned since then has a Waytes." I ran a few cross-references. "All of whose postings match date-to-date perfectly, as well as his ascent through the ranks." I trailed off into silence.

"Oh come on, that's ridiculous," said Caroline.

"This from the girl who wants us to locate Newton and Pepys' leprechaun horde?"

"The existence of a cache of gold is perfectly plausible; the suggestion of alchemical origins is immaterial. But you're suggesting that Commander Waytes – one singular Waytes, the same one we've both met in the flesh – has been on the books with the Navy since the time of Trafalgar, like the Count of Saint bloody Germain?"

I opened another browser tab. "Since before then," I said, pointing. "Signing off or mentioned in passing on Admiralty paperwork almost as far back as the stuff exists."

Caroline looked troubled. She turned back to her own machine, started typing furiously. "Look up what ship Waytes was posted to in 1843, will you?"

"Uh... HMS Erebus. Why? What've you found?"

"You'll see in a moment. And where was he serving in 1836?"

"HMS Beagle... seems to have been on a lot of the great exploratory voyages, doesn't he?"

"Right. Particularly ones that stopped at Ascension Island."

"Any ship down that way was bound to call into Ascension, it's the only port for hell knows how far."

"Both of those stopped there for quite a while, not just a fleeting visit. Both of them carried home biological scientists who'd go on to be influential and powerful men."

"Darwin I know; who's the other?"

Caroline spun her laptop to face me; a thoughtful and slightly cunning-looking young man in round glasses peered out at me from a shadowy portrait on a Wikipedia page. "Joseph Dalton Hooker, director of Kew Gardens. The guy who suggested that the Navy ship trees and other botanical matter to Ascension in what was technically the first terraforming experiment ever conceived."

"Look, this is getting stupid," I said. "We're both acting like the cranks we answer queries from at our day jobs. Look hard enough at any big data-set, and weird coincidences crop up."

"What, like a centuries-old still-serving Naval officer with a Lovecraft mania?"

"The Navy Lists are notoriously inaccurate," I snapped. "For all I know this could be some long-running departmental gag with the records clerks. The writer's equivalent of sending someone to the quartermaster's stores to ask for a long..." I trailed off again.

"A long *wait*?" Caroline asked sweetly.

Cold wet mud seeped into my trainers as I paced, John Cleese style and soaked to the skin, through a glistening flowerbed.

Though Clapham Common's charms are many, they are absent during a rainstorm at 3am. Once Caroline had cracked the location – some combination of acrostics and transposition cyphers, apparently, or so she told me when she woke me up – she was determined that we should go find the gold ourselves. The rain drumming on the windows wasn't the only thing to prompt my protests.

"I thought we were going to tip off the authorities, let them handle this? And now you want us to traipse across Clapham Common at night and dig a bloody great hole?"

"If we tip off the authorities, we'll never see it. We'll never know if this really was Newton's Philosopher's Stone!"

How we'd be able to tell alchemical gold from chocolate money in this downpour was beyond me, but I was still excited; there was something Enid Blytonish about it, I suppose. I finished off my count, stamping my heel into the grass a few meters from a tall brick wall.

Caroline had been following close behind, and wasted no time in setting to digging with her garden spade, tugged out from concealment in an old sports holdall. Tension radiated off her like heat, and her enthusiasm was infectious. The bag provided me with a rusty entrenchment tool, and I pitched in as well. Half an hour and three feet of topsail later, I had my Indiana Jones moment as the entrenching tool hit something that replied with a wooden *thunk*.

Caroline squealed like a little girl at a pony sanctuary, elbowed me aside and began prising the thing out. The rain had eased off as dawn approached, so I stripped off my filthy gloves and attempted to roll and smoke a cigarette as she worked. Caroline hardly stopped for breath; with the box dragged to the surface she stood tall, spade raised above her shoulder, and took a hard swing at the padlock, which burst with a dull clatter. She fumbled open the lid, gasped, fell to her knees in the mud.

It was just like that scene in *Pulp Fiction*.

Okay, so it wasn't actually glowing, but as that boxful of pencil-length pieces of pure gold caught the wan light of the rising sun shouldering its way through the clouds, it was the most luminous thing I'd ever seen. Caroline and I reached our hands toward the gold almost as one.

"Don't touch it, Mister Raven." The voice emanated from a flowerbed. Waytes stepped out. "It'd be more than your life was worth."

"You've got a nerve," I called out, though I pulled my hands back as he approached. "Was putting me through all this really necessary?"

"It was, yes, but not for the reasons you think."

"Oh, we know why, Waytes," I replied. "Ascension Island? Hooker?" I gestured at the gold. "This whole business has been so weird I'm beginning to think this stuff really is a magical experiment gone wrong."

"I don't believe that at all, Mister Raven. But you're still in grave danger."

I laughed. "Why? Because you're going to sacrifice me to Cthulhu?"

"No," said Waytes, "because you're kneeling next to a ruthless antiquities thief with a pistol in her hand."

I felt something cold and hard on the back of my neck. "He has a point," Caroline muttered.

I felt myself flush with anger. "Well, what the hell did *you* need to drag me into this for?" I demanded. "You could have got the ledgers without my help, digital or physical."

"Consider yourself my false trail of evidence, if it makes you feel any better. Stand up." I obeyed, and found myself acting as human shield between her and Waytes. Smart girl.

"Let him go, Caroline," called Waytes. "If this ends now – no deaths, no theft – things will go a lot better for you."

"Nonsense. I think it'll go a lot better for me with you dead, the gun in this geek's equally dead hand, and the gold in a safety deposit box in a São Paulo bank, don't you?"

"The theft will be traced to you eventually."

"But it'll take a while, won't it, without you around to explain your own false trails? Look, if you let me go, you and Swampy here" – she nudged me in the neck with the pistol – "get to live. Or you can try to stop me, and you both die. No big deal either way for me at this point, really, though I'm in something of a hurry."

"Hey," I said, panic rising, "don't I get any input here?"

"Shut up while the adults are talking," she snapped, and returned to trading threats with Waytes.

That was the final straw. My blood sang with adrenaline, and in my brain – strung-out from stress and lack of sleep – I felt something give. After two days of being led around by the nose like a sacrificial goat, my inner eschatologist recognised one last chance for agency before the dying of the light as Caroline removed the gun from my neck to point it directly at Waytes. I raised my right leg, and stamped down and backward as hard as I could onto the arch of her foot.

Things get fuzzy at this point; Hollywood does nothing to prepare you for just how loud a modern handgun sounds when it's fired within centimeters of your ear. As my legs jellified and I collapsed downward, Caroline's shot was closely followed by another. I have no idea how long I was out – maybe only seconds – before coming to laid foetal on the ground, my eyes scrunched shut, listening to the pink noise patter of the rain on the moist turf slowly reasserting itself through the high whine of tinnitus.

"Any chance of a hand over here, Raven?" came Waytes' plaintive voice. "Don't worry, she's down."

I uncurled a little, glanced left and right, flinched away from the ruin of Caroline's face lying no more than a meter away, right between me and the box of gold.

"That was about it really," the Raven concluded. "I was cleared of all charges and offered my old job back, but, in a particularly bookish kind of post-traumatic response, I found I'd had enough of working for the Navy. So Waytes helped me secure a position out in Civvy Street."

"Hang on a sec, you can't leave it there," Jocelyn objected.

"Quite right," said Dr Steve. "You've avoided clarifying the most tantalising aspect of all."

"Oh?" The Raven feigned innocence.

"*Is* this Waytes character really an immortal or not?" Crown Baker gave voice to what we were all thinking.

Or nearly all of us, at any rate. "Preposterous nonsense," Professor Mackintosh was heard to mutter.

The Raven gave a mischievous smile. "Ah, now that would be telling."

"Oh, come on!"

"Well, perhaps with enough Old Bodger inside me I might be persuaded to overlook the requirements of the official secrets act just this once…"

There was a mad scramble towards the bar.

The Story Bug

James Lovegrove

I usually pitch up at Fountain at around the same time – half sixish. On this particular occasion I turned up an hour before that; not through kind fortune but deliberately so. Eric had emailed asking if I could be there at half five, as there was someone he wanted me to meet. I enjoy Eric's company and don't get to see him as often as I like, so, as there was nothing urgent that afternoon, I was happy to oblige.

The 'someone' proved to be another writer – an individual I'd actually met once before, though only briefly. I won't mention his name for fear of embarrassment, but suffice to say that I would never have recognised him from our previous encounter. He looked to have aged significantly and had lost a fair bit of weight, while there was a nervous, restless air about him.

"It's funny, being back here again," he muttered. The significance of the comment eluded me at the time.

Once we'd all settled in with a pint, Eric turned to me and said, "I know how much you enjoy a good story, just wait till you hear this!"

With that, our guest began.

I'm not much of a one for hanging out with the science fiction crowd. Truth be told, I find most other writers a bore and a chore – and I'm under no illusion that the feeling mightn't be mutual.

I do, however, count three SF authors as close friends, and it was with them one evening that I was weaving my way, none too steadily, through the back streets of central London, a little to the east of Soho. We had just attended a publishing function of some sort – book launch, annual back-pat, whatever – which had ended at the disgracefully early hour of 8.30, and we were heading in search of further refreshment in the company of seven or eight of our colleagues, brother scribes, along with the all-important editor. I say 'all-important' because he had the expense account and the company credit card and had rather foolishly promised us their use. He might as well have given us the keys to the Bank of England and told us to go and help ourselves.

The leader of the pack, Richard, whose books unfailingly courted controversy and unfailingly sold well, swore blind he knew of a pub round these parts that was famous for being the haunt of several key British SF novelists of the 1950s. Eric, of course, insisted that he knew of a splendid watering hole in this very area, but Richard would hear none of it. So we were busy looking for his pub, in a kind of quest-cum-pilgrimage. The fact that Richard couldn't recall the name of the place, or even the name of the street it was on, was neither here nor there. He was determined to find it, and beta males that the rest of us were, we were determined to follow him.

After marching us confidently down countless insalubrious side streets and into and back out of countless dead ends, eventually Richard located the pub tucked away in a narrow street that led off Chancery Lane. Or at any rate, he was adamant that it was the place we'd been looking for, and we were too footsore and, more to the point, too thirsty to dispute the matter. It was getting on for 10 o'clock by then, and with only an hour left 'til last orders, any drinking establishment would do.

Eric, though, seemed perplexed. "This is the bloody place I was talking about," he muttered to me. "Why wouldn't that idiot listen? I could have brought us here hours ago!"

The pub in question, the Fountain, seemed decent enough. Olde worlde, to be sure, but warm inside, and clean, with horse brasses and framed sepia prints vying for space on the flock wallpaper and that strange tinge in the air which only traditional pubs have, even in this smokeless age – a hazy, almost tangible miasma that I can only call, for want of a better word, atmosphere.

We settled in, the dozen of us tidily doubling the total of customers already present. I arranged it so that I was sharing a table with my three friends – Adam, Roger and Eric – and was insulated from some of the less desirable members of our party. Among the latter I included the bestselling American fantasy-saga author who was over in the UK on a promotional junket and couldn't stop boasting about his lissom twentysomething girlfriend (what she saw in this middle-aged, balding, self-important multimillionaire, I can't imagine). I also included the composer of space operas whose epic tomes were as girthsome as their progenitor, and as resistible, and the purveyor of "high concept" malarkey that was impenetrable to any reader lacking a masters degree in astrophysics.

Once orders had been taken and drinks had arrived, the four of us – our own little subgenre, you might say – put our heads together and chatted about almost anything under the sun *except* SF. Everyone else focused on that subject and no other, marvelling at so-and-so's lucrative three-book contract and commenting enviously on whatchemacall's seven-figure Hollywood deal and dissecting, rather gleefully, the critical drubbing doled out on whoozit's new offering in the latest *Interzone*. Our quartet, by contrast, preferred to cast the conversational net a bit wider. Talking shop is tedious. Writing is a dull and mechanical act when practised on a regular basis, and publishing is a business like any other and no more intrinsically interesting for having some sort of creative endeavour as its foundation stone. More to the point, there's more to life than science fiction. Heresy, but true. Surely if SF has taught us anything, it's that.

"A government has a responsibility to protect its citizens. Of course it has."

So said Adam. We four had strayed, probably unwisely, into the briar patch that is politics.

"The question is," he went on, "where does that responsibility end? How far should our leaders be prepared to go in ensuring our continued sovereignty, and how far should we let them? What is and is not allowable when it comes to defence of the realm?"

In physical appearance Adam is like Beaker, hapless lab assistant to Professor Bunsen Honeydew in *The Muppet Show*, only handsomer. The resemblance is never more marked than when he is pontificating, as he was then, forefinger in the air.

"Some would argue anything and everything is allowable," I said.

"Up to and including torture?" said Roger. As well as being a writer, Roger is a dentist by profession. Perhaps understandably, then, torture is seldom far from his thoughts. "But, if we use so-called coercion techniques to extract information from our enemies, doesn't that transgress international law?"

"Doesn't it also invalidate the information we get?" Eric chipped in. Eric is that rarity, a softly-spoken, self-effacing Yorkshireman. "A suspect will say anything to make the interrogation stop. So ninety per cent of the intelligence obtained using torture will be dodgy to say the least, if not downright false."

"But the ten per cent that isn't could save lives," I said. "That, surely, makes it worthwhile."

"The point I think we're missing here," said Adam, donnishly, "is that if our side commits acts that are unconscionable to all right-thinking people, not only do we concede the moral high ground, we give the other side licence to commit acts which are even more heinous. Setting a good example is paramount, whatever it costs us. Otherwise we're simply inviting greater hatred and atrocity down on our heads. Come the revolution –"

"Oh God, here we go," I groaned.

"Come the revolution," Adam reiterated, "when we're all living in anarcho-syndicalist harmony, our behaviour as a society will be a shining beacon to the rest of the world. All of us will be equal and alike, treated fairly by our elected representatives."

"And we won't have enemies any more," I drawled, "because other countries will see what a utopia we have created and want to join in and emulate it. Soon the entire planet will be one happy, joyous Soviet wonderland; men, women and children holding hands, striding forth in dignity and strength, and nothing bad will ever happen again."

"Exactly!" declared Adam, pounding the table.

Roger gave a wry laugh, while Eric merely shook his head and took a swig of beer.

"Long live that day," said an unfamiliar voice from nearby.

We all turned.

There was an old man sitting alone at the next table along. I'd barely noticed him when we came in, other than to feel a slight pang of pity for him that his evening was about to be ruined by a gaggle of SF types colonising his corner of the saloon and intruding on his quiet introspection with their garrulousness. He had pinched cheeks and rueful eyes, evidence of a life that had seen its fair share of sorrows. In all, his face seemed as bitter as the pint of bitter facing him.

"But until it comes along," he continued, "our rulers will carry on abusing us and others, all in the name of freedom and domestic security. And I should know."

"How?" I asked, casually, not that interested. "How would you know?"

"I'm one of their victims," the old man said.

"Oh." There wasn't much else one could say to that.

"Yes. You are looking at someone who has suffered at the hands of the governing elite, suffered grievously, and has received nothing in the way of recompense – not even an apology."

"Well, you don't look too bad on it, if you don't mind my saying so," said Adam.

"Appearances can be deceptive, my friend. Not all injuries leave visible scars."

"Can you tell us what happened?" Eric enquired.

"I thought you'd never ask," replied the old man. "Although – the price of enlightenment is customarily a drink." He drained his glass at a gulp. "And I am, as you can see, in need of a refill."

It just so happened that requests for the next round were being taken. We sneaked in an extra pint for the old man. Those expenses weren't going to tot themselves up on their own accord now, were they?

"Thanks," he said, and introduced himself as Henry Purbeck.

We in turn introduced ourselves, and Purbeck asked if we were all SF writers, and we confirmd we were, and he said he hadn't heard of any of us but he used to meet a lot of SF writers here, at this very watering hole, back in the day. The greats. The ones who genuinely could write and, what's more, were sticklers for their science."

"Can still find a few of us here even in this day and age," Eric murmured to me, "and we're not *that* bad."

"Knew how to keep a novel short, too," the old man said, clearly not having heard Eric's aside. "Books are too inflated these days. I blame word processors. They encourage verbosity. When everyone used typewriters, writing was laborious. All that redrafting and retyping – it obliged you to be concise. You had to make every word count. Now, all anyone cares about is the word count. People pad beyond belief, and beyond endurance, SF writers especially, because it's easy to. That's why I don't read the stuff anymore."

"Well, that's our careers dismissed in a few short sentences," I said, and Adam kicked me under the table.

"Still," Purbeck said, "my story should be of personal interest to you. It's about writing, in a way. Any of you heard of a place called Chilton Mead?"

Blank looks all round.

"No reason you should have, I suppose. It's a top secret MoD research facility in Wiltshire."

"'Top secret' would imply we're not meant to have heard of it," Roger pointed out.

"Indeed," said Purbeck. "But secrets have a way of leaking out. No security system is perfect, and Chilton Mead has had a fair few lapses in the recent past. They've been hushed up, kept out of the newspapers, but word of mouth is less easily restrained. I was just wondering if it had got as far as your ears, you being men of some level of intellect who appear to be plugged into current affairs. Obviously not. Never mind. Chilton Mead, at any rate, may be found in the countryside not far off the A481."

"Hold on, should you be telling us where it is?" I said. "If you've been there you must have signed the Official Secrets Act, meaning you're forbidden from revealing anything about it."

Purbeck gave a sardonic chuckle. "After what they did to me there, frankly the Official Secrets Act can bugger off! Besides, I wouldn't be surprised if the place has been shut down by now. Economic crisis, budget cuts, all that. Chilton Mead never produced much that was of practical application to the military, mostly a string of duds, misfires and own goals and, since it wasn't too costly to run, that would have made it an easy target in a savings drive. Much less controversial to close a facility that receives a few million quid per year in funding than one that receives tens or even hundreds of millions. Especially when it isn't producing appreciable results. So by all means go looking for it if you wish. I doubt you'll find it. They've probably removed the fence, razed the above-ground structures, scoured the endless levels of basement of all reusable material, then dynamited the site and filled in the hole. There'll be nothing there except a rough patch of earth, maybe a mound like a tumulus or barrow, hiding an empty grave. A burial place for mad dreams."

"Why would we *want* to find it?" Adam wanted to know.

Purbeck shrugged. "Curiosity? You're better off not trying,

though, take it from me. Just in case it still exists." He took a pull on his ale. "So, when I was there – this was back in the late 'nineties – there was lots going on. Busy little hive, Chilton Mead was. Buzzing with scientists, and presided over by an army officer queen."

"Don't ask, don't tell," I remarked.

"Metaphorical queen," said Purbeck. "Colonel Nutter, the unfortunate fellow's name was. A prophetic name too. He wound up insane, consigned to the booby hatch, whether as a result of accidental exposure to an experiment gone wrong or simply too much time spent in the company of deranged eggheads, I don't know. This Nutter, back before that, when he was more or less sane, phoned me up out of the blue one day and invited me to come to Chilton Mead in a consulting capacity. I have some expertise in the realm of far-out science, where cutting edge meets off-the-wall, and the colonel wanted to tap it. In essence, he wanted me to audit the many different forms of research that were going on under his aegis and decide which had potential and which were on a hiding to nothing. Then he would be able to concentrate everyone's attention on the areas likely to bear fruit and discard the fallow yields, and thus increase the chances of obtaining something useful to show to his paymasters. The colonel was a desperate man. Chilton Mead was a career cul de sac and, having been stuck there for years, he was keen to be provided with treasure with which he could buy his way out.

"I set to work. First I waded through reams of paperwork, test results and the like, sorting wheat from chaff. Chilton Mead specialised in weapons, but not the conventional kind. It created things that could subtly destabilise our opponents, make it impossible for them to function in a theatre of war, and thwart their efforts to spy on us. But not missiles or guns or electronic countermeasures, nothing so crude. Abstract, scalpel-like devices that could finely and surgically achieve the desired effect, with minimal loss of life.

"To give you an example, one professor was working on a

graffito that could engender insanity in whoever looked at it – a tin-pot dictator, say, some Third World tyrant causing his populace untold misery. The graffito need only be spray-painted on a wall near the victim's home, where he would see it every day, and eventually its peculiar, distinctive shape would embed itself in his thought processes and develop into an obsession. He would fancy he saw it everywhere and that it was somehow a cryptic message intended just for him, from some otherworldly entity perhaps. Debilitating loss of faculties would then inevitably ensue."

"How very Lovecraftian," Adam observed. "Or is it Langfordian?"

"To give another example," Purbeck said, ignoring the interruption, "a selection of pop-hit songwriters had been assembled and tasked with coming up with a phrase of music which would lodge in the minds of all who heard it, remorselessly, indelibly. The purpose was twofold. The phrase could either be deployed on enemy forces, to sow confusion and lessen combat effectiveness, or under different conditions used on our own forces, to reinforce the comradely bond and create an army of semi-hypnotised soldiers, all marching fearlessly in lock step, nodding along to a unifying tune."

"Zombie iPod shock troops," said Roger, and Eric sniggered.

"Then there was the Fatal Philology department," said Purbeck, "where they were attempting to isolate a word that could kill. You know the saying about sticks and stones? Here were people doing their utmost to prove that words were far from harmless. If you think how bad some insults make you feel and how offensive certain pejorative terms are to certain religious communities and ethnic minorities, then surely a distillate of all those words – verbal hatred refined to the nth degree – might prove lethal. They did in fact succeed in inventing a single monosyllable that could induce instant death by brain haemorrhage in the hearer and the beholder. The only problem was, no one could actually say it out loud or write it down without dire consequences for himself. It was, quite literally, unrepeatable."

"Well," I said, "it's good to know that our taxes aren't going to waste."

"Who are you kidding?" Eric retorted. "You and I are full-time writers. We don't earn enough to pay tax."

"Come the revolution," said Adam, "there'll be no taxes at all. Instead, the workers will be invited to make voluntary contributions towards a central fund, each according to his means, and –"

"Adam," said Roger, "I think you're due to see me for your annual check-up shortly, aren't you? There's that upper left molar I'm rather concerned about. Particularly tricky to drill into, upper molars..."

That shut our resident Trotsky up more effectively than any ice pick.

"Over the course of several weeks," Purbeck resumed, "I gave Chilton Mead a thoroughgoing, head-to-toe health assessment. I visited each and every laboratory on the premises. I observed countless experiments in progress, and was forced to witness the sometimes terrible fates of the subjects of those experiments. At Chilton Mead, after all, there was no way that testing could be carried out on mice or even primates. Lower species of mammals were no use. Only humans would suffice, and none of them was a willing volunteer, either. Prisoners – persistent offenders, guilty of the worst crimes – were press-ganged into submitting to the not so tender mercies of the scientists. Tramps were kidnapped off the streets and 'conscripted'. Sink estates were trawled for tearaway youths. Society's undesirables were spirited away to become lab rats, and not all of them emerged unscathed or even alive. In that respect, I suppose I could consider myself lucky."

"What did happen to you?" I asked.

"Here we get to the nub of it," said Purbeck. "I found

myself one day in the presence of a Professor Wargrave. A sombre surname for a man who was in fact rather bright and chirpy, almost birdlike in his lightness of speech and gesture. Wargrave was developing a debriefing technique that would enable spies and informants to furnish accounts of what they knew or had discovered, in such a way that there would be no self-contradiction and inaccuracy. Military data-gathering is frequently hampered by the unreliability of sources on the ground. If you can't completely trust a witness – and you can't, because memory is a defective implement – then you'll be advancing into a hostile situation of which you have no clear picture, and catastrophe is the likely outcome. If, on the other hand, your intel is faultless and delivered to you in a readily appreciable form, the benefits are obvious.

"And what better form is there for imparting and taking in facts than a story? See, I told you this would be of personal interest to you. You are creators of fiction, and this is, at heart, all about stories.

"What Wargrave had done was fashion a substance that would compel anybody exposed to it to relate an utterly honest and complete account of any event or scene their interrogator requested."

"Like a truth serum, you mean?" said Eric.

"Similar but so much more. This was no mere chemical concoction. This was a biological agent harvested from the DNA of some of the greatest novelists and poets alive. Samples had been covertly collected from hotel rooms around the world – hairs, saliva, sweat, blood – and screened and evaluated, and the relevant bits of genetic code had been snipped out and inserted into the genome of a virus, and that tiny organism, a germ not unrelated to the one that causes the common cold, had duly replicated itself and was now the vector for Wargrave's agent."

"You think there's any of *us* in that bug?" I wondered.

"I would guess they gave the four of us a wide berth," said Eric. "Probably the whole science fiction community, come to think of it."

"But authors tell lies," Roger said to Purbeck, reasonably. "What is a work of fiction but a lengthy and elaborate tall tale? We trade in make-believe. So why would this Wargrave use authors' DNA if what he was after was a means of extracting the unvarnished truth?"

"Ah," said Adam, "but isn't fiction actually just a vehicle to convey fundamental truths, the facts of life decked out in narrative form? The medium may be an artificial construct but the message it conveys is pure."

Purbeck let us debate the issue for a few moments, until we reached the conclusion that, in principle at least, what he was claiming was acceptable, perhaps even plausible.

"And then there was a mishap," he said. "There's always, it seems, a mishap at Chilton Mead. It's par for the course. And who do you think was standing there when Professor Wargrave – quick-moving, as I said, but also clumsy – dropped the cylinder which held his agent in aerosolised form? Who was sprayed with the agent when the cylinder landed on its nozzle and released a spurt of its contents? Who inhaled microscopic quantities of the agent – trace amounts, but enough to be infected by it?"

"You," I said.

"Me," he confirmed, nodding. "And the upshot is, I have a story to tell, and thanks to that agent I can't stop telling it. No matter where I go, whom I meet, I end up recounting my experiences at Chilton Mead, at the slightest provocation. The Official Secrets Act is meaningless to me. I have no choice. Wargrave's 'story bug' is permanently in my system, and what's in me *must* come out – narratively structured, all irrelevant details omitted, pared to its purest plot and true in every part. I am, like the Ancient Mariner, obliged to buttonhole strangers and tell them my sorry tale. You, gentlemen, have been my Wedding Guests this evening, and I am grateful to you for that, and also apologise. Now, I have detained you for long enough, and I'm sure you'd like to get back to the discussion you were originally having before I forced my attentions on you."

So saying, Purbeck dashed down the rest of his pint, rose stiffly, and made to leave. Just before he went, however, he paused, and a queer, pained look came over his face. This was followed by a tremendous sneeze which almost perforated my right eardrum and which his cupped hand failed to confine fully. A small amount of dampness sprinkled my cheek, and I fixed him with a dirty look, which Purbeck was oblivious to as he was already making a beeline for the exit.

After that the four of us were silent for a time, while our colleagues beside us jabbered on.

Then Adam, jerking a thumb towards Purbeck's table and empty, froth-marbled glass, said, "So, what do we reckon?"

"Barking," I said.

"Fibber," said Roger.

"Lonely and a bit sad," said Eric.

"He managed to scam a drink out of us, though," Adam said. "Respect to him for that."

With that, we dismissed Purbeck and his weird little anecdote and resumed our banter until chucking-out time came round and we were back on the streets of London. Goodbyes were said and I made my way hurriedly towards Victoria in order to catch the last train home.

As the carriages sauntered southwards through the dark I had leisure to ponder Henry Purbeck again. Idly I hoped that, if his tale was true and he *had* contracted some kind of storytelling bug, it wasn't communicable – especially by sneezing.

At East Croydon several passengers got on, including a woollen-wrapped, grey-haired granny who took the seat opposite me. She fired me a brief, friendly smile, then opened up her Sudoku book.

Just as she was applying pencil to grid, I was overcome by a sudden and at the time inexplicable urge. I tapped her on the knee and said, "Excuse me, ma'am. I can't help noticing you're doing Sudoku."

"Ye-e-es," she said, still friendly, but wary.

"Well, here's a puzzle for you. Would you like to hear it?"

Her nod was even warier, but it was all the encouragement I needed.

"Let me know what you think," I said. "Tonight, you see, this old chap in the pub told me a story. It went like this..."

And before I knew it, I was giving her a full report of our encounter with Henry Purbeck and his misfortune at Chilton Mead. I used all my narrative skills, such as they are, to make it interesting. I streamlined the storyline, in order to make sure I didn't lose her attention. I provided thumbnail sketches of the main characters, dropped in some foreshadowing, and even quoted dialogue as though it were in inverted commas, complete with said-bookisms. I built to a dénouement, and when I was finished I sat back feeling both relieved and somewhat surprised at myself. I'm simply not the sort to strike up a conversation with complete strangers, and certainly not to spin them a reasonably lengthy yarn.

Or at least, I *wasn't*. I didn't use to be.

The horror crept slowly through me. As the old woman, who'd patiently heard me out, returned her attention to her Sudoku, I felt a terrible dread stirring, and I couldn't stamp it down or rationalise it out of existence.

Had I caught the bug? Had Henry Purbeck infected me?

If so, how many more times would I be compelled to tell the story of him? How long for? For ever? And who to?

To everyone I might meet?

To everyone I know?

To you?

No sooner had our guest voiced those final, chilling syllables, than the not-inconsiderable form of Brian Dalton loomed above us, having just arrived.

"Hello, guys, you're early aren't you?"

Crown Baker appeared hot on his heels with Jocelyn in tow

— a forensic chemist he'd recently introduced to the group. "Who's for a drink then?"

Our guest took the opportunity to say his goodbyes. I invited him to stay on and join us for the evening, certain that the group would make him welcome, but he refused, claiming a prior engagement.

The best part of an hour passed before I was able to catch Eric more or less alone and ask, "What did you make of all that, then?"

"I really don't know," was his reply. "He didn't sneeze on you, did he?

"No," I said.

"Thank God for that."

"And Weep Like A|exander"

Neil Gaiman

The little man hurried into the Fountain and ordered a very large whisky. "Because," he announced to the pub in general, "I deserve it."

He looked exhausted, sweaty and rumpled, as if he had not slept in several days. He wore a tie, but it was so loose as to be almost undone. He had greying hair that might once have been ginger.

"I'm sure you do," said Brian Dalton.

"I do!" said the man. He took a sip of the whisky as if to find out if he liked it, then, satisfied, gulped down half the glass. He stood completely still, for a moment, like a statue. "Listen," he said. "Can you hear it?"

"What?" I said.

"A sort of background whispering white noise that actually becomes whatever song you wish to hear when you sort of half-concentrate upon it?"

I listened. "No," I said.

"Exactly," said the man, extraordinarily pleased with himself. "Isn't it *wonderful?* Only yesterday, everybody in the Fountain was complaining about the Wispamuzak. Professor Mackintosh here was grumbling about having Queen's "Bohemian Rhapsody" stuck in his head and how it was now following him across London. Today, it's gone, as if it had never been. None of you can even remember that it existed. And that is all due to me."

"I what?" said Professor Mackintosh. "Something about the Queen?" And then, "Do I know you?"

"We've met," said the little man. "But people forget me, alas. It is because of my job." He took out his wallet, produced a card, passed it to me.

Obediah Polkinghorn

it read, and beneath that in small letters,

UNINVENTOR.

"If you don't mind my asking," I said. "What's an uninventor?"

"It's somebody who uninvents things," he said. He raised his glass, which was quite empty. "Ah. Excuse me, Sally, I need another very large whisky."

The rest of the crowd there that evening seemed to have decided that the man was both mad and uninteresting. They had returned to their conversations. I, on the other hand, was caught. "So," I said, resigning myself to my conversational fate. "Have you been an uninventor long?"

"Since I was fairly young," he said. "I started uninventing when I was eighteen. Have you never wondered why we do not have jet-packs?"

I had, actually.

"Saw a bit on Tomorrow's World about them, when I was a lad," said Michael, the landlord. "Man went up in one. Then he came down. Raymond Burr seemed to think we'd all have them soon enough."

"Ah, but we don't," said Obediah Polkinghorn, "because I uninvented them about twenty years ago. I had to. They were driving everybody mad. I mean, they seemed so attractive, and so cheap, but you just had to have a few thousand bored teenagers strapping them on, zooming all over the place, hovering outside bedroom windows, crashing into the flying cars..."

"Hold on," said Sally. "There aren't any flying cars."

"True," said the little man, "But there were. You wouldn't

84

believe the traffic jams they'd cause. You'd look up and it was just the bottoms of bloody flying cars from horizon to horizon. Some days I couldn't see the skies at all. People throwing rubbish out of their car windows... They were easy to run – ran off gravitosolar power, obviously – but I didn't realise that they needed to go until I heard a lady talking about them on Radio Four, all 'Why Oh Why Didn't We Stick With Non-Flying Cars?' She had a point. Something needed to be done. I uninvented them. I made a list of inventions the world would be better off without and, one by one, I uninvented them all."

By now he had started to gather a small audience. I was pleased I'd grabbed a good seat.

"It was a lot of work, too," he continued. "You see, it's almost impossible *not* to invent the Flying Car, as soon as you've invented the Lumenbubble. So eventually I had to uninvent that too. And I miss the individual Lumenbubble: a massless portable light-source that floated half a metre above your head and went on when you wanted it to. Such a wonderful invention. Still, no use crying over unspilt milk, and you can't mend an omelette without unbreaking a few eggs."

"You also can't expect us actually to believe any of this," said someone, and I think it was Jocelyn.

"Right," said Brian. "I mean, next thing you'll be telling us that you uninvented the space ship."

"But I did," said Obediah Polkinghorn. He seemed extremely pleased with himself. "Twice. I had to. You see, the moment we whizz off into space and head out to the planets and beyond, we bump into things that spur so many other inventions. The Polaroid Instant Transporter. That was the worst. And the Mockett Telepathic Translator. That was the worst as well. But as long as it's nothing worse than a rocket to the moon, I can keep everything under control."

"So, how exactly do you go about uninventing things?" I asked.

"It's hard," he admitted. "It's all about unpicking probability threads from the fabric of creation. But they tend to be long and tangled, like spaghetti. So it's rather like having to unpick a strand of spaghetti from a haystack."

"Sounds like thirsty work," said Michael, and I signalled him to pour me another pint of Old Bodger.

"Fiddly," said the little man. "Yes. But I pride myself on doing good. Each day I wake, and, even if I've unhappened something that might have been wonderful, I think, Obediah Polkington, the world is a happier place because of something that you've uninvented."

He looked into his remaining scotch, swirled the liquid around in his glass.

"The trouble is," he said, "with the Wispamuzak gone, that's it. I'm done. It's all been uninvented. There are no more horizons left to undiscover, no more mountains left to unclimb."

"Nuclear Power?" suggested 'Tweet' Peston.

"Before my time," said Obediah. "Can't uninvent things invented before I was born. Otherwise I might uninvent something that would have led to my birth, and then where would we be?" Nobody had any suggestions. "Knee-high in jet-packs and flying cars, that's where," he told us. "Not to mention Morrison's Martian Emolument." For a moment, he looked quite grim. "Ooh. That stuff was nasty. And a cure for cancer. But frankly, given what it did to the oceans, I'd rather have the cancer.

"No. I have uninvented everything that was on my list. I shall go home," said Obediah Polkinghorn, bravely, "and weep, like Alexander, because there are no more worlds to unconquer. What is there left to uninvent?"

There was silence in the Fountain.

In the silence, Brian's iPhone rang. His ring-tone was The Rutles singing 'Cheese and Onions'. "Yeah?" he said. Then, "I'll call you back."

It is unfortunate that the pulling out of one phone can have such an effect on other people around. Sometimes I think it's because we remember when we could smoke in pubs, and that we pull out our phones together as once we pulled out our cigarette packets. But probably it's because we're easily bored.

Whatever the reason, the phones came out.

Crown Baker took a photo of us all, and then Twitpicced it. Jocelyn started to read her text messages. Tweet Peston tweeted that he was in the Fountain and had met his first uninventor. Professor Mackintosh checked the Test Match scores, told us what they were and emailed his brother in Inverness to grumble about them. The phones were out and the conversation was over.

"What's that?" asked Obediah Polkinghorn.

"It's the iPhone 5," said Ray Arnold, holding his up. "Crown's using the Nexus X. That's the Android system. Phones. Internet. Camera. Music. But it's the apps. I mean, do you know, there are over a thousand fart sound-effect apps on the iPhone alone? You want to hear the unofficial Simpsons Fart App?"

"No," said Obediah. "I most definitely do not want to. I do *not*." He put down his drink, unfinished. Pulled his tie up. Did up his coat. "It's not going to be easy," he said, as if to himself. "But, for the good of all..." And then he stopped. And he grinned. "It's been marvellous talking to you all," he announced to nobody in particular as he left the Fountain.

The Ghost in the Machine

Colin Bruce

"I knew a man who built a mind-reading machine that really worked," said Eric thoughtfully.

We all looked at him. Jocelyn, who had been in full flow about the uselessness of brain scanners in courtrooms, gave a loud snort.

"What's more," Eric continued unabashed, "the basis was so simple, I can describe how to make one in five minutes. And if you can sincerely tell me it wouldn't work, *I'll buy you all a drink.*"

Never in the Fountain have I heard such a pin-drop silence fall so fast. It wasn't so much the prospect of a free pint (though one or two of us who happened to have full glasses started sipping them quickly and inconspicuously) as the shock factor. It was the most unexpected statement I've ever heard in that pub, and that's saying something. If a tourist had wandered in from the street at that moment, he might have thought he'd taken a wrong turn and found himself among Madame Tussaud's waxworks.

"There was this chap in my doctoral year who had two obsessive interests – well, three really, but the third went unfulfilled. The first two were conjuring tricks and computers. The third would have been girls, but his lack of success on that front rather followed from the first two.

"But at the first two he was good. You know the old trick where somebody hides an object (with the conjurer out of the room, obviously) and the conjurer takes someone's wrist and forces them to guide him to it 'telepathically'? What he's really doing is feeling your pulse: the closer you get, the more you tense up and the faster your pulse beats, it's quite hard to suppress. The technique was invented long before the lie detector, but it works just as well, especially if the conjurer has a good line of patter that makes the subject just a little bit nervous, and Cedric was good at that.

"He was also a whiz at computer programming. However, on the third front, there was one particular girl he fancied, who unfortunately was profoundly uninterested in either conjuring or computing. He would have remained her wistful admirer from afar, had she not had the misfortune to be mugged one evening. One of those less than subtle crimes, some thug who just grabbed her handbag and ran, not even trying to hide his face.

"We took Alicia out for a drink to console her, and she described a futile hour spent at the police station trying to reproduce the attacker with that photofit system they use, where you pick out the right eyebrows and nose and mouth and so on and put them together. It rarely produces anything useful, unless the victim happens to be a professional portrait painter with a photographic memory.

"As she described the process, Cedric got a thoughtful look in his eye. It was only a couple of days later that he hammered on my door, in remarkable contrast to his usual diffidence, and practically dragged me across the corridor to see a computer program he had written.

"I was deeply unimpressed when I first saw the screen. It held an incredibly crude cartoon of a face, the kind of thing a five-year-old might have drawn, but Cedric insisted on sitting me down and fastening something to my wrist. I'm sure it was one of those medical gizmos you can get quite cheaply from a catalogue, probably a pulse counter with a couple of electrodes to measure your skin conductivity to see if you're sweating, a so called stress monitor.

"'Tell me,' said Cedric very seriously, 'which person in the world are you most afraid of?'"

"I had no hesitation. At that time it was unquestionably Professor Walsh. A tyrannical old don who would probably not be allowed to teach undergraduates nowadays – someone would sue him for post-traumatic stress disorder, with considerable justification. He would regularly reduce students to tears with his sarcastic questions: in a couple of sentences humiliate you in front of your classmates, destroy your self-confidence, make you wish you could just crawl into a hole and die quietly. Cedric also attended his classes, and seemed unsurprised by my choice.

"'Close your eyes, please,' he said. 'Now, imagine that you're sitting in his lecture theatre, with everyone in the world whose good opinion you value there in the audience. You know you should understand what he's saying, it sounds easy, but somehow you can't quite grasp it. Then he asks a question, you've no idea what the answer is, you've got to hope he doesn't pick on you, doesn't see you. Now' – his voice became subtly menacing – 'open your eyes and look at the screen.'

"I looked. The face on the screen was writhing in a nauseating manner. It quickly became more like a human face, but blurred, as if a veil were in front of it, melding rapidly from one shape to another, the features gradually becoming more stable. Then the face became three dimensional, turned to left and right; the eyes seemed to look about - and suddenly the veil disappeared, and Professor Walsh was looking right out at me, his mouth twisted in contempt. I actually jumped in my seat.

"That's a neat trick!" I admitted. "Was that from last week's lecture? Brave to bring your camera into the theatre without him spotting you, I know how furious he gets if he thinks anyone's messing about with gadgets while he's talking"

"Cedric shook his head. 'I promise you, I've never taken such a photograph,' he said seriously. 'And that wasn't off the Internet, either. You did this all by yourself, just tensing up whenever the picture looked more like him, and relaxing whenever it got less good.'

"Come on, Cedric-"

"'Okay, I might have guessed you would pick Professor Walsh. So think back into the past, before I knew you. Who were you most afraid of when you were, say, eight?'

"Within seconds, the program had run again, and Mrs Morgan, the most intimidating teacher at my primary school, was staring out at me. It took several more runs to convince me, but when we got to age fourteen, and Joanna's face materialised, I was convinced. I'd never let on to *anyone* what a crush I had on her, and how terrified I'd been at the prospect of talking to her, which I never got up the nerve to do. Cedric couldn't possibly have known that!

"Cedric, this is seriously good stuff," I told him. "Get yourself down to the Patent Office, then to Scotland Yard. I'll help you with the sales pitch.

"I was already wondering what it would be like to be one of those Internet start-up millionaires. But Cedric wouldn't listen. What he wanted me to do first was persuade Alicia to come and try the machine. He knew she thought he was creepy, and wouldn't accept an invitation direct from him.

"And so we discovered the machine's great limitation. It needed a subject with good mental self-discipline, who could focus their mind to an exceptional degree."

Eric smiled modestly. "I'm sure you can see why *I* didn't have any trouble. But it only produced the desired result with about one person in four – and that was among us graduate students, obviously far better mental subjects than the general population."

He ignored several heavy coughs.

"In Alicia's case, a very common problem occurred. It drew a face quickly enough – but one that was recognisably Cedric's! The most immediate threat in her mind was not the mugger, but the alarmingly intense fellow-student who had wired her up to his strange device. In a way I can't blame her, Cedric did look a bit deranged at the best of times.

"We proceeded to try it on the rest of our year. They were

quite impressed, always conceding that the face drawn triggered some deep emotion in them, even if they couldn't recognise it as a specific person. It really did feel as if the machine were dipping into their subconscious: an eerie experience. But that was the only consistent feature. Even when it did draw the intended person, it tended to produce a sort of impressionistic or montage version, more like a skilled cartoonist or portrait painter's work than a standard photograph. Interesting, but hardly what was needed for a police line-up.

"The idea seemed destined for that great scrap heap of inventions which sort-of-work, but not quite well enough to be useful. However, word got around, and out of the blue Cedric got his first client: a Jesuit priest. He expressed intense scientific curiosity – the Jesuits have been famous for that for centuries, of course – and wanted to see the machine demonstrated on a subject of his choice. In due course an appointment was arranged, and Father Jules turned up with a young man who he said would be an ideal subject, who we afterwards discovered was his curate.

"Father Jules insisted that he should be responsible for explaining the machine to the subject, the crucial patter to focus the man's mind on the desired target. If only we had known what he had in mind! But really, how could we have guessed? When all was ready, Father Jules bent down and spoke in his curate's ear in a threatening tone.

"'This is a wonderful machine, Anthony. You have heard how scientists have traced the areas of the brain responsible for religious experience, conscience, and much else? This device can look deep into your soul. I have put you forward for the priesthood. I believe that you are the sincere young man you seem to be. But always in such decisions I am haunted by doubts. I am human and fallible. How many times have I been wrong? Now there is a way to know for certain.

"'Look at the screen, Anthony. If your soul is pure you have nothing to fear, the machine will pluck from your mind the image of the face of God. But if you are seeking the priesthood for the wrong reasons – perhaps even planning to abuse the trust placed in you – then it is the face of the Devil himself that you will see!'

"The young man stared at the screen, obviously scared. I am sure *we* all think him naïve, but after all we are not priests-in-training, are we? Father Jules stared intently over his shoulder. After a few seconds the expressions of both men started to change, and to become similar. At first I could not be sure whether it was awe, or even ecstasy, that they were experiencing. In a way the extremes of joy and horror are strangely similar. But soon there was no doubt: it was not wonder but fear that clutched at both men, fear turning to an extreme of terror. Father Jules seemed to try to speak, but only a terrible choking noise came from his throat, flecks of saliva on his lips. And the look in both their eyes!

"I was the first to react. I could not reach the computer itself, but I managed to grasp the cable and pull the plug out of its socket. But it was too late. Both men were shuddering, gasping, desperately trying to breathe but without success. And within moments the rest of us became witness to the fact that it is indeed possible to die of fear. The coroner said heart failure, a million-to-one coincidence, but I know what I saw."

Eric paused and sipped his beer regretfully. "It was a tragedy, of course. Yet there is one almost incidental feature I still regret. If only I had been able to reach the switch on the monitor, rather than turning the machine itself off. For now no one will ever know – *what was it they saw?* What does the authentic face of the devil (insofar as such can ever be defined from the point of view of an atheist like myself) actually look like?

"But the image was gone forever, and so the next day was Cedric. He had quit his studies, and taken all copies of his unexpectedly powerful program with him."

There was a long silence before someone said: "I suppose overcome by remorse he destroyed the program, and never returned to the field of computing."

Eric frowned. "You know, that is exactly what I assumed myself, until a few weeks ago.

"I had gone down to the country to visit my aunt for a few days. A duty her nephews and nieces share conscientiously. Finding her conversation on the exclusive subjects of birth, death and spiritualism a trifle tedious, I was relieved to hear that on Sunday a fête was being held on the village green. Not my usual entertainment, but at least a couple of hours distraction.

"There was the usual skittles and tombola and so forth, but my eye was drawn to one particular tent outside which a queue of young girls, some of them remarkably pretty, had formed. I asked the nearest, purely out of curiosity of course, what was to be found inside?

"She giggled. 'It's this amazing machine, sir. My friends have tried it already. The man wires you up to a computer and sits you before it. And in a little while, a veil parts and you see the face of your perfect mate, the man you subconsciously want to marry.' She giggled again. 'Or the man you want to do something with, anyway,' she said saucily.

"Now it may seem quite a leap for me to have thought that it must be Cedric and his machine in there. But you see, I had jokingly suggested this very application to him as a fall-back, reckoning that in the throes of romantic desire, young women would queue up to use the machine even if it turned out not to work!

"I would have gone on into the tent to verify my suspicions, but moments later my aunt suffered one of her turns – I believe she had received an unfortunate tarot reading – and I never had a chance to follow the matter up. I don't mind telling you that it rests considerably on my conscience."

Dr Steve shrugged. "Surely a fairly harmless deception, no worse than palm-reading and the like?"

"Oh, it's not the deception angle," said Eric sourly. "It's the thought that quite often the machine will inevitably draw some kind of artist's impression of Cedric himself. Not a photographic likeness of course, and not every time – the girls would hardly fall for that. No doubt sometimes the machine even performs as advertised, but I suspect that quite frequently when one of the girls later sees Cedric outside his tent in the sunlight, having already consciously forgotten his rather forgettable features, she may well be struck by a deep intuitive conviction that here is the man she subconsciously desires. And be most vulnerable to being taken advantage of!"

There was a gob-smacked silence as we contemplated the thought of Cedric spending his days always upon some sunny village green, with always a queue of attractive young ladies queuing up for his attention. All this to the rustle of ten-pound notes which the taxman need never be bothered about. While we, infinitely his betters, slaved away at our keyboards and taught Physics 101 to freshmen. I think it's fair to say the bile rose in our throats. But Crown Baker – it would be Crown, of course! – was thinking on more constructive lines.

"Shocking!" he said. "And of course we should really feel sorry for Cedric, deprived of his true intellectual fulfilment by the temptation of more, er, immediate rewards. But tell us more about his program. I'm inclined to think that with just a few more clues it could be reconstructed quite easily. I'm sure I have read in some reputable context that thirty or so parameters are sufficient to describe the human face very adequately. I suppose the program used a genetic algorithm, to hunt through the space of all possible faces efficiently?"

Everyone leaned forward. Apparently, we were all keen to improve our knowledge of algorithms.

Eric shook his head firmly. "I really don't remember the details. But frankly, it should take any competent programmer just a few days' hard work to get on the right track, using what I've already told you."

Alas, as so often in the Fountain, the words 'hard work' acted as a kind of counter-spell. Moments later our little group had shrunk, and Bogna behind the bar was (as usual) the only person there you would possibly have associated with the concept. But to this day I can't help wondering whether for once – and quite irrespective of whether his story had been even faintly true – the device Eric described would actually work, should you feel inclined to build one.

A Bird In Hand

Charles Stross

Perhaps you've gathered the impression from my colleagues' stories that our little social group that meets at the Fountain is, shall we say, a trifle stuffy, and excessively interested in the nuts and bolts mechanics of space flight, astrophysics, and the like. Not to say oestrogen-deficient. Well, you'd be mostly right – but not entirely so.

As it happens, we harbour a secret cabal of biologists, geneticists and paleontologists. There is the formidable Laura Fowler – a poster-child for nominative determinism, running her very own research group in avian phylogenetic taxonomy. There's Graham O'Donnell, who spends most of his time bossing servers around these days – he's a secret master of bioperl ninjutsu – and whose hobby is updating his tick-list, kept in a remarkably dog-eared copy of the *Good Beer Guide*. (Rumour has it that in his spare time he's working on an evolutionary taxonomy of brewer's yeast strains...) And there's Bogna, although precisely which area of the biological sciences she worked in before hearing the call of the hand pump remains a closely guarded secret to most.

And there are the single Tuesday polymorphisms (as the geneticists call them) who turn up for a single session then disappear again. Like Kayla Martinez, a skinny blonde with the pallid complexion of the post-doc researcher who has gone too long without exposure to sunshine, whom Prof Laura brought along one evening.

"For God's sake don't risk the ploughman's," Laura warned her new protégée: "the cheese is unpasteurized and as for the pickle, Graham's sure it's recycled from an experimental growth medium for GFAJ-1 –"

"GFA-what?" chirped up Prof Mackintosh, looking mildly dyspeptic.

"The arsenic-tolerant extremophile from Lake Mono." Graham twitched slightly and peered at his nail beds. "You can never be too sure."

"Have new lunch," volunteered Bogna: "duck liver pâté and salad."

"That sounds interesting!" Laura paused. "What is it?" She asked with evident concern; for our new visitor, Kayla, had turned even more pale than before.

"*Duck*!" Spat Kayla. "Oh God!" She raised her glass and chugged back a good solid mouthful of the Old Stoatmangler that Dr Steve had placed in front of her, presumably to help with her anaemia. "Duck!" She hiccupped. "M'sorry." She covered her mouth.

"Duck?" Laura looked puzzled. "I thought you liked the Anatidae? Wasn't your thesis on –"

"The role of short interfering RNA sequences in controlling POU transcription factor expression in <u>Cairina moschata</u>." Her face wrinkled in an expression of infinite disgust. "Not actually a member of the Anatidae, but close enough for government work."

"Anatidae?" Prof Mackintosh echoed. "Would someone care to translate?"

"*Ducks*," the Raven volunteered sepulchrally, eliciting another shudder from our delicate visitor. "Isn't Cairina moschata the Muscovy duck?"

"Yes, yes it is," said Laura. "And Kayla here knows more about what goes on during the first four days inside a Muscovy's shell than just about anyone else on the planet." She turned concerned eyes on her protégée. "What happened? Was it something to do with that Kansas fellowship you took?"

Kayla nodded mutely. "Oh God," she mumbled. "*Ducks*."

The word seemed to resonate with horror for her. "I'm going to have to find a new area," she added disconsolately. "I just can't face them any more, after what happened. I mean, I've got full-blown ornithophobia. Panic attacks, cold sweats, the lot." She pulled a wadded-up tissue from the sleeve of her cardigan and honked mournfully into it. "I can't even face down a piece of pâté: too many bad associations. I know it's irrational, but..." She trailed off. There was a faint mutter of *she's clearly quackers* from over the hubbub of the bar, but nobody showed any sign of noticing it.

"The contract didn't renew?" asked Laura. "And you're back here now -- are you applying for any posts?"

Kayla shrugged. "I'm trying to catch my breath. Thinking about what to do next. Maybe move sideways into mammalia..."

"What about dinosaurs?" Dr Steve asked brightly: "I hear there's a lot of money in trying to breed — did I say something wrong?"

He trailed off, staring after Kayla's trail — for he'd barely started on this fertile line of enquiry when our visitor departed at high speed in the direction of the Ladies, hand clutched over her mouth.

"Birds are a specialized sub-group of theropod dinosaurs," Laura said slowly. She turned and stared at Dr Steve with narrowed eyes. "The one remaining family of dinosauria that didn't go extinct at the end of the Cretaceous. Did you *mean* to trigger her phobia or did you just let it slip out by accident?"

"Birds? Are *dinosaurs*?" Steve looked genuinely perplexed. "Are you kidding me?"

Prof Mackintosh rolled his eyes. "Even *I'd* heard of that!" he announced. "There was something in the comics about it just the other week — Tyrannosaurus rex apparently had feathers, did you know that? And it laid eggs. Probably quacked like a duck, too." He prodded the brick of pinkish paste balanced on the edge of his plate. "I wonder what a pâté de foie Tyrannosaur would taste like?"

"Don't," advised Prof Laura, her eyes tracking towards the flight path to the Ladies loo. "I suspect she could tell you a story or two."

"Why Kansas?" Graham chipped in. "I thought it was overrun by fundy nutters of the evolution-denying persuasion?"

"Excuse me." It was Kayla. Somehow she'd returned from her hurried nose-powdering excursion without taking the obvious route back from the lav: she looked pale but determined. "I really ought to be able to handle it better, I'm afraid. I'm sorry, everyone."

"Sorry for what?" Asked Dr Steve.

Kayla sighed. "It all started with the Demon Duck of Doom and the American televangelist." She paused to wet her whistle: "Not many people know this, but back in the middle Miocene, the Australian outback was home to a gruesome predator. The current thinking is that modern neornithines survived the K-T event – the great extinction that killed off their cousins, the dinosaurs – because they were small flyers. They could breed fast and fly long distances to scavenge for food while the food chain the big cousins depended on collapsed in disarray for decades or centuries. But in the millions of years afterwards, they radiated; new lines appeared, including big, flightless birds. Like *Bullockornis*. Think of a duck that stands two to three metres tall, weighs a quarter of a ton – about the same as a male African lion – and has a beak like an axe-blade. *Bullockornis* was a predator, a giant flesh-eating *duckckck*." She made a choking noise with the final word, and paused to take deep breaths before continuing.

"Frank Kottleman was a preacher-man from Wichita. He was on a revival tour of Australia when he went round a museum in Darwin, of all places, and saw a mounted *Bullockornis* skeleton. It was a 'know thine enemy' scouting expedition; he was looking for chinks in the enemy armour, because Frank was a rock-ribbed young-Earth creationist. And I think *Bullockornis* caught his imagination. Especially the display copy, which described it as the Demon Duck of Doom – it's the sort of thing that sticks in a young child's memory and gets them interested in paleontology, I guess. Frank was one of the trustees of the Kansas Biblical Dinosaur Museum – you've heard of them? Lots of dioramas of Jesus riding a big raptor, Adam and Eve feeding their family from a single Apatosaurus egg, that kind of thing."

"Biblical Dinosaurs," mused Prof Mackintosh: "do you suppose they're kosher? If they've got feathers and beaks –" His mouth shut with an audible *click*, then he glared at the Raven pointedly: "Ouch."

"Excuse me." Kayla swiftly necked the remains of her beer. "Oh god, the memories." She held her glass up.

Such signalling is stock in trade among the thirsty post-doc: Bogna had it out of her hand in a split second, before plonking down the pot of Puddles' Old Mouthwash IPA that Graham had sportingly paid for while she was holding forth on the subject of giant flesh-eating Australians. "Aha," she said appreciatively, taking a mouthful. A moment later her lips crinkled appropriately. "Where was I?

"I didn't know this back then. All I knew was that I was an unemployed post-doc, and then this letter arrived inviting me to a job interview in Kansas, with a business-class return attached. It was pitched from an outfit called Witchita Taxonomics, who keep a very low profile and mostly look – from the outside – like a biotech company. And nobody at the interview asked me anything about evolution," she said, a trifle defensively. "I was really pissed off when I got there and found out who WT was mostly working for, but by then it was too late. And I needed something to do before the next round of research funding back home."

"Would you like to tell everyone what the job was about?" Laura prompted.

"Oh, all right. Kottleman and his fellow creationists aren't totally stupid. They run this bible museum with animatronic Ceratopsians, but they know it's not going to convince everybody that they're right. What they *really* want to do is to show *real* dinosaurs living cheek-by-jowl with human beings – and to bring their dinosaurs to life without any need for evolution. If, they reason, you can transform a bird into a dinosaur by epigenetic phenotypic modulation – by controlling which developmental genes are expressed and in what sequence, rather than by crudely hacking new genes into the thing – then they think they've got a disproof of Godless Darwinism to point to, as well as a really cool (hence profitable) museum exhibit." She paused.

Dr Steve was looking a trifle vacant, his jaw adrift in full-on flycatcher mode. "Whut?"

"They don't understand evolution *or* genetics," she said, a trifle crossly. "They're hung up over a book published in the 1860s – they haven't got a *clue* about the state of genomics today, they just know they don't hold with it. And the only model they've got is as obsolete as classical Newtonian physics. No, worse."

"Would you care to explain?" asked Prof Mackintosh. "What obsolete model are they using?"

Kayla paused for a moment, then launched into her explanation: "Back in the 1940s, when Franklin, Gosling, Watson and Crick worked out the structure of DNA, the general layperson's understanding was that the genome was like a construction blueprint for a cell; that each base pair corresponds to an amino acid at some sequential point in a protein molecule's polymer chain. But that's actually wrong. A bit later, we discovered introns – sequences of 'junk' DNA separating the exons that code for proteins. Much later still, we worked out that the introns are actually a mess of different things, ranging from endogenous retroviruses hitching a ride on our replicators to anchor points for short interfering segments of RNA that control whether a particular gene is switched on or not. And we've got far fewer genes than anyone imagined; only about thirty thousand, rather than the third of a million to million originally posited. Genes are, if I can steal a computing metaphor – well, at first we thought the genome was like a computer program which, executed on the machinery of a cell, would generate another cell and copy itself. But then we realized the genome is actually more like the statically declared data embedded in a *running* program, and a cell is actually the executing state vector of that process. If you look at it, you're seeing a snapshot. All the DNA does is hold the initialization state of a bunch of variables –"

Dr Steve's mouth was a-droop again. "Are you calling my cells a computer?"

"That's an imprecise metaphor." Kayla frowned. There was fire in her eyes and colour was returning to her cheeks. "The point is, the genome is just a bunch of templates for polypeptides. How the genome is expressed – which bits are switched on or off – is the important thing in determining how an organism develops. You can build a whole bunch of different phenotypes – different sets of physical traits -- using the same chromosomal toolbox, just by switching different bits on or off using epigenetic switches. Which is what they wanted me for: to turn a Muscovy Duck into a phenotypic replica of a *Bullockornis*, and to use the *Bullockornis* to incubate the eggs for a T. rex."

Prof Mackintosh: "So you're saying that a duck has all the right genes in place, you just need to express them in the right sequence and it'll grow up into something different but related? If it walks like a duck, and quacks like a duck, it must be a Tyrannosaur..."

"Sort of."

Kayla looked pained but Laura was nodding. "You need to knock out some key developmental genes, and possibly insert a couple of additional ones, but it's like humans and chimpanzees; 99.4% of our genome is identical! What makes the difference is how the gene expression is modulated, the whole epigenetic structure that keeps them coordinated."

Kayla took a long swallow of mouthwash; for a moment she looked as if she was about to gargle and spit, but she swallowed convulsively. "The difference between *Cairina moschata* and a workable phenotypic *Bullockornis* turns out to be less than 0.2% of their genome. We added pathways to express some digestive enzymes looted from the bald eagle, but mostly it was a matter of rearranging the POU transcription sequence -- that's where Wichita Taxonomics comes in. They've developed an expert system for redesigning avian epigenetic modification – given a complete genome sequence and a partial map of the short interfering RNA space for that organism you can turn Bird A's offspring into something resembling Bird B. And most of the time it'll breed true. They made Kottleman and his investors a small fortune by breeding a commercially viable strain that expresses sex-specific pigmented beaks before hatching, which allowed their biggest battery farm customers to deploy computer vision systems in the Texan Turkey-sexing wars; when they hired me, they were pitching for a fat DARPA contract to breed mine-hunting penguins for the US Navy – but they had bigger goals."

She sighed. "I didn't get to work on the cyborg velociraptor program for the USMC. Didn't *want* to, for that matter: bad enough using animals to go after improvised explosive devices, but wiring up their brains... no. However, *Bullockornis* was an interesting intermediate step to what Frank really wanted. Which was a T. rex. Which we delivered."

Dr Steve's mouth flapped, uncharacteristically speechless for a moment. Then he gathered himself with some aplomb. "I don't believe a word of it," he said with stiff dignity. "Fundamentalist theme parks with Tyrannosaurs? They'd never get it past the insurance company. And anyway, we'd have been reading about this in the tabloids! You –" He pointed a shaky finger at Kayla "– are trying to gull us!"

"It's clearly a flap about nothing," Prof Mac added.

Kayla clearly didn't share their love of the pun sublime. But she hadn't come unarmed. Sliding a hand into her bag she flipped a glossy card on the table. It landed face-down, and Graham reached out to flip it rightside up.

"Tyrannosaurs had *feathers*?" Croaked Dr Steve.

"You can see it in the fossil record," Kayla replied sharply.

"*Yes*, Tyrannosaurs *did* have feathers."

"But... magenta? And *pink*?"

"We're not sure about the pigmentation," she admitted. "We've recovered fossilized melanosomes from Sinosauropteryx and other theropods, but the evidence for T. rex is patchy. So we had to take an educated guess." She tapped the picture and the e-ink card came to life: the flanks of the sleeping monster rising and falling slowly as it lay atop an examination table big enough for a small elephant. "This is Janet, our first juvenile. As you can see, they pack on weight fast – from a five kilo hatchling to three hundred kilos of bad tempered biteyness in eleven months – but take a while to mature to reproductive age." She pulled out another e-card. "Here's Brad, our second." She swallowed queasily. "Actually, he was called Sheila when he first hatched. Nobody's too clear about how to sex juvenile Tyrannosaurs, which is why we had the, uh, accident."

"Sexing Tyrannosaurs –" Dr Steve tried hard to regain his grip on the conversation before it slid into surrealism. "Why would you want to do that?"

"Because Kottleman was trying to breed them," Kayla explained. "The current young-Earth creationist theory is that if they can demonstrate something that walks like a Tyrannosaur, quacks like a Tyrannosaur, and breeds true but is actually derived from a present-day duck, then they can plausibly claim that the theropod dinosaurs were simply hit by a viral pandemic during the Fall from Eden and turned into birds overnight, as if by magic." She pulled a face. "That, and the biblical dinosaur show is a huge fund-raiser. But first you've got to get them to breed true."

She drained her glass and held it up. This time it was Prof Mackintosh who shambled tipsily barwards to obtain a pint of Penguin Bitter.

"The trouble with dinosaurs is that nobody knew what the soft tissue arrangement really looks like, and nobody could even guess at their mating behaviour. Birds and lizards don't have a separate vagina and anus, they have a cloacal orifice and the eggs and sperm pass through this – in fact, most male birds don't have a penis; they produce sperm and store it in the seminal glomus, a pouch just inside their rectum. To fertilize a female they need to insert the sperm into her cloaca –"

"Are you telling me that all dinosaurs are *godless sodomites*?" demanded Prof Mac; then in his best high-kirk sermonizing voice, as practiced on countless hordes of bored undergraduates, he added, "and what, pray you, does yon Baptist minister of religion say to *that*, in the name of all that's holy?"

"I think he'd have said that God moves in mysterious ways, especially in the men's room at the leather bar he hung out in on bear nights. Allegedly." Kayla's cheeks were fading back towards their former paleness. "World's worst-kept secret: those ministers of religion who preach loudest and shrillest against teh ghey are probably that way inclined themselves. But yes, sodomy definitely goes together with dinosaurs. Ahem." Another mouthful of beer disappeared into her mouth. "Anyway, we needed to sex our Tyrannosaurs and collect sperm samples. Now, bird testes and ova are internal, and, as I mentioned, most birds don't have penises; even those which do, like the Anatidae, store them internally until they've mounted a female, at which point the organ everts – all but turns itself inside-out – often very fast. The problem we had at the Dinosaur Museum lab was that the reproductive organs are soft tissues, so they're murderously hard to X-ray. Avian penises in particular are usually small and hard to find. Nobody's built an MRI scanner big enough for a half-ton of juvenile raptor, and you can't even sedate the beast and stick your arm up its anus to sex it by palpation – until they've gone through an entire life cycle and we've had a corpse to dissect we won't know enough about Tyrannosaur anatomy to be sure if we'd got it right. All we could go by was comparative blood titres of testosterone and other androgens. Which is how we figured out that Brad was probably male, and should have a sack full of sperm to milk.

"Well." She put her beer down. "We had a meeting about it on the Friday, discussing ways and means. Frank sat in on it – as our customer and the owner of the Museum he had every right to – and I should have realized he was taking notes. *Why don't you stick a shocker up its back passage?* he asked. *That works for most poultry.* Which got us onto some reminiscences from when he was growing up on his dad's farm, where they bred Muscovy Ducks. And then onto some, um, strictly non-professional speculation of an increasingly prurient nature. As you can imagine, Frank was a man of god rather than science; his concern was strictly that we couldn't use male stock in the proposed Jesus rodeo, lest the ladies and wee ones in the audience see something they shouldn't. And he took a startlingly in-depth interest in the topic at hand." She frowned furiously. "That should have tipped me off. But anyway, we agreed to try electrostimulus first, using a stimulator sized for bison. And to sedate Brad on Saturday – they tend to be very docile once you've fed them a twent- kilo turkey loaded with a quarter of a gram of oxazepam – in preparation for the exam the next morning."

She swallowed another mouthful of beer.

"I blame myself," she said softly. "When you're working with lab animals someone has to go in and feed and medicate them every day, clean the cages or animal enclosures in the case of the bigger beasts. It's a lot like running a zoo. So it's a seven days a week operation. I went in to check on Brad on Saturday, and he was fine. A one year old adolescent Tyrannosaur isn't something you'd want to be alone with if he's hungry, but with a turkey in his stomach he's about as docile as a well-fed alligator. Although a lot cuter, with the colourful chick-down just beginning to give way to adult plumage, and the disproportionately big eye orbits – they're not as lizard-like or scary as the movie recreations make out. Baby Tyrannosaurs aren't totally independent; they rely on their mother to bring food to the nest, so for the first couple of months they squeak and hold their mouths wide and jump up and down, flapping their forearms, which are disproportionately big when they're young. I'd taught Brad to sit up and beg, because this made it easier to feed him: you'd lean over the viewing balcony in his stall – which was three storeys high and about the size of a small aircraft hanger, to accommodate adult growth, but as a chick he was lost in it – and drop chunks of cooked turkey right down his throat. Even as an adolescent, all of four metres long from beak-tip to tail, he was pretty hard to find.

"Anyway, when I left on Saturday, Brad was sacked out in his nest, snoring off a Thanksgiving-grade tryptophan binge. Not to mention the Serapax. I filled out his daily worksheet, updated the logbook, and went home for the evening."

She took another long drink, lost in thought.

"When you're running an animal operation there are some things you do and some things you don't do. You don't ever go and work with a big carnivore on your own – anything that weighs more than you, basically. You make sure there's always someone who knows where you are. And there's a key control system to get access to the animal rooms. But the flip side is that, if it's a private institution, nobody's going to say 'no' to one of the directors on an inspection tour. As far as we could establish afterwards, Frank had got a little bit too curious about certain aspects of theropod soft tissue anatomy, and he decided to go down to the lab and see what was on the slab. Doubtless he figured that while Brad was doped up to the nictitating membranes and still weighed less than a Siberian tiger he'd be safe to poke. Not to mention to stroke. Frank had heard about the birds and the bees, but obviously this hadn't entirely satisfied his curiosity: that, or he had decided to trade in his ministry for a place in the Guinness Book of World Records and a permanent seat on the talk show circuit. So he went into Brad's enclosure on his own, some time on Saturday night, wearing nothing but leather chaps and carrying a king-sized bottle of lube and a remote-control vibrator."

She shuddered again.

"Wait a mo." Prof Laura stared at her with an expression of dawning, profound horror. "I thought you said you'd used a *Bullockornis* to produce the eggs? And you'd bred them from *Muscovy Ducks*?"

Kayla nodded.

"What's so bad about Muscovy Ducks?" Asked Dr Steve. "I thought they were good for eating..?"

Prof Laura turned to him. "Better put down your beer, dear." She nodded at Kayla. "Is what's coming what I think it is?"

Kayla nodded again. "Muscovy Ducks are weird even by bird standards. Unlike most aves, they *do* have a penis – two-thirds the length of their body and corkscrew shaped, because Muscovy Duck sex would get any of you gentlemen who tried it life and a minimum twenty-year tariff. Sex among the Muscovy Ducks is a lot like rape, so there's a biological arms race in train – the females have bizarre oviducts with lots of dead ends, to make it harder for the rapists to fertilize them. Because penetration is forceful the males are noted for their rapid, even explosive, eversion – they can go from fully internally retracted to money shot in two hundred milliseconds."

She paused for a few seconds, her gaze turned inward. When she started speaking again, her voice was shaky. "I found them the next morning. Frank and Brad. I called an ambulance, but it was too late. Brad was... we had to shoot him with a sedative dart before we could get the vibrator out. It wasn't pretty. The Kansas animal protection league threatened to sue the Museum into a smoking hole in the ground when the news got as far out as anyone was willing to let it. They're not as big on animal cruelty as we are here in England, but bestiality pushes their buttons. And as for Kottleman's New World Ministry, they wanted nothing to do with it. There was a security CCTV in the stall, but the contractors cheaped on it. Like Muscovy Ducks, a T. rex can go from fully retracted to erect so damn *fast* that it happens between frames. Even a juvenile like Brad – well, when the dildo started to vibrate, Brad reared up. And Frank, standing in front of him, got it in the face – full force, like a boxing glove with Mike Tyson behind it. Brad's erection punched Frank's lights right out. And then Brad did what comes naturally, and ejaculated.

"Which gave rise to an office memo that did the rounds the next morning, and some very bad taste jokes. Starting with, what do you do when you see a Tyrannosaur coming?"

Dr Steve: "Duck?"

"You got it." Kayla paused for another mouthful of beer. "Resulting in the issue of a memorable health and safety memo announcing the discovery of a new hazardous practice which was to be avoided: inhalation of dinosaur semen. Which, ladies'un'gennelmen, is why I am back in the UK and looking for a new research post, and why I confidently predict that you will *not* see dinosaurs in zoos any time soon – or at least until appropriate safe handling procedures are developed. Even though the autopsy report concluded that death by fowl play was everted!"

The Hidden Depths of Bogna

Liz Williams

Everyone always talks about landlords. Okay, they're important – critical, even – in the great scheme of things. They're one of the great British archetypes – never mind Britannia, or Queen Elizabeth, it's the British landlord that has attained such a crucial Jungian role in the national psyche. Mine host – jolly, rubicund and hail-fellow-well-met, an avatar of John Bull. What's not to like?

But the landlord is only half the story of any British pub. The other half is the barmaid. What do you think of, when I say the word 'barmaid'? Betty Turpin, perhaps, her name redolent of highwaymen, that 18th century ring? A woman who continues to remind me of the late Les Dawson. Or Corries' Bet Lynch, with a blonde pompadour that would put most of the Sun King's court to shame? I'm inclined to bet that the image that first comes to mind when I utter the word (especially if you're a bloke) is: peroxide, buxom, cheery, and probably a whole host of vague thoughts that involve stockings and the music hall.

It was these sorts of thoughts that were going through my mind on an icy night in January, just after New Year. It was ingrained in my memory as also being the night before the flood. And those thoughts were inspired by Bogna. But not, however, as one might assume…

"…knew a barmaid in Rhyl, back in the late seventies," Crown Baker was saying. "Face like the offspring of a stoat and a hatchet. Used to get out the Flit at half past ten and polish the tables with a thin-lipped glare. God help you if you were halfway through your pint."

"Some people shouldn't work behind the bar," Ray Arnold agreed. "A bad barmaid's even worse than a bad landlord. At least the landlord isn't always there, but the barmaid is."

"So what's the worst barmaid you've ever known?" I asked, opening the floodgates to a slew of horror stories involving Presbyterians, Dobermans, beer that was actually poisoned, and the Welsh.

"Thank God," Dr Steve said in heartfelt tones that, I feel sure, were echoed in every heart around the table, "Thank God the Fountain's always been lucky with their employees."

There was a moment of almost religious silence while we all ruminated on the bar staff of the Fountain, past and present. There had been June, in place for many years before her eventual retirement to Bournemouth. She might have been built like a Sherman tank but she'd had the proverbial heart of gold. There had been Tracey – tiny, elfin and surprisingly posh – who had supplemented a meagre grant at UCL for a couple of years by working behind the bar of the Fountain, and who could be relied upon to provide an encyclopaedic knowledge of the works of every philosopher from Plato onwards. My personal favourite had been Cassandra, now running a voodoo Botanica in New Orleans. (One Tuesday, a customer who had obviously been some kind of minor celebrity had made the mistake of pushing in front of a regular and asking 'Don't you know who I am?' Cassandra had furiously rung the last orders bell and, when silence fell, had demanded of a packed bar, in a penetrating Cardiff accent, 'Does anyone know who 'e is? He's for-gotten. *Senile.*')

Figures out of legend. And now, we were equally blessed with Sally and Bogna. Sally was a mainstay of the pub – quiet, efficient and charming – and none of us knew anything about her, despite persistent enquiries. We didn't even know which part of London she lived in, although one assumes that Michael had contact details. Not wishing to seem like stalkers, we didn't pester, and Sally continued to serve us with quiet, efficient charm.

We knew a lot more about Bogna. At least I thought we did, until the night of the flood.

Polish, we all knew that. Came, she once told me, from Wroclaw, which is an industrial city in the south. It has, she also told me, a famous steelworks. Her father was a chemist; her mother died when she was young and Bogna herself had followed her dad's scientific lead and done a degree in biology before coming to England 'for adventure, also money' and getting a job behind the bar of the Fountain. It's hard to say what she looked like: she had what I always think of as a typically Slavic face, rather dramatic, with prominent cheekbones, and her hair colour changed pretty much every week. At the time of the episode which I am about to relate, it was, indeed, peroxide blonde, but given what I've said above, it would be a mistake to think of Bogna as bubbly. She was, after all, a Slav.

During the barmaid discussion, Bogna's name was obviously brought into the conversation.

"Then there's Bogna," Brian Dalton remarked. "I mean, you can't see a girl like that working behind a bar for the rest of her life. She's obviously destined for greater things."

"Well, of course she is," Professor Macintosh replied. "She's got a biology degree. She's only over here to make a bit of money, like most hard-working young Poles. She's saving up to do a doctorate. She wants to apply to Imperial."

"How do you know that?" Brian asked.

"She told me." The Professor looked briefly smug. "Bogna tells me things."

After that, the conversation necessarily lapsed, as Bogna herself came from behind the bar and began to clear away the welter of empty pint glasses and crisp packets. It was, after all, close to closing time, but Bogna was, as I think I've said, one of the good barmaids, who never hustled you out. I know Michael had, on occasion, spoken to her about altering a somewhat Soviet telephone manner (namely, the need to answer the Fountain's phone with, "Good evening, this is the Fountain, how can I help you?" rather than barking *What?"* into the mouthpiece), but other than that she took a cavalier attitude to things such as making customers leave, the times in which food was supposed to be served, or enforcing the smoking ban ("In Wroclaw, smoking compulsory, keeps pollution from lungs, biological fact"), and it was for this that we loved her.

"Hello, Bogna," the Professor said now. "How are you?"

"Good." She nodded, as if for emphasis. "I am good today."

"Excellent," Brian replied.

"But I have feeling." Bogna's Slavic countenance grew darker, brooding. "I have feeling that will not last."

"Don't say that!" the Professor said. We'd become used to filling in the occasional noun/verb gaps in Bogna's discourse. "It's a New Year."

"Never-the-less," Bogna said with care, endowing the word with several more consonants than it should have possessed. "Never-the-less."

We should, I suppose, have known she was right.

Tuesday evenings are sacrosanct, but I'm an irregular visitor to the Fountain on other nights. The day after this conversation, however, I found myself up in Holborn again, seeing a web client. We holed up in his offices during the morning. The temperature had risen significantly overnight, producing a thaw in the unseasonal weather that had blanketed the capital, and turning what would have been yet another snowfall into thick, sleety rain. When I left my client, it was lunchtime and the prospect of ploughing across London in the dank muck that was currently descending from the heavens filled me with gloom. I ducked into the small alley on which the Fountain was situated, and sought refuge in the pub.

At least, I would have done if I hadn't stepped over the threshold into about 3 inches of water. Michael was standing in the middle of it, wearing Wellingtons, wielding a mop and bucket.

"Dear God, Mike. What happened?"

"We have," the landlord said, peevishly, "rather obviously had a flood."

"Burst pipe?"

"Yes. It must have frozen during the snow and, when the temperature started going up last night, it cracked. I came in this morning to find water pouring through the ceiling. We've turned the supply off, but…"

"Well, look, man, if there's anything I can do to help."

"Is help," Bogna said, behind me. She, too, was Wellington-clad. She thrust a mop at me. "This."

So I spent the afternoon mopping grimy water out of the pub. Luckily for Michael, the floors are wooden, and apart from the legs of tables and chairs, there's nothing really at that level that would be affected by flood damage. By four o'clock, we'd got most of it up and the pub looked cleaner than it had for weeks.

"I am appalled," Michael said to me, "by the fact that we appear to have been living in a welter of filth. Still, at least there's less dust."

"Blessing in disguise, perhaps."

"Nie." That was Bogna. "Water unhealthy. Can contain bacteria. Biological fact."

Michael grunted. "I'm going back upstairs to phone the insurance man again. Thanks for helping out. I owe you a pint."

By that time, I was ready for one. But alas, it was not to be.

"Water also in cellar." Bogna's face floated at the top of the narrow stairs like a small moon.

"Oh no! It must have gone through the floorboards."

"Has damaged pumps."

"Surely not!"

Bogna gave an emphatic shake of the head. "Pump not work."

"I'll take a look at it."

She gave me a look best described as 'dubious.' "You?"

117

"Yes. I used to work for Allied Domecq before I went into I.T. Trust me. I know what I'm doing."

I could tell she didn't believe me, but I followed her down the stairs to the cellar. I'd never been in the Fountain's cellars before and, down here, the age of the building was plain: it must have gone back two or three hundred years. Ancient beams stretched above our heads and the lighting was, to say the least, dim. As I was going to suggest to Bogna that we find a torch, the lights sizzled and went out.

"Bogna? You all right?" There was no reply. "Bogna?"

Warily, I splashed forwards. The water sloshed around my ankles as I shuffled, not wanting to move too quickly in case I fell over something. If Michael's basement was anything like the rest of the Fountain, it would not be a minimalist space...

Reaching out, my hand encountered rough wood. I groped in my pocket for my mobile phone and, by its wan light, saw that I'd reached a doorway. I scanned the room, but the light was too feeble for me to discern anything except a lapping pool of water. Surely this was too much to have come from a burst pipe? Frowning, I made my way through the doorway and found myself in a network of rooms.

"Bognaaaa!" - but there was no answer. I went along the wall, feeling my way, until rough brick turned into stone beneath my fingertips. The water was, by now, around my knees, but it didn't seem to be getting any deeper. I was, however, unnerved by the possibility that there might be a sudden drop – and it had already occurred to me that I'd walked a greater distance than the boundaries of the pub's walls could have accommodated. Like a lot of these old London pubs, it went back a long way, but surely not quite this far....? Well, I thought to myself, somewhat guiltily, let's see how far this actually does go back.

By the time I'd sloshed through what felt like a quarter of a mile, I started getting a little nervous. I even checked to see if there was a phone signal down here, but, as I'd suspected, there was not. So, I had a choice, to go back, and tell Michael what he presumably already knew – there was a cavern of Tardis-sized dimensions under his pub – or go forward and investigate. No choice, really.

I was almost relieved when I came to a barrier. It was not, as I'd expected, a full wall, blocking off a couple of cellars, but a low barricade of bricks, and I could hear the sound of water, too. In the light of the phone it looked old, slightly crumbling, and I was cautious as I peered over it.

A river ran beneath and all at once I realised what this was. The old river Fleet had run close to here. This must be one of its tributaries, which the city had long since closed over. I wondered what lay above us – presumably one of the small backstreets which interlaced through Holborn. Glancing around by the phone's light, I saw that the little balustrade arched away to the left. I went carefully around a corner. Below, rough steps led to the river, and water was gushing from a spout in the wall. Closer examination revealed that this was in the form of a lion's head. It looked extremely old. The splash sounded very loud in the darkness.

"A fountain!" I said, aloud.

As if in response, there was a slippery, rustling hiss. My feet shot out from under me and I went down, scrabbling for purchase on the rough stones. I found myself being pulled over the parapet and into the basin onto which the fountain poured. Dark water closed over my head. I spluttered and splashed. This happened so quickly that I was startled rather than frightened, but reflex took over and I kicked out, striking upwards into an unexpectedly bright light. I felt a hand clasp firmly around my wrist and I was hauled up to the parapet and over. I lay, gasping, on the stones. Michael was blinking down at me.

"Are you all right?"

"I think so." I hadn't been under for long enough to inhale much water. Coughing, I sat up. "What the hell happened? And where's Bogna? She was down here, too – is she Okay?"

"It's damn dark down here, even with a torch." Michael

gestured to the large maglite which he'd placed on the parapet. "I saw you lose your footing and go over."

"But…"

"Easily done," Michael said, smoothly. "This floor can be like glass when it's wet."

"What about Bogna?"

"She's up in the bar," Michael said, looking slightly puzzled. "She's been bailing out for the last half hour."

"But —" I stuttered, again. Unless there was another way out of here, then the barmaid had certainly not come past me.

"Let's get you into the warm, or what passes for it. I'll even get you a single malt on the house," Michael said.

Half a bottle of the Macallan later, ensconced in front of a gas fire in the landlord's upstairs front room, I was recovering somewhat from my sudden immersion when there came a knock on the door and Bogna came in with a plate of sandwiches.

"Bogna! I thought we'd lost you in the cellars."

"Nie," the barmaid muttered. She seemed to be having trouble meeting my gaze. "I came back."

"How did you find your way back upstairs? I didn't see any other passages."

"Is like maze down there," Bogna said, but her cheeks were flushed.

"Bogna?"

"Will you… tell?"

I frowned. "Tell who? What?" But I was remembering that rustling hiss, and the sheer strength of whatever had dragged me into the fountain. I knew I hadn't fallen. And suddenly I was equally certain that Bogna had not been scrubbing out the back bar all that while.

"Is reason," the barmaid said, "Why I study biology."

"Okay…" I began.

"Is also reason," Bogna went on, "why I not like cellar."

"What are you telling me, Bogna?"

"Is dark. And old water."

120

"Well, I can quite understand how claustrophobia might –"

"Is not claustrophobia. Is… something else."

She held out her hand. Her skin was, I noted, very pale. "In Poland, is legend. About rusalki – you know word?"

"Aren't they some kind of water spirit – oh. But you're not –"

"Spirit, not. Is legend, but is true, also. Biological fact. Different kind of human. Mother is not dead. Gone. This is why I study biology, to know. To understand family history. In Poland, are lot of lakes, also caves. Light does not reach. Combination of water and darkness… causes change."

"Causes you to change, you mean? Into some kind of predator? Into a rusalki?"

"Rusalka," Bogna said. "Singular."

I stared at her. I might have thought this was a wind-up, but she wasn't the type. Her broad face was quite earnest… and besides, I knew something had dragged me under that lightless water.

"I won't tell," I said. "And at least now we know why it's called 'the Fountain.' Just don't ask me to help you change a barrel, though!"

After Bogna left me there in front of the fire, I reflected on what had happened. *A Rusalka? Really?* Either way, this was going to make a great tale for next Tuesday night. Except that I'd promised Bogna, and, besides, no one would believe me. Even if they did, they'd only want me to show them by going back down there… and I'd rather drink a pint of Heineken than face that again.

On second thoughts, I think this is one story I might keep to myself.

In Pursuit of the Chuchunaa

Eric Brown

I look forward to Tuesday evenings at the Fountain with a degree of anticipation most people might think inordinate. I *do* get out from time to time – to bookshops and supermarkets, mostly, and to the odd publisher's event and book-launch – but I'm a freelance writer and I spend much of my time shackled to my desk. I pen science fiction for a living – a genre I love with the degree of obsession the rest of the human race seems to reserve for its detestation... and perhaps that's part of the attraction. I belong to a group of aficionados who know, in their hearts, that SF is the true quill.

So where better to mingle with these like-minded oddities than a public house? And not just any old pub. The Fountain is hidden in a maze of backstreets and alleys off Chancery Lane, a cosy bolt-hole which is almost impossible to find and which has a certain fame among the cognoscenti.

This particular Tuesday night, the first in November, was memorable for two reasons – the especially bitter onset of winter, which brought six inches of snow to the capital for the first time in years, and the arrival at the Fountain of Eva Shavinsky.

All the regulars were present when I pushed into the snug, along with a blizzard of snow like a theatrical effect. Professor Mackintosh stood clutching a pint of bitter in his right fist; clamped in his jaw was the full-bent pipe he'd recently taken up as his not-so-subtle protest at the smoking ban. He was listening to Dr Steve and Ray Arnold, who were discussing the latest extra-solar planetary discovery, along with almost a score of writers, scientists and fans. It was a while before I managed to fight my way through the scrum to the bar.

Imagine my delight when I found that the guest beer was Timothy Taylor's Landlord. What better? One of the finest ales in the world *and* the company of fellow writers... I was a happy man.

I was about to turn from the bar, having secured my pint of foaming, when I noticed a small woman at my side. She seemed to be having difficulty attracting the barmaid's attention. Now, it's not in my nature to pick up women in pubs, nor to assume that they need my help, but in this particular instance I decided to set aside my scruples.

"Sally," I said, catching the eye of the barmaid. "I think you have a customer."

The woman squeezed past me with a quick smile and peered dubiously at the beers on offer.

"Could do worse than the Landlord," I suggested. "If you like bitter."

"Bitter?" I could tell, just from the one word, that she was foreign.

"Bitter beer, an English speciality."

She nodded and said to Sally, "One glass of Landlord bitter, please."

"You a fan, or did you find yourself here by accident?" I asked.

She smiled. She was a tiny woman, very pale, with ice-maiden features and bleached blonde hair scraped back from a high forehead. I wondered if the Nordic Midget Ballet Company was on tour.

"Me, I am a writer of Ess Eff, as you say here."

"Just a minute..." I said. I racked my failing brain. I was sure, now she'd mentioned the fact she was a writer, that I'd seen her photograph somewhere. I was determined to impress her with my knowledge. "Got it! Eva... Eva Shurinsky?"

Her smile widened. "Shavinsky," she corrected me, and offered her tiny, cold hand, which I shook with care.

"You had a story in *InterNova* a couple of years ago," I said. "I proofed the non-British tales. I remember yours for a couple of reasons. It didn't need many corrections at all, and I thought it a great story."

She beamed. "That is so kind of you to say so."

I introduced myself, and she nodded and said, "You are a writer, too, no?"

"For my sins. Look, follow me and I'll introduce you to some writers worthy of the title."

I ploughed through the drinkers and Eva followed in my wake. When we emerged in the corner of the room where my usual gaggle of friends and drinking partners were uncharacteristically silent, I presented Eva and said, "Eva Shurinsky, all the way from Russia. Eva had a cracking tale in the second issue of *InterNova*."

"And what brings you to these benighted shores?" Ray inquired.

"Oh," Eva said, grinning at me, "I just had to come so that I could taste this famous English bitter beer."

A second of amazed silence greeted this, and then we laughed.

"Welcome to England," Professor Mackintosh said, and we raised our glasses as one. We relocated to a table beside the blazing fire.

"Actually," Eva went on when we were settled, "I came to England because my government is... how do you say...? chasing me?"

Ray stared at her. "Chasing you?"

She nodded matter-of-factly. "That is so. To tell the truth, they want me dead."

I exchanged a glance with Dr Steve. Now we do get our fair share of crackpots and fringe cases in the Fountain, especially on Tuesday nights, but Eva didn't appear to fit into either category.

She looked at each of us in turn, then said, "I have heard about this pub is famous. You come here to tell stories, no?"

The professor smiled. "Well, one or two tales have been told in the Fountain."

"That is good," Eva said, "because I have a story to tell. Really I have told half already – in the *InterNova* story. That is what alerted the authorities to what happened." She bit her lip. "I think I was a little foolish to publish the story, but at the time I had no idea of the consequences."

I recalled Eva's story, about a group of anthropologists looking into reported sightings of the Siberian Wildman...

"One moment," Dr Steve said, noticing that several of our glasses were almost empty. "We can't listen without drinks, can we?"

He brought another round and then, replenished, we returned our attention to the diminutive Eva.

"At the time I was working at the Moscow State University as a lecturer in anthropology," she said. "My specialism was anthropology, and I was particularly interested in Neanderthal Man. We have a few sites in the former Soviet Union where Neanderthal tribes lived – dispersion points, from where they spread across to Europe and the southern Caucasus. My particular interest was in attempting to piece together their social structures, their tribal hierarchies, from the little archaeological evidence we had to hand."

"A tall order," Ray said.

She smiled. "A little evidence goes a long way, in my field. I had sufficient findings from field trips I'd done during the past year – this was 2007 – to keep me busy at my desk for years. I had my future all planned out. I would interpret my findings, publish my results in a number of papers, then write them all up in a monograph. I calculated this would take me five years, at least. And after that..." She smiled. "Well, I really hoped that the quality of my work might gain me a post in a Western university."

I took a sip of bitter and wondered if this was why she was over here.

"However," she went on, "fate intervenes, does it not, to lead you down unsuspected paths?"

"It most certainly does," said a chess player at the next table, a prolific hack writer of over a hundred space operas. "I was all set to become a grand master when the need to earn an honest living turned me to the typewriter."

"An *honest* living?" quipped Dr Steve.

The chess player smiled sadly and returned to the game.

I said, addressing Eva, "What happened?"

"One of the other departments in the Institute, the modern anthropology unit run by the infamous Professor Kharkov, was short staffed. I was seconded to join them on a field trip to Siberia as nothing more than a glorified secretary. I cannot describe how angry I was. But —" she waved "— what could I do about it? Kharkov was senior, very senior: he was in with that villain Putin and his cronies, so the rumours went. If I valued my career at the Institute, I had to accept the secondment and put a brave face on the situation. I would be away for over a month – a month when I could be doing my own valuable research! – and the thought of spending weeks in Siberia at the start of winter..." She gave a theatrical shiver. "Believe me, your English winters are like summer by comparison! But I accepted the post with bad grace, as you say, and joined the expedition. We travelled by train from Moscow deep into Siberia, and while on the long journey I struck up a friendship with a young research fellow, a Bulgarian named Ana Hristova. She was a veterinarian, and her specialism was the study of primates. Now Professor Kharkov had outlined very briefly why we were travelling to Siberia – to investigate sighting of the infamous Siberian Wildman – but he had left the details vague. On the train, Ana filled me in."

Dr Steve, never one to allow anything to delay the replenishment of an empty glass, called time out and repaired to the bar for another round. Eva had drained her pint and ordered a second, and I silently admired her fluidic capacity.

Dr Steve returned with a tray of beer and sufficient food to keep even Eva's Siberian expedition going. (That's what I like about the Fountain, to digress somewhat: the beer is excellent and the range of victuals second to none – with the exception of Michael's infamous ploughman's, of course.) We helped ourselves to a variety of nuts, pickled eggs, pork scratchings, salted crisps and Bombay mix. Only then did we return our collective gaze to Eva.

"According to Ana, our destination was a small village two hundred kilometres north of the town of Konsk, the railway station where we would alight. Just a few hundred people lived in this village, named Bratensk, mainly loggers, trappers, fur-dealers and various traders. These places are very odd, as you might expect, and their inhabitants are very strange, too. They spend much of their time alone; living alone, working alone... and drinking too much alcohol."

I looked into my glass and observed, "Now, why does that sound so familiar?"

"Shut up," said Ray, "and listen."

Eva went on, "Ana told me that that summer a hunter was out in the forest a few kilometres from the village. He was returning after a day's hunting, carrying the carcass of a deer he'd shot that afternoon. The sun was going down, and he was hurrying home before darkness fell. He heard a sound behind him, the soft padding of careful footsteps, and before he could turn to see what it was, or take cover, something knocked him to the ground. The odd thing was, it didn't attack him. He fell, dropping the deer, and he heard grunting and then running footsteps. When he dared look up, whatever had knocked him over had fled – taking the carcass. The hunter suspected a fellow hunter – there were several in the area with whom he had differences of opinion, let's say – and he insisted on calling in the police. There was no police force in Bratensk, so they had to be summoned from Konsk, the closest town. They came and investigated the attack and the theft, and went away again without having found the hunter's assailant, even though it could only have been a fellow villager.

"So... the enigma remained, just another unsolved incident in a region of Earth where crime is rare but mystery abounds." She took a long drink, then continued, "One month later, a trapper was returning to his cabin in the forest when he saw a shambling figure emerge from the building and disappear into the forest. When he reached the cabin, he found that it had been ransacked. He had no possessions worth stealing, but several cuts of dried meat were missing. Again the police were called in and they questioned the trapper about the figure he'd seen running into the forest, and he was quite adamant: the figure was not human, he said. It was a chuchunaa, a Wildman."

Eva paused and smiled at our various rapt expressions. "I think now I must go quickly to the rest room."

We directed her to the ladies' loo, and while she was away I recalled Eva's story in *InterNova*, in which a group of Moscow anthropologists travelled to Siberia, led by the curmudgeonly Dr Kharkov (renamed in the story), to investigate sightings of the chuchunaa. What had followed was the central character's meeting with a Wildman and her narrow escape from its clutches. Stated like that, the story sounds trite, even formulaic, but what had made it special was the quality of the writing – beautifully turned phrases and exquisite psychological insights – and the haunting sense of loneliness she managed to convey: the sequestration of the village, the isolation of the creature itself, which was the last of its kind, and even the melancholy insularity of the first person narrator. Very Russian, I had thought at the time. I wondered now if Eva had been writing about herself.

On her return, Eva took up her beer, fuelled herself with a gulp, and resumed. "The police searched the surrounding forest, of course, but not very thoroughly. They had better things to be doing than investigating the theft of meat, and they departed the same day, leaving a village in fear. The locals were well aware of stories about the chuchunaa – many had claimed even to have seen a big, hirsute figure stalking the wilderness.

"We arrived just before the onset of winter, leaving the train at Konsk two hundred kilometres away and hiring four-wheel-drive vehicles to take us the rest of the way. The idea was to comb the forest while the weather held, then spend a month studying our finds, if we found anything at all." She shivered. "Bratensk was... bleak, so bleak. One road, a collection of tiny cabins – old, log cabins and ill-repaired temporary structures. Some people were even living in freight containers they'd fashioned into crude dwellings. We took over two old cabins, made what repairs we could, and then hired a local trapper to guide us into the forest... I was so, so cold. All the while I could only think of my warm Moscow apartment, my desk at the Institute, and all the work I had to do on my own research project. I was pretty low, to be honest, and not at all excited at the prospect of running through the snow after a Siberian Wildman!"

Ray asked, "You didn't believe in the creature?"

She gave a thin-lipped smile. "Of course not. I thought they were stories dreamed up by lonely alcoholics to add spice to empty winter nights...

"Anyway, the day after we arrived, we left on foot and followed the trapper into the forest. I tried to forget about my personal discomfort and appreciate the beauty all around me: the snow-laden fir trees, the brilliant blue sky, the way the snow wasn't just white but many colours, from brilliant dazzling white to a kind of electric blue...

"We found nothing on the first day, nor on the second or the third, but on the fourth day the trapper came across what he said was a trail – this was deep under cover of fir trees, where the snow hadn't fallen. We followed him for kilometres and eventually came to an outcropping of rocks set into a hillside. The trail led to a shallow cave, and I must admit that even though I was sceptical, I felt a certain fear at the thought of entering the cave. Kharkov went first – claiming to be frightened of nothing – and then the rest of us followed." Eva pulled a face, remembering. "The most amazing thing about the cave was the stench. You cannot imagine the smell! A mixture of sweat and faeces and rotting flesh... I had to run out, with Ana, both of us..." she mimed a palm to her mouth, "... how do you say, gagging? I was almost sick in the snow.

"The trapper claimed that the cave was where the chuchunaa made its home, and as he said this I felt the hairs on the back of my neck rise, as if we were being watched by something as we stood in the snow. We took it in turns to return to the cave (I tied a handkerchief around my mouth and nose) and collect samples of faecal matter, hair and bone, which we took back to our base.

"Then we began the slow process of analysing our finds."

In Eva's fictional account, I recalled, a few days later her Bulgarian friend, Ana, came to her and told Eva that she'd made the acquaintance of a strange old woman who lived alone in the village. The woman, according to Ana, knew the current whereabouts of the chuchunaa.

The denouement of the story had Eva and Ana visit the old woman, who took them deep into the forest to the underground lair of the chuchunaa, from which the women had a narrow escape...

Now Eva was saying, "... and so that night I went, with Ana, to the old woman's cabin. You cannot imagine the conditions in which she lived. These people are poor beyond belief. How they exist on the little food they scrape from the forest, and barter with traders... I do not know. And the filth! It is true to say that the stench in the old woman's cabin was almost as bad as that of the cave in the forest. The woman herself – her name was Olga – was as fat and as pale as a ball of lard, wrapped in layers and layers of shawls and headscarves. Only her round face peered out, and I recall that her grey eyes were as cold as ice. She offered us a precious nip of vodka – but seeing the condition of the glasses, I declined. Ana asked her about the chuchunaa.

"The woman told us that she had known the creature – she

called it the *uten-ekhti-agen*, 'the one who wanders in the forests' – for more than seventy years, and she was now eighty-five. She had first seen it while chopping wood at her grandmother's house, even deeper in the forest. And she told us that her grandmother had known about the creature for a number of years. The old woman even claimed to have met the creature on several occasions... Ana and I exchanged a glance at this, and I said, 'But weren't you scared of so fearsome a beast?' The woman laughed, and wiped tears from her eyes, and replied that the creature was gentleness itself, and would never hurt even so much as a mouse.

"Ana said, 'But this summer it attacked a hunter from the village.' And to this the old woman replied that it had pushed the hunter to the ground and escaped with a carcass – hardly the actions of a 'fearsome beast'.

"Then Ana asked if the woman might take us to meet this famously 'gentle' creature... and the woman nodded and said yes."

I stared around the group, which sat mesmerised by Eva's story. She had us in the palm of her hand, hanging on her every word, notwithstanding the far-fetched – excuse the terrible pun! – nature of the tale.

"And you went?" Ray wanted to know.

Eva nodded. "We went."

"And met the creature?" I asked.

She smiled at me, took another swallow of beer, and went on, "At the dead of night, when all our colleagues were fast asleep, the old woman led us through the trees, our way illuminated only by the intermittent moonlight. We penetrated deeper into the forest, in the opposite direction from where the trapper had led us on the first occasion. We must have walked about three kilometres before the old woman stopped by a small hillock and demanded we sit on a fallen log and listen to her story. So sit we did, and we listened.

"First of all, the woman said, we had to understand that the creature was not the chuchunaa we were seeking – and she proceeded to tell us a story first recounted to her by her grandmother, back in the twenties of the last century, when the old woman was a little girl. Her grandmother had told her that twenty years earlier, in 1908, in the region of Siberia two hundred kilometres north of Bratensk, there had been a great explosion in the sky one morning, an explosion that flattened forests over a vast area, and destroyed buildings, and killed animals and even a few trappers and hunters. Tunguska, of course... No one could even guess at the cause of the explosion, though later scientists said it had been a falling meteorite. Then, one day a few years later, the old woman's grandmother was in the forest seeking mushrooms, when she came across a strange silver object, about the size of a smallish cabin. It was much battered and covered in lichen and moss, but she made out the outline of a hatch in its flank...

Eva looked at us each in turn, and said, "Then the old woman gestured to hillock before us and said, 'Hidden under those branches, you will find the silver cabin.' Ana and I just stared at the woman as if she had taken leave of her senses. But before we could express our disbelief, something within the hillock moved, and the old woman said, 'It wishes to meet you, Ana, Eva...'

"'Meet us?' we replied, too shocked by what was happening to do what we should have done, and fled. 'Meet us? But why?'

"'Because the creature is lonely,' the old woman said, 'and wishes to meet the educated citizens of this world. It has been here for a long time, with only itself for company, its only contact being my mother, who brought it food from time to time.'

"I was staring at the mound, and watched as a creature emerged from behind a swatch of branches. It was perhaps two metres tall, and very broad, and a jet black pelt covered its body. Its face... its face was not human, not at all... and not animal, either, in that it resembled no earthly animal: it had great, black, round eyes, and a disconcerting concavity where its nose should have been, and only a thin line for a mouth. And as we stared, it gestured for us to follow, and then retreated back into the mound. Ana followed, and seconds later I joined her, overcome by the conviction that the creature was indeed gentle.

"We pushed past branches and clods of earth until we came to an oval aperture through which we made out the lighted interior of the... vessel. The creature was seated at the far end of the small chamber, holding out its hand as if beseeching us to enter.

"We did so, and sat on the silver floor, and looked around us at the banked consoles, the oddly configured walls and bulkheads, contorted into shapes like nothing on any human vessel.

"And then the being spoke to us. Only... we did not see its lips move at all, but we heard its soft voice in our heads as it greeted us and told us not to be afraid.

"And for the period we were with the creature – perhaps an hour – we listened in awe as it explained that it hailed from a planet which circled the star we knew as Zeta Ophiuchi; that it and its fellows had been on a mission of exploration to Earth, and had been overjoyed when they discovered sentient life here... only for that joy to turn to horror when the landing manoeuvre went tragically wrong and their ship's nuclear drive exploded. Only it, the being before us, was close enough to an escape capsule to get out in time... And one hundred years ago it had come to rest in the forest near Bratensk, where it had lived alone ever since."

I wanted to break the spell of her tale and glance at my friends, perhaps in order to convince myself of their scepticism, but such was the power of Eva's delivery, the spellbinding content of her narrative, that I could not take my gaze from her.

"Then Ana asked the creature if there was any chance it might be rescued by its people. The alien replied that a rescue craft would take another four hundred Terran years to reach Earth, and that it could expect to live only another two hundred years at most.

"Then I asked the question which had been uppermost in

my mind since we had entered the alien's vessel: what did the creature want with us?

"The alien took a while to reply. I stared at its great sad eyes, and felt waves of melancholy emanate from the being from the stars. At last its word entered my head: 'I wanted to tell you my story. Communication, to my people, is of vital importance, the modus operandi, you might say, of our existence. Reality, to us, lacks essential quiddity until we have shared it...'

"I was aware of its hesitation. I sensed that there was another reason we were here. Then it gestured with an outstretched hand. 'Also,' it said, 'once every one hundred year we... change, we transform ourselves somatically... On our homeworld we change as a way of survival, to confound predators. It is a slow and painful process. Now, I wish to transform myself into the semblance of a human being, and for this to take place I needed to meet educated, worldly creatures so that I might have a... *template*... on which to base my metamorphosis. I wish to go abroad, to travel planet Earth, to experience its wonders...'

"And then I felt a strange sensation in my mind, as if my every thought and feeling were privy to the probing of the alien – and suddenly I was aware that I was alone – I turned, but Ana had fled. I had never felt such terror as I did then. I too took to my heels and ran outside. The old woman was no longer outside the mound, and we had to find our own way back to the village. It took us two long hours, but at last we arrived at our cabin. We said nothing to our colleagues about what we discovered... I for one did not want all the glory to go to the arrogant Dr Kharkov, and nor did I want the world hounding the creature from the stars. One month later we left Siberia: the samples we discovered in the cave turned out to be nothing more than the deposits of a brown bear...

Eva gestured with her empty glass. "A year later, I decided to write a story based, partly, on my experiences in Siberia. A big mistake, I think. The authorities questioned Ana, and shortly after that I heard no more from her. That is when I decided to leave my country..."

She shrugged, smiled around the group of listeners, and whispered, "Please, excuse me one moment," and she eased through the crowd towards the loo.

"Well," I said into the ringing silence that followed, "I think that might have been the best tale I've heard in here for some time..."

"She can certainly spin a yarn," Dr Steve said.

"Utter tosh," opined Professor Mackintosh, "every word of it. But entertaining, I'll grant you that."

"Just a tic," Ray said. "She claimed she was being chased, that the authorities back in Russia wanted her dead... A trifle extreme, no?"

We mulled this over for a while, and I said I'd question her on this point when she returned.

Perhaps ten minutes later I glanced at the door of the ladies' loo. When Sally the barmaid squeezed past us collecting glasses, I said, "Could you pop into the loo, Sal, and see if our friend is okay? She's been in there a while now."

Sally deposited the empties on the bar and pushed into the ladies' toilets. She came back seconds later, shrugging. "Empty. There's no one in there."

"How on Earth...?" I began.

Ray laughed, and ever the rationalist said, "She snuck out when we weren't looking. The Landlord obviously didn't agree with her!"

"I wonder..." I began.

Ray fixed me with his gimlet stare. "What?"

I shook my head. "She said the alien wanted to transform itself into human form, to go abroad, travel planet Earth, experience its wonders... And why did she tell us the story of her discovery if the Russian authorities were after her? What did she say the creature had said: that reality lacked... *essential quiddity*... until his people had shared it?"

Ray clapped me on the back. "You've had one Landlord too many, sir!"

"Speaking of beer," Dr Steve said, "whose round is it?"

So Eva's story was relegated to a matter of subsidiary importance beside the pressing matter of recharging our glasses.

"I'll get this one." I said, and as I moved to the bar I considered the story Eva had told. A work of fiction, obviously, to rival the version I had read a couple of years ago...

Obviously.

Behind me, I heard Professor Mackintosh laugh out loud and declare, "Now, my friends, that reminds me of a certain incident that happened during my time at Yarlsbury..."

The Cyberseeds

Steve Longworth

The credibility of any tale told at the Fountain may be estimated by the gallon. Professor Mackintosh's stories are usually rated at a quart, requiring the listener to consume no more than two pints of Old Bodger before yielding to the Professor's erudition and conceding the total plausibility of whatever fantastical concoction has just rolled elegantly from his silver tongue.

Brian Dalton likes to push the boundaries a bit, so he generally favours a half-gallon yarn. But when Dr. Steve starts with, "You'll never believe this…" you know for sure that you won't, unless you've consumed the full eight pints.

It was a quiet early Tuesday evening, courtesy of the latest round of industrial action by the operatives of Transport For London, and many of the regulars were still struggling manfully across a chilly, gridlocked cityscape. The prof and I had been at a meeting within easy walking distance of the Fountain and were off to an early start.

"Slow tonight," I commented to Bogna as she poured my first pint of the evening.

"I say this to Michael just last week," she replied. "I tell him we should have karaoke competition on Tuesday night."

"*Karaoke?*" spluttered the Professor, his facial expression that of a Pontiff who had just stumbled across a condom machine operating in the Sistine Chapel.

Fortunately, before he succumbed to total apoplexy, a soothing pint of his favourite ale was thrust into his hand, at

139

which point Dr. Steve arrived and joined us at the bar.

"You all right, Prof?" he asked, a look of genuine concern on his face. "Do I need to go back and get my medical bag?"

"Bad tidings," muttered the Professor, "the spectre of kara-bloody-oke stalks the saloon bar. I think I need a whisky chaser."

"Well here's a story about how to react to bad news," said Dr. Steve. "You'll never believe this…"

"Bogna," said the Prof, indicating the twelve-year-old single malt, "if he's off on another one of his medical anecdotes you'd better make that a double."

"So anyway," began the good doctor, "my mate Nick Baines was the on-call obstetrician one evening at a provincial hospital in the West Midlands when there's an urgent call to the delivery suite. He gets there to find a group of Midwives crowded round a newly arrived bundle of joy. Well, it doesn't take Nick long to see what the problem is. The little fella's been born with six digits on both hands and feet. 'Who's going to tell his mum?' asks Nick, then realises from the way they're all looking at him that this is why he's been called. So, accepting that this is what they pay him the big bucks for, he goes and knocks on the door of the mother's room where he finds her already recovered from the birth and watching Eastenders. 'Congratulations,' he says, 'I'm pleased to say that your baby is absolutely fine… except… that he has an extra finger on each hand and an extra toe on each foot.' 'Oh, right,' says the mother, completely unfazed, not even taking her eyes from the telly. Well, my friend was rather taken aback by her apparent indifference. 'If you don't mind me saying,' he says, 'you're not as upset by the news as I'd imagined you'd be.' 'Well,' she says, gaze still fixed on events in Albert Square, 'at least now I know who the father is.'"

As we all laughed and raised a glass to fatherhood (however random) we were joined by Ray Arnold. Encouraged by the response to his last story, Dr. Steve launched straight away into a follow-up.

"Nick Baines' family lived in a remote cottage in Cumbria. His dad passed away some years ago, and his younger brother, Jack, was still living at home with their mum. Jack, who wasn't as bright as Nick, lived a pretty dull and uneventful life, until he bumped into a US Air Force pilot on secondment at the RAF base where Jack worked as a handyman. You'll never believe this…"

"Bogna," said Ray and I simultaneously, "another Old Bodger please." This had all the hallmarks of a full gallon story.

A few more Tuesday night regulars had straggled in and settled down with a drink to hear the doc, who was now getting into his stride.

"Jack Baines was a lad who never really reached his full potential. If he'd pulled his finger out he might have had a crack at emulating his older brother, but he was far too interested in video games, girls and the pub."

An empathetic murmur rippled around the bar.

"So Jack left school with a handful of modest GCSEs and little ambition. He drifted into a number of occupations where he picked up the basics of woodwork, plastering, painting and decorating, plumbing, that sort of thing. Eventually, he ended up not far from home at RAF Spadeadam in the Lake District, in a civilian job as the base handyman. He had a number of girlfriends but was way too comfortable living with his mum, Diedre – Dee to her friends – who never charged him a proper rent. He was far too disorganised to save up so they led a fairly hand to mouth lifestyle.

"Well, one day Jack comes up with this bright idea. He's going to buy a burger van, but instead of overcharging the punters for a heart attack in a bun he's going to sell healthy-option, low-fat venison burgers and make his fortune. Trouble is, he's broke, but his mum has something set aside for a rainy day. Before he died, her husband had bought a wodge of shares in an obscure new American computer company called Microsoft, and the rest, as they say, is history.

"'Take these into town and go see a stockbroker,' she tells Jack, handing him a sheaf of share certificates. 'The money you get for them should set you up nicely.'

"Jack goes to work the next day intending to leave early in the afternoon to sell the shares in town, but before he sets off he decides to visit the base canteen for lunch, and that's where he bumps into the Mysterious American Pilot.

"Jack's half way through a Ginsters when this flash-looking Yank in a flying jacket and mirrored sunglasses walks up to his table and says 'Mind if I join you?' The canteen's pretty full, so Jack shrugs and the stranger takes a seat. Anyway, they fall into conversation and the guy introduces himself as Major Majic Dossen — Serbian ancestry, apparently — from Groom Lake air force base in Nevada."

"Ah!" said Ray Arnold. The rest of us looked at him in expectation. Ray's interjections are usually highly illuminating. He grinned at us. "You've all heard of Groom Lake, of course."

"Have we?" asked The Raven who had now attached his singular presence to the steadily accumulating congregation.

"You have," replied Ray emphatically. "Except I'm sure that you'll know it better as Area Fifty-One."

There was, of course, a general dropping of pennies, this being a gathering of individuals well aware that Area 51 was where they took the captured flying saucer and carried out the alien autopsy in 1947 following the Roswell Incident.

"In fact," continued Ray, furrowing his brow, "the whole Roswell business was allegedly managed by a secret committee established by President Harry S Truman called The Majestic Twelve." He glanced at the medical raconteur. "Or was that the Magic Doz...?" But with the long practice of someone who daily inserts a tongue depressor, Dr. Steve silenced Ray with an expertly placed pork scratching.

"So anyway, Jack and the Major get chatting, and the visitor lets slip that he's come over to England on secondment to recover from a bout of nervous exhaustion induced by flying experimental aircraft over the Nevada test range at Groom and the Mojave Desert out of Edwards. Jack expresses his surprise that a senior pilot would need a break from flying, as most sky-jocks of his acquaintance had nerves of tempered steel. The American shakes his head and replies in a whisper, 'But did any of them ever fly a plane reverse-engineered from a crashed UFO?' Well, at this point he's got Jack's undivided attention, but not wanting to seem a total country bumpkin Jack expresses a degree of scepticism.

Somewhat affronted, Major Dossen asks him, 'What, you want proof?' and after looking furtively round the room he slips something out of an inside jacket pocket. Angling his hand so that only Jack can see what he's holding in his palm, he slowly opens his fingers to reveal five bean-sized, oval, metallic objects that seem to throb gently with an eerie green glow. 'What're they?' asks Jack. 'We're not too sure,' says the Major, 'but they seem to be critically important to achieving escape velocity in the alien space vehicle. We just haven't figured out how yet.' Jack was entranced. What he'd give to own those alien artefacts. 'What I'd give to own those alien artefacts,' he says, as Dossen slips them back into his pocket. 'Well one day, some bright guy's gonna figure out what these things are and how they work, and that guy's gonna become a billionaire.' Jack likes the sound of that. He clears his throat. 'Look, I don't suppose there's any possibility you might want to sell those things?' Major Dossen laughs so loudly that half the diners in the canteen turn to stare at him. 'Son, these things are priceless. Anyhow, what could you possibly have to offer me in exchange?' Jack reaches into his tool-bag and pulls out the wad of shares. As soon as the American sees the name 'Microsoft' his eyes bulge behind his mirrored lenses. 'Jack – can I call you Jack?' 'Oh yes, definitely,' says Jack. 'Jack,' says the Major again, pulling his chair up closer and putting an arm round Jack's shoulder, 'I suffered a bit more than nervous exhaustion. Flying a plane made from alien technology is a deeply disturbing experience. Everything you think you knew about handling an aircraft goes straight out the window. We had crashes; one in particular where a couple of my close buddies…' He tailed off and slipped a finger and thumb up under his glasses to rub his eyes. 'Well, let's just say that it got to me, and I developed some pretty dysfunctional coping strategies. Booze. Gambling. Jeez, those internet poker sites. Fact is, I'm in deep financially and my credit card company's giving me some serious heat.' He taps the pile of Microsoft certificates. 'You serious about this? I mean, are these shares genuine?' 'I swear on my life,' replies Jack. 'On my mother's life.' Dossen pauses for a long moment then slowly reaches back inside his jacket, withdraws the objects of Jack's desire and places them on the table. 'You really sure you wanna do this?' 'Done,' replies Jack, snatching up the alien quintet. 'Done,' replies a smiling Major Dossen, calmly gathering up the shares. 'Yes indeed.'

"Jack wastes no time and races straight home to share the good news. His mother, Dee, is of course, furious. 'You idiot! That burger van was going to be our cash cow,' she yells at him, 'and you've gone and swapped it for a handful of Majic's beans. Whatever will become of us now?' and she bursts into tears. So Jack promises he'll try to get the shares back and he phones RAF Spadeadam, but no one's heard of an American Major called Dossen who's on secondment from Nevada. 'Perhaps he's undercover and using an alias,' Jack suggests to his mother, at which point Dee demands of the Gods how she could possibly have given birth to a son so deficient in common sense. In a fit of fury and frustration, she grabs the alien artefacts and chucks them through the open kitchen window into the back garden.

"So, that evening, thoroughly ashamed by his own naïve gullibility, and eager to escape from Dee's on-going torrent of invective, Jack slinks off early to bed. He sleeps badly, partly because of a huge thunderstorm, and partly because of strange groaning and creaking noises from outside, which he puts down to the thunder and heavy rain. In the morning he wakes somewhat disorientated because the room is so dark. Thinking the sky must still be full of storm clouds, he pulls back the bedroom curtains and his jaw hits the floor."

At this point the cleverly confabulating clinician paused strategically for a refill. In the honourable tradition of the Fountain a pint of Old Bodger already waited at his elbow.

"There in the back garden," continued our suitably fortified physician, "is a giant metallic tower, lit with the same eerie green glow that he'd seen only the day before in Major Dossen's palm. Jack quickly dresses and dashes out into the garden, where he finds Dee standing at the base of this monstrosity, staring up into the sky. The tower's circular, about ten feet in diameter and it stretches up as far as the eye can see and disappears into the clouds. Jack cranes his neck but can't see the top of this thing, so he dashes out of the back garden and up the hill at the back of the cottage to see if he can get a better perspective. When he turns back to look his jaw hits the floor again. The tower's disappeared! He dashes back to the cottage, and as he gets to within twenty feet of his mother, who's still standing there staring slack-jawed into the sky, the tower suddenly reappears! Jack stops, walks back a couple of feet – tower gone; steps forward again – the tower's back! Now I have to say that of all the aspects of this tale, this is the one I really don't get."

"Easy," said Professor Mackintosh. "Metamaterials."

"Meta-what?" said someone.

"Fabricated structural elements with a refractive index less than zero. From certain angles this would render the structure invisible."

"I know what you mean, dude," said a random youth who was picking up a bottle of Taiwanese lager from the bar. He was covered in Lord of the Rings tattoos and designer acne. "Like in that film."

"What film?" asked someone else.

"Oh yeah, man, what was the name of that Schwarzenegger movie with the invisible camouflage suit worn by the predator?"

"Er," I began, "that would be Pre…"

"Total Recall," said Ray Arnold.

"Conan the Barbarian," said Paul the Librarian.

"Kindergarden Cop," said Michael.

Our group has its own ruthless and subtle way of punishing outsiders who interject when an anecdote is in full flow; especially those who say 'dude'.

"Anyway," said Dr. Steve with a reproachful glare at the back of the retreating interloper, "Jack and his mum were not suddenly interrupted by the Police, RAF, SAS, 'Men In Black', or whatever, because the damn thing's," with a grateful nod of acknowledgement to the Prof, "invisible; metamaterially dematerialised. They live miles from anyone else, so there are no nosy neighbours, and they don't have a milkman or paperboy that visits them in their splendid rural isolation.

"'Blimey, Mum,' gasps Jack, 'what the hell's *this*?' Resisting the urge to berate her son again for being so dim, Dee spells it out for him. 'That American pilot – he was telling you the truth! This tower must go up all the way into space! Look, here's a control panel, or something,' and she reaches up to prod a recessed button on the side of the tower. A door slides silently open; but a door clearly intended for someone about ten feet tall. 'Wait here,' says his mum, and dashes back into the cottage. Minutes later she's back with a fully laden rucksack, a rolled-up sleeping bag and a couple of bulging handgrips. 'Better get the old chemical toilet out the shed,' she tells Jack. 'Why?' asks Jack, by now totally bewildered. 'Where are you going?' She looks at him fondly, and with the patience possible from only a mother, tells him, 'It's not for me, dimwit, it's for you! You're going to see what's at the top of this thing. If you'd ever bothered to read any of your dad's Arthur C. Clarke books you'd know that this is a space elevator, and it's going to take you several days to get to the top. So here's enough camping gear and food to last you for the journey up and down. Please don't make me explain why you'll need the chemical toilet.' 'But how do I operate this elevator?' pleads Jack, lugging over the portaloo. 'Just get in there,' insists

Dee, giving him an encouraging shove, 'and see what happens. It's probably automatic.' 'How will I get ba...' But it's too late, the doors swish shut and Jack suddenly starts to feel a lot heavier as the lift begins to accelerate upwards."

"Hang on," said Ray Arnold, "a space elevator would only work if it was situated on the equator, otherwise you couldn't achieve geostationary orbit, and anyway..." but just then his mobile phone rang and he nipped out of the bar to answer this.

"Well," said Dr. Steve, slipping his own mobile back into his pocket and cancelling the call to Ray's number, "Jack spends the next three days travelling rapidly upwards. His quick-thinking mum had stuffed enough grub into his luggage to feed a small army. She'd even thought to pack his games machine to keep him occupied on the journey. Eventually, the elevator starts to decelerate. Then, most disconcertingly, the walls gradually become transparent and he feels as if he's floating in space. He can see the tower, because it is ever so slightly angulated, stretching out for hundreds of miles below him, and above him the lift is heading towards a platform, evidently the terminus. Suddenly, from behind the moon a small bright star appears and accelerates toward him. As he gazes moonward the star resolves into a brightly lit flying saucer, spinning and winking and growing bigger and bigger until his view of the moon is completely blocked out by a truly monstrous spaceship. Just as the flying saucer docks with the platform, the elevator reaches the terminus and the lift door swishes open."

"Missed call from a withheld number," muttered Ray as he re-entered the bar, gazing glumly at his cell-phone. "I don't recognise the number and whoever it is isn't picking up."

"Tsk, tsk," sympathised Dr. Steve. "So, in his haste to get out of the lift, Jack slips on the pile of discarded food wrappers strewn over the lift floor and falls and cuts his hand on the lid of an empty tin can. Cursing his clumsiness, he ties a hanky around the cut on his hand but not before he's stepped out into the terminus and dripped some blood on the floor. Immediately an alarm sounds, a great whooping up-and-down noise accompanied by a strange deep voice repeating the same incomprehensible message over and over again. 'That's torn it,' thinks Jack, 'I'd better find somewhere to hide.' He rushes down the corridor… and skids to a sudden halt as he almost bumps into the back of heavily armed, giant alien cyborg. Jack's standing there, paralysed with fear, when a hand grabs hold of his collar and yanks him into a room off the corridor before the hideous creature can turn round and spot him. He finds himself face to face with a gorgeous blonde, made up and dressed like a femme fatale from a nineteen forties film noir and wearing what looks like a Bluetooth ear pod. She has a forefinger over her lip. Jack gets the message. They wait until they hear the alien stomp down the corridor. 'You sure screwed up,' says the girl in a Texan drawl. 'They know you're here. You set off the alarm. Take this,' and she pulls another ear pod out of her pocket. 'What is it?' asks Jack. 'Universal translator,' she replies, slipping the device in to his lughole. She flicks a switch on the pod and immediately Jack can understand the message booming out over the alarm.

"'Intruder code three-five-four-one, olfactory sensors detect Anglo-Saxon haemoglobin; apprehend viable or terminated for osseous disintegration and nutritional recycling.'

"Wait a minute," said Ray Arnold. "Three-five-four-one? That sounds like Fee-Fi…" but with a deft flick of the foot Dr. Steve removed the beer mats holding up the back of Ray's barstool and he toppled into the Raven.

"Steady on, Ray, bit too much Bodger tonight mate," said the Liberally Lancinated Librarian, grabbing Ray under the arms to keep him from sprawling across the floor.

"'I'm Jack Baines. What's your name? And what the hell are you doing here?' Jack asks the girl. 'Henrietta Gold,' she replies, fluttering her eyelashes at him, 'but you can call me Goldie. Those giant robot-creatures abducted me from Houston, Texas in nineteen forty-seven. I'm a WAG.' Jack was flustered. "You're a footballer's wife or girlfriend?' 'No, I'm a Willing Alien

Groupie. Hey!' she exploded, taking in the shocked look on Jack's face, 'A girl's gotta do what a girl's gotta do to survive around this place. I've seen the cover of *Amazing Stories*, I know what these guys want. They mean business. To them, we're just a tasty source of nutrients. They were planning an invasion when their scout ship, sent to plant the cyberseeds, crashed in Roswell, New Mexico. We've been in suspended animation on the far side of the moon ever since, waiting for the space elevator to be activated. Well, three days ago we suddenly woke up again, and,' she spread her hands, 'here we are!' 'Cyberseeds!' says Jack, 'so that's what those things were!' Imagine his shock on learning that his mum had accidentally triggered a full-scale Earth invasion! 'So what do we do now?' he asks. Well, Goldie's an all-action Texan gal and she grabs him by the arm and shoves him back into the corridor. 'We gotta get back down before they do. Come on!' And she drags him towards the space elevator. Just as they dash through the elevator door one of the giant alien cyborgs arrives outside and points its death ray at them. 'Halt, resistance is usel…' but the quick-thinking Goldie kicks over the chemical toilet into the path of the onrushing giant alien, which promptly slips base over apex. 'Blimey,' says Jack, stepping forward to get a better look at the stool studded sentinel, 'and I thought it was us who were in the shit,' but Goldie pulls him back into the elevator, touches the wall to reveal a hidden control panel, and hits a button. The doors close and the elevator starts to accelerate back to Earth. She pulls off her shoe and smashes the stiletto heel into the controls. 'That should prevent them from stopping us. Now, what're we going to do for the next three days?' she asks, glancing sideways at the sleeping bag and raising her eyebrows.

Dr. Steve paused for a mouthful of Old Bodger. "I will draw a polite veil over the events on the return journey. Suffice to say that it was a good job Jack's mother had stuffed his rucksack with high-energy snack bars. Well, eventually the lift returns to Earth, the doors open and a somewhat dishevelled and slightly sheepish pair of intrepid space travellers emerge to face a rather startled

Dee Baines. 'And who's this?' she demands of Jack, arms akimbo, eyeing up the somewhat anachronistic girlfriend. 'No time for that,' replies Goldie. 'We've got to spike those suckers,' and she pulls what for all the world looks like a golden egg out of her ample cleavage, tosses it into the elevator and presses the button to close the door. 'What was that?' asks Jack. 'You never mentioned it on the way down.' 'Dark matter bomb,' replies Goldie. 'A girl has to keep something for a rainy day. Watch this.' Just then there is a dull 'crump' and with a bright flash of light the tower starts to rapidly disappear from the ground upwards, like a flame running along a fuse towards a stick of dynamite. 'That'll fix 'em!' whoops Goldie, 'This'll only take a few seconds.' High above the Earth there's an immensely bright twinkle, then nothing. 'What was that?' asks Jack. 'A flying saucer being smashed like a piece of old crockery,' replies Goldie with a grin. Dee Baines looks the pair of space warriors up and down, goes to ask a question, thinks better of this and says, 'You'd both better come inside and tell me all about it.'"

"And I suppose that Jack and Goldie got married and lived happily ever after," said Ray Arnold.

"No, two weeks later she left him for a techno-pirate from an alternative reality who'd materialised on the back of the trans-dimensional shockwave caused by the dark matter explosion in Earth's orbit."

"So poor old Jack came away from the whole adventure with nothing," I said.

"Not quite," said Dr Steve, draining the last of his pint. "He still had the universal translator that Goldie had stuck in his ear. Imagine how much that must be worth. Unfortunately, Jack had no imagination whatsoever, so he saved up and bought a burger van. I hear he's doing very well, selling low fat venison burgers to the high fat Americans who pass through RAF Spadeadam."

Dr. Steve pulled on his overcoat. He'd spun his story out all through the evening and now it was almost closing time. "So thank you for listening to my Jack and Dee Baines talk," he said with a wink. At which point there was a collective groan and people started throwing beer mats and peanuts. "Hey," said the medic, slipping his coat off again, "there *is* a post-script. Jack had a sister, a petite redheaded hoodie who lived in one of the Yorkshire Ridings. She once had a scary, lycanthropic adventure with her megadentulous mum's mum..."

"Sounds like a furry tail to me," said the Prof, adopting a broad Bradford burr.

"Time gentlemen please," called Michael. "As Professor Moriarty said to Dr. Watson – haven't you got Holmes to go to?"

Feathers of the Dinosaur

Henry Gee

"A pint, and quickly."

Michael looked up from behind the bar, his face white with shock. Not at the peremptory tone of the request, nor even at the distinctly un-Fountainlike demeanour of the customer, but at the choice of beverage. The last time Dr Laura Fowler had demanded an alcoholic drink Michael had been equally shocked. On that occasion it had been a white-wine spritzer, and Michael's expression suggested that either he'd never heard of one or he thought La Fowler had asked him to remove his trousers and do handstands on the bar.

"Straight up? A pint?"

"No, in a tankard. Sometime today would be nice."

"Any particular pint?" asked Michael. He was beginning to sound hurt.

"Old Bodger," puffed Graham O'Donnell, squeezing his way to the bar. "Two pints, one for me and one for Dr Fowler – and a pint of whatever you're having, Michael."

"Now you're talking" said the landlord, suitably mollified. Oil, if that's what it was, had been poured on waters which, if not troubled, had shown signs of incipient turbulence.

By then, of course, the slow and slightly sodden susurrus of Paradise Bar chat had sputtered into silence as everyone turned towards the source of the recent rise in emotional temperature. Not that those of us gathered on that particular Tuesday – all male as it happens – regretted the sight.

I think we all recall the evening Laura Fowler first joined us at the Fountain. She was a bit of a show stopper. Slender, in perfectly tailored grey woollen skirt and jacket; immaculate, form-fitting white silk blouse showing off a poitrine that made up for in elegance what it lacked in bulk; legs that went up to wherever legs go up to; long, unfeasibly shiny and well-styled brown hair and big, flashing brown eyes, she looked as out of place in the Fountain as a giraffe might riding a unicycle. In fact, 'Tweet' Peston quipped on that debut evening that she looked as if she'd walked out of a hair-care commercial and asked if she thought she was 'worth it'. That was the first time anyone crossed La Fowler, something few have dared since. Not while sober, at any rate. She'd said nothing, but then, she didn't need to. Her eyes had turned on Tweet like twin petawatt lasers. Poor Tweet shrank visibly, probably trying to solve differential equations in his head to avoid his brain actually imploding. Whether Dr Fowler's withering glance squeezed any excess neutrons out of him is not recorded. The pints in here have foaming heads, but bubble chambers they are not.

Oh yes, Dr Fowler made quite an impact. There's no question that in terms of sartorial elegance she is without equal among our august group. Not even Professor Mackintosh can match her, though he always dresses smartly in polished brogues, tweeds, trousers with razor-sharp creases, and the ever-present tie – something I enjoy ribbing him about. His is the smartness of another age.

Oddly, Graham O'Donnell, Laura's frequent companion, tends towards the opposite end of the fashion scale. The evening he appeased Michael with a drink was an especially windy one, and many of us looked a little unkempt on our arrival, but Graham looks that way much of the time. Tuttle-Derby once whispered to me that this was probably due to the hours the man spent twitching, under hedges and on windy cliff tops etcetera. Who's to say he didn't have a point?

The shock for all of us, I think, was that on this occasion Laura matched him. She appeared – and there's no easy way of putting this – dishevelled. Her clothes were as smart as ever, but they looked as if she'd slept in them. Her hair was all over the place. And her eyes were punctuated not by expertly applied mascara, but by dark rings, like bruises.

"Is everything all right, m'dear?" asked Professor Mackintosh, as space was made for Fowler and O'Donnell. Fowler looked at him, but her gaze looked inward rather than outward, and she said nothing. Her eyes were focused on her pint which she picked up, and drained in a single draught. O'Donnell signalled Michael for a refill.

"I take it this is for medicinal purposes?" said Dr Steve, once the new drink arrived. He was doubtless totting up the units that petite brunettes could safely drink in one go without running the risk of instant liver failure. Fowler drained this second pint, rose, and disappeared to the Ladies'.

By now the company was visibly concerned, if only in its enforcedly avuncular manner.

"I'm sorry," said O'Donnell, "Perhaps I should explain." the bar fell silent.

The floor was his.

"I'm afraid Laura's had a bit of a shock. You know she works on bird evolution. Well, we've just come from the Natural History Museum..."

"I knew it. That 'Fossil Birds from China' exhibition," I said.

"Been meaning to pop along myself," said Crown Baker. "Any good?"

"Yes, it's great," said O'Donnell, "but Laura, being a professional, went behind the scenes. I tagged along behind, and, well, it's a tale." Looks were exchanged. Crown Baker sighed: it was his round, and he knew it. He waved towards Michael who, in the tic-tac between experienced barmen and regulars, raised an eyebrow back at him. He knew what to do.

"It's like this. Twenty years ago, nobody really knew how birds evolved. There was Archaeopteryx, and that's really pretty much it. And even that looked reptilian. Apart from the feathers, of course."

"A missing link?" said Crown Baker.

"Well, perhaps, but don't let Laura hear you say that," said O'Donnell. As if on cue, the lady in question reappeared, looking much more composed. Her arrival coincided with Michael and a tray of pints. Laura took one without waiting to be asked and set to it as if she were dying of thirst.

"Now, these days we'd say that Archaeopteryx was just another dinosaur with feathers," O'Donnell continued, "But twenty years ago it was all different. Feathered dinosaurs hadn't been discovered. Although people like Thomas Henry Huxley had speculated that dinosaurs and birds were related, nobody took that very seriously".

"Why not?" asked Dr Steve.

"Because Archaeopteryx lived in the Jurassic, tens of millions years before the dinosaurs it most resembled – small, running-abouty things like Velociraptor – had evolved. And yet, here it was, pretty much fully formed, a bird, in the Jurassic, long before Velociraptor."

"Velociraptor and its friends and relatives lived in the Cretaceous, didn't they?" asked Crown Baker.

"I always thought that film didn't have the right name," I said.

"Ah! Jurassic Park!" said Crown Baker. "I guess Cretaceous Park didn't have the same ring to it."

"I've a theory about that," said Professor Mackintosh. "Jurassic rhymes with Boracic. Potential for low-budget remakes, you see. There's a corner of Hollywood that's forever in the sound of Bow Bells." He winked. Only later did I twig he'd been trying to cheer Laura up, and that she looked up at him then, thin traces of a smile on her lips, their perfection marred only by a beery moustache.

"So, there it was," continued O'Donnell, oblivious to any body language flickering around him. "The evolution of birds was a complete mystery. People thought that birds probably didn't evolve from dinosaurs. Maybe their ancestors were some nonspecific crocodiley thing, back in the Triassic".

"Now, hang on," said Dr Steve, "birds look even less like crocodiles than dinosaurs."

"Sure, but that's crocodiles now," said O'Donnell. "Back then, before the dinosaurs really got going, there were lots of crocodile-like reptiles of all shapes and sizes. Some were quite small, some even walked on their hind legs, and, with a bit of a following wind, some were maybe even a bit birdlike."

"So, you're saying that birds evolved from crocodile-like things in the Triassic?" said Dr Steve.

"No, that's not what he's saying." Laura's voice, quiet, contralto, yet emphatic, filled the room. "Graham is saying that nobody had any idea where birds came from. The default was some unspecified group of reptiles. But we already know birds evolved from reptiles. You just have to look at a chicken to realise that. So, saying that they evolved from some group or other in the Triassic is like you physicists saying 'x = x'. No wonder all the so-called scientific creationists are physicists. And, not only that, men. Honestly." She turned back to her pint.

O'Donnell, perhaps driven by an abhorrence of vacuums, rushed to fill the uncomfortable silence. "The problem was that there was no convincing group of fossils in the Triassic that looked like birds. There were a few claimants, but nothing that would really stand up in the proverbial court of law. The few palaeontologists making a case for a bird-dinosaur link had a similar struggle. Then, in the 1990s, fossils of dinosaurs with feathers started coming out of China, making it clear that dinosaurs had been feathered for a very long time -- back into the Jurassic or even further – and that Archaeopteryx was just another dinosaur with feathers. The bird-dinosaur link seemed well-established. Only..."

"Only?" prompted Crown Baker.

"Well, there were a few blowhards who continued to agitate against the bird-dinosaur link. They appeared at conferences with button badges that said BAND -- Birds Are Not Dinosaurs. But they kind of faded away with time." O'Donnell sighed and took a manful swig. Laura had finished her third pint by now, and, slumped in her seat, gazed across the table with a thousand-yard stare.

"Graham's given us a fine hors-d'oeuvres, m'dear." This was Professor Mackintosh, twinkling at Laura and trying to meet her gaze. "What say you to giving us the main course? My round? Hmm?" Laura brightened visibly in the attention, as the Professor signalled to Michael behind the bar.

"Oh, well, if I must," she sighed, sitting up and leaning forward slightly, as if about to impart a secret. The rest of us leaned forward too, partly for this shared sense of conspiracy, but also, if we're honest, to get a better view of her decolletage. I'm not ashamed to say that we're a pretty prehistoric crew, us Paradise Bar regulars. Paradise it may be, but there are far too many Adams and not nearly enough Eves.

"You know I work on the evolution of birds, right?" she began.

"Right!" we panted, sycophantically.

"But I don't usually work on fossils. It's all genes. By comparing the genetics of lots of modern bird species, and making a few assumptions about the rate of evolution, you can get a fix on when modern groups of birds evolved. But there's a problem. You need external calibration. Some independent marker of when points in evolution happened. That's where fossils come in, and Archaeopteryx has always been that marker. Because of Archaeopteryx, we always thought that birds had evolved by the end of the Jurassic at the latest."

"But Graham said that Archaeopteryx was just another dinosaur with feathers," said Dr Steve, unwisely, as Michael arrived with another tray of Old Bodger.

"I was coming to that," snapped Laura, pausing only to sup from her pint. I could have sworn I saw ice form on mine. "It wasn't just feathered dinosaurs that came out of China – a lot of fossil birds came out, too – birds that were much more birdlike than Archaeopteryx. At last we had some decent fossils we could use to calibrate the rate of evolution. The story was clear. There were lots of birdlike dinosaurs around, and even some dinosaur-like birds, all the way back into the Jurassic. But birds of a more modern type – birds I could use to reference the evolution of modern birds – didn't get going until after the K/T Boundary."

"Who's this 'Katy Boundary'?" interjected Dr Steve. For a doctor, he hasn't much idea about his own safety. This time it was Professor Mackintosh who came to his rescue.

"The Kay-Tee Boundary. Cretaceous, Tertiary. And, yes, I know 'Cretaceous' starts with a 'C' but there you have it. The mass extinction. Sixty-five million years ago last Tuesday. You know, asteroids and whatnot. Put paid to the dinosaurs."

"Anyway," Laura continued, "that's the reference point I've had ever since I was a graduate student. Solid as a rock. Until..." she began to waver. Silence fell upon the company, and none dared break it. Laura smiled wanly, took a gulp of Old Bodger and continued.

"Until... well, today."

"Ah, yes, we come to it at last!" Crown Baker ventured.

"I'd heard rumours, of course," said Laura, "So I was quite excited when we – that is, Graham and I – got to the Museum."

Graham took that as a cue to interrupt. "The exhibition was well away from the crowds, in a side gallery. We had to pay extra to get in, so we had the place pretty much to ourselves, and..." Laura scowled at him.

"Yes, well, the exhibition contained what I expected," she said. "But I had an appointment in the palaeontology department. Alexa Mallard – the curator of fossil reptiles and birds – had told me she had something that I might find interesting.

"So, there we are, in her office, high up in the southeast tower of the Museum, looking down at the traffic in Cromwell Road, but, you know, not looking, because this thing on Alexa's display monitor was..."

This time the pause could only have been for dramatic emphasis.

"You know, it's hard to put something into words – something completely unexpected, something you've seen for the first time. At first, though, it didn't look so strange. On Alexa's screen was a high-def picture of a fossil bird. And it was perfect, down to the beak, the feathers, the wishbone, the stubby tail with a fan of feathers: I swear that if I'd just been passing I'd have put it down as roadkill – a pigeon, maybe, or a crow, freshly squashed by any passing bus. It looked that modern. No fingers on its wings, no teeth, no dinosaur sickle-claw, this was a bird, no question.

"So Alexa asked me what I made of it, and I... I... well, I told her what I've just told you. And I'll never forget what she said next. 'That's what I thought you'd say', she said. 'When I first looked at it, I couldn't believe it. I just wanted another pair of eyes, calibration if you like, someone who knows all about birds but who isn't a palaeontologist'." Laura took a long pull at her pint. She placed the tankard slowly and carefully on the table. The dull clunk filled the room like the footsteps of doom; such was the collective holding-of breath, held more intensely when Laura unfastened one button on her blouse. "Is it just me or is it hot in here?"

Professor Mackintosh smiled at Laura and gave Crown Baker a sharp nudge. He took the hint and opened a window, letting some breezy London evening air into the fervid fug. The 'breeze' was sufficiently strong to soon shut it again.

"That's when Alexa delivered her bombshell," Laura continued. "'You'd better sit down,' she said, so Graham and I sat on the sofa in her office. 'The thing is', she went on, 'this thing is Triassic. And what's more, very early Triassic.' Alexa's words took some time to sink in. I stammered something about being sure, and Alexa said the age determination was absolutely certain, the geology was unimpeachable, the fossil came from a site in Inner Mongolia, well researched, she'd been there herself, all above board. The picture was from a paper she'd been sent in confidence, to peer-review by a journal, and at first she thought it was a fake. But – well – it's not. It's for real."

"Sorry," said Dr Steve, "I don't get it. Triassic, Early Triassic, Late Triassic, Boracic, what's the difference? Am I just being thick?"

"Afraid so, old man," I said, making my way to the bar. It was my round. Having some distance between me and the table allowed a certain perspective. There they were, the Fountain Regulars, clustered around Laura Fowler like supplicants before the Cross, the massed empties before her luminous form playing the role of votive candles. Our Lady of the Divine Bodger. For her part, Laura seemed so stunned by the implications of her story, of what she was about to say, that she was unable to continue. Evidently, her brain wanted to give utterance, but her mouth and vocal chords simply refused. Either that or it was the beer. Laura had just drained her fourth pint of Old Bodger, a quantity which has been known to make people dance naked in fountains and do silly things with road cones. Rugby players. Medical students. People with twice the body mass of Dr Laura Fowler. The lady remained remarkably composed withal.

"The thing is," said Graham, with rising heat, "this is a bird, a proper bird, an honest-to-goodness, twitchable bird. I know a bird when I see one, and this one was as birdishly birdlike as any bird I've ever seen, and..."

"And your point is...?" said Dr Steve, waspishly I thought, but then there was all that beer. We'd matched Laura pint for pint, though none of us were as yet under the table. Graham O'Donnell snorted. Dr Steve growled. We all felt the ground shake, and it wasn't continental drift. Only Professor Mackintosh looked unchanged, unperturbed, a smile on his face, making almost microscopic adjustments to his tie.

"My point is," said Graham, "that birds like that don't appear in the rock record until after the dinosaurs have died out, that is, the K/T boundary..."

"I was wondering when we'd hear from our friend Katy Boundary again," said Dr Steve, looking at his watch, and getting to his feet.

"...to find a modern bird in the earliest Triassic. Well? Do you see the significance of that? Do you?" Graham O'Donnell was now on his feet, matching Dr Steve, eye to eye. "Back in the earliest Triassic, dinosaurs hadn't even evolved! It can mean only one thing..."

That's when Laura found her voice. "It means that birds didn't evolve from dinosaurs, after all. It means that..."

"Ah, I get it," said Professor Mackintosh, "dinosaurs evolved from birds. How remarkable..." He moved closer to Laura. "I can see this'll mean rejigging quite a bit of your earlier work, m'dear. Happened to me with string theory. I'll tell you what to do..."

At that moment the door slammed wide. It was still blowing a gale outside, and a very wind-blown Jocelyn Sparrow staggered in, accompanied by a gust that had us all calling for her to 'shut that door!' During the flurry of activity caused by Jocelyn's arrival, both Prof Mackintosh and La Fowler slipped away – I didn't see them go – leaving Graham O'Donnell to his own devices, although he didn't seem too disconcerted.

"So what have I missed?" asked Jocelyn as she settled down with drink in hand.

"It's a bit complicated to explain all over again," I said to Jocelyn.

"Oh very well! Serves me right for being late."

That didn't stop the rest of us discussing it, though, and Jocelyn probably caught the general gist soon enough. Dinosaurs evolved from birds? Now there was a concept to rock the scientific world.

The following week, we awaited Laura's arrival with considerable anticipation. As for Professor Mackintosh, he seemed somewhat evasive about what had happened after they left us.

"Well, I escorted the good Doctor back to her place in a taxi. She was distinctly, shall we say, bodgered."

"Did you help her indoors?" asked Dr Steve with a leer in his voice.

"Of course," replied Professor Mackintosh. "I am a gentleman. And, being a gentleman, I then departed promptly."

Soon after, Laura herself turned up, with Graham in tow.

"Get me a lemonade," she told him.

"Not a pint of Bodger?" enquired Dr Steve.

La Fowler grimaced. "Never again! Not after the hangover I had last week."

"The consequences," I pointed out, "being proportional to the cause, namely a revolution in our notions of evolution? If you'll pardon the rhyme."

She stared at me hauntedly. "I went back to the Museum, you know. I had to see that photo again! The whole journal submission…"

"And?"

"Alexa Mallard is no longer with the museum. She's apparently accepted a very lucrative job offer in America, one which had to be taken up immediately. Her colleagues seemed quite puzzled. Fortunately, I remembered which journal she was peer-reviewing that paper for. So I phoned the editor, for all the good that did me. He denies indignantly that any such paper has ever been submitted, or been sent anywhere for peer-review."

Tweet Peston burst out laughing. "So you were pulling our legs all along!"

"Well done you," said Dr Steve. "I fell for it."

I disagreed. "Four pints of Bodger says she wasn't."

"Is that a bet?" asked Tweet.

"No, I'm talking about the emotional state she was clearly in last week."

We looked at Graham, who shrugged. "I don't know what to make of it all."

Professor Mackintosh took it upon himself to intervene, in

elder statesman fashion. "Suppose – just suppose – that a time machine could ever exist, now or in the future, and suppose that an experimenter sent his pet parrot – just for example – back into the past to test said machine, and now suppose that this parrot somehow escaped and subsequently got fossilised. Just one birdy, mind you, so there'd be no descendants. Well, if that fossil were ever discovered, providing actual evidence of such a time machine, I reckon any sensible government would crack down on it, keep a tight lid, at least pro tem, pending further investigation."

I stared at the Prof. "You're not seriously suggesting…?"

He shrugged. "I merely say suppose." He smiled knowingly, and tapped the side of his nose.

"I've changed my mind," Laura called out to Graham, who was still at the bar. "I'll have a pint of Bodger!"

"Hair of the dog?" asked Dr Steve.

"No," Laura said, as serious as you like. "Feathers of the dinosaur."

Book Wurms

Andy West

Unusually for the Fountain, conversation around the table fizzled out. Partly due to the fact that the last topic lacked novelty, it being little more than a rerun of something discussed the previous Tuesday: the imminent (1.5 million years hence) far-too-close visit of the orange dwarf Gliese 710 to the Sol system. Also, people were pausing to get their heads around the latest guest beer: Brain Teaser.

Although tending towards a ruby ale in colour, Brain Teaser had a malty foundation with an overtone of leather, which one felt should belong to a much darker and more robust beer. Above this comfortable sofa of flavour sat hints of liquorice and chocolate, like a sweet stout, not to mention a slight metallic after-taste that left the pallet feeling cleansed between sups, reminiscent of an IPA. How someone had combined these attributes from across the spectrum of ales in one brew was indeed a brain teaser.

I sometimes found myself in the role of de-facto host for our Tuesday gatherings, and in this capacity I was about to dish up a reserve tale I'd kept back for just such a quiet moment, when the ratty-faced man stepped forward. That was my name for him anyhow; I'd seen him once or twice before, hanging around at the edge of the group, listening to our debates and stories with obvious attention yet never interacting. He introduced himself as Günther and said he had an interesting story. To hear him talk, apart from a slight accent, you'd never have realized that his first language was German or anything other than English.

"Please, go ahead," I urged, glad that I wouldn't need my reserve, which in truth was mostly cribbed from the Internet. This was bound to reduce its appreciation, originality being highly prized.

"It can't be *just* a story. The theme has to be scientific you know," Professor Mackintosh pointed out, rather sharply I thought. Perhaps the prof didn't like Günther's unkempt look.

Günther smiled patronisingly and somewhat mysteriously, as though the dark of his brown eyes hid some secret knowledge.

"Oh, I think you'll find this qualifies."

Günther could hardly be less Germanic. The long nose and thin face inspiring my nick-name were of dark eastern-Mediterranean hue, possibly Turkish, and his receding hair was black and greasy. The cut of his threadbare suit did have an Austrian look though.

After clearing his throat and taking a large sup of Brain Teaser, Günther began.

"This happened to... to an acquaintance of mine. A young man, early thirties, married but with no kids. One Saturday he and his wife popped into a little shop that sold antique and second-hand books, here in the city. They were just browsing you know, not likely to buy. While the man, Tom, was checking out volumes on old motorcycles – a hobby of his – Eve looked at the art section. A large and rather curious book caught her eye. It was a hand-crafted work, apparently by an amateur and packed full of bizarre pictures, brightly coloured and rather primitive yet at the same time intricate and fascinating. There was apparently no structure or linking theme to the work, drawings and paintings and crayon illustrations all ran into each other seemingly at random. Strange symbols and lines and dots competed for space too, as did writing; *lots* of writing. Some of the latter was in type-fonts of various kinds, some was hand-written, much was in tiny script and covered whole pages – spilling over the artworks – whereas elsewhere words pressured the edges of pictures yet didn't cover them. 'Must be a million words or more,' Tom estimated when he sauntered over. '*The conflict with Hell cannot be engaged by Man, even the most clever,*' read out Eve from one small section. '*Computers multiply, while communication diminishes.* What a weird book!' Many of the pictures and symbols seemed religious in nature: gory crucifixions, saintly figures striving against darkness, inverted crosses and such, though the full subject matter varied widely. The book made Tom feel uncomfortable somehow, but Eve purchased it, apparently on a whim.

"Within a couple of weeks, Tom was feeling a lot *more* uncomfortable about that book. Eve had taken to reading it obsessively; late into the night, during meals with it propped by her plate, even in the toilet. She developed a haunted look, with dark rings under her eyes. Her work as a teacher was impacted; heck, their sex life was impacted! Yet whenever Tom tried to talk about the problem, she was highly defensive, aggressive even. She started clutching the book to herself or locking it away, perhaps afraid that Tom might dispose of the one thing that now inspired her in life."

Günther paused for another sup at the complex tastes of Brain Teaser.

"Now Tom was an atheist and consequently he didn't believe in evil as a living entity, but the book made him doubt. Seriously doubt. On the odd occasion when Eve was less guarded, he'd glimpsed lurid pictures of the devil and alarming symbols of Witchcraft inside it, and often Eve unconsciously mumbled things at breakfast, such as: '*When first Satan the black bow bent, and the moral law from the Gospel rent...*' or '*Eternal damnation faces those who do not write the message...*', the latter which she'd sometimes repeat over and over. And Tom recalled the upside-down crosses too."

Professor Mackintosh frowned at this point and swept imaginary hair across his balding pate. "I hope this isn't going to be a ghost story or some silly Satanic Bible nonsense. Because by definition it *cannot* then have any basis in truth!"

The rest of us were all engrossed in the tale by now, except perhaps for the Raven. He had been obliviously fiddling with his mobile in the corner, but looked up sharply at the words *Satanic Bible* and stared at Günther's back.

Günther's eyes smouldered yet he gave a thin-lipped smile. "I assure you, this is true, sir. *Gospel Truth*." I signalled him to go on.

"Well, Tom was out of his depth. He saw his doctor, who talked about Prozac and depression. Then, in desperation, he went back to the bookshop. The proprietor shrugged his shoulders. 'Looked harmless to me. I'd say it was an attempt to emulate the works of William Blake. I've seen similar efforts both old and new; that one's at the better end of the spectrum but clearly still an amateur work. I'll be happy to provide a refund if you bring it back'. Tom had only a passing familiarity with Blake's work, but felt that... ehm... the bookseller was holding something back. Yet, short of threat, what could he do? He'd never felt so impotent; his Eve was being sucked into some kind of religious hocus-pocus and he had no way of fighting for her!

"When Tom returned it was to a pleasant greeting shouted by Eve from the dining room. His heart rose, and rose still further when he rushed in there to find her *not* reading the book! Although *it* was there, open on a corner of the table, Eve was humming to herself and scribbling on a piece of paper. 'Hey, we could go out tonight,' he offered. 'We haven't done that for a while.' But Tom's hopes were premature. 'Far too busy,' Eve replied. His spirit was crushed still lower when he saw she was writing strange text, and that on other pieces of paper that were scattered about she'd evidently practised drawings of bearded prophets and pentangles and strange trees."

Professor Mackintosh grumbled and tapped his pipe loudly against the hearth, signals studiously ignored by Günther.

"Despite himself, Tom was surprised at the quality of the work. 'I didn't know you could draw,' he commented hollowly, for the sake of something to say that might keep her engaged.

'I've always wanted to' was her odd reply. Then she mumbled rhymes in some foreign tongue while frantically filling a page with tiny though curiously neat text. Tom picked up a discarded sheet and saw a bleak yet complex tree under which there was some decorative prose: *Science is our tree of Death, Art is our tree of Life, Post Normal Science is our Escape.* Then he edged around the room and glanced casually at *the book*, hoping not to evoke Eve's defences. *Mary had a little lamb, its fleece was white as snow, but within a few years snowfall will become a rare and exciting event. Children aren't going to know what snow is.* This peculiar version of the nursery rhyme was written around a sketch of an intense sheep-headed man, whose coat bore the initials 'Dr V'. Another rhyme intersected: *In books or work or healthful play, I would be busy too, for Satan finds some mischief still, for idle hands to do.* Surrounding both rhymes were lines of ugly children, or perhaps dwarves, whose intersecting shovels caused an optical illusion that made Tom's eyes hurt."

I noticed a flicker of acknowledgement pass between Mackintosh and Dalton, who both now looked a little wary, but I'd no idea what in Günther's tale had triggered this. Tuttle-Derby's cherubic face revealed only entrancement.

"Well," Günther went on after another sup, "things got steadily worse for Tom. If Eve had been distracted before, she was doubly so now. She assembled inks and paints, crayons and draughtsman's tools and even an old typewriter. She worked constantly on producing strange material like that in *the book*, to the exclusion of almost everything else. She was fired from her school, she became dirty and lost weight, much of the time she was barely coherent. Belatedly her family and friends rallied round, but to little effect. Eve paused only for her mother, but restarted work the moment her parents drove away. From Tom's perspective even this minor victory was a dubious benefit, because ultimately Eve's mother blamed Tom and not *the book* for the problem, claiming that he'd never properly supported her daughter. To Tom's now constant pleading, Eve would answer only that all would be well again once her work was finished."

"A curiously powerful book," I commented, "for all its apparently simplistic phrases."

"Yes, yes," enthused Günther, his eyes shining, "very powerful, very." He pulled a couple of folded sheets from inside his suit and handed them to Tuttle-Derby. "Examples."

"Hey, this dragon's moving!" Tuttle shoved a sheet at Dalton.

Günther smiled toothily. "Quite safe, quite safe! Just an optical illusion, you know."

The pages were highly engaging, featuring strange patterns that attracted yet confused the eye, and more of the odd truisms, if such they could be called. Two that stood out were: *'We look at more and more images, but see less and less'*, and *'Satan has more knowledge but less wisdom than any other creature'*. Others were: *'True Life cannot be measured by the number of breaths we take, but by the moments that take our breath away'*, and, *'In 2035 AD the rivers of India will fail, to the peril of millions, for the Great Himalayan Glaciers will be no more'*. The Raven sidled up to the group but I noticed that he was careful to stay behind Günther. The group was strangely subdued, with none of the usual banter, and the atmosphere was rather tense. Raven took the pages being passed around as though they were a loaded gun, glancing at them obliquely and taking care not to stare directly at the artwork. I began to feel a little uncomfortable myself, especially as the sheets demonstrated that there might be some truth in the weird tale of Tom and *the book*.

"Nonsense! Drivel!" declared Dr. Steve, who'd drifted in just after Günther got started. Nevertheless he stared at the sheet in his hand, until Prof Mack pulled it from him.

"Ahem," voiced Günther by way of restarting. "Tom researched William Blake on the Internet: 'the Book of Urien', 'The Song of Los', 'Urizen' and 'Jerusalem' and 'the Daughters of Albion'…"

"I'm familiar…" murmured Dalton.

Günther grunted. "Yes. Strange, inspired. Cartoon-like, yet

not so. Emotive, proud and prophetic. Despairing. Wisdom or mad scribbling? Blake's work was certainly reminiscent of *the book*, but this didn't help Tom any. So he took advantage of Eve's increasing exhaustion. Early one morning, while she slept with her head on the dining room table after working all night, Tom stole *the book* from under her hand. On the open page he noticed the image of a missile and a sour-faced man with green skin and red ears. *'We have guided missiles and misguided men'*, ran the inevitable phrase. In between its lines ran another in a tiny font: *'Be it remembered, that incidentally the temptations of Satan are of Service to the people of God.'* In jumbled colours on her laptop screen was more. Eve had taken to fashioning a few basics on this machine before adding the rest by hand, though her lack of computer skills seemed to cause great frustration. *'Ours are the days of healthy profits and unhealthy relationships'*, Tom read.

"Now Tom didn't destroy the book; his intent was to find the source of its hold on Eve, so he returned to the bookshop once again. But the bookseller was very clever. Tom tried anger, despair, pathos, even threat and trickery, but received only calm and innocent responses; which told him nothing. But this man *had* to know something. Tom ended up getting his money back, but *his Eve* was what he really wanted back, so finally, *finally…* Tom became clever too. He returned to the shop late in the evening after it had closed. He reached the rear of the building via a back-alley, and crept into the yard, hoping maybe to break in and find out for himself what the bookseller wouldn't reveal, though in truth he had no idea what to look for."

"A vampire cell?" suggested Tuttle-Derby, his eyes wide. "Somehow they've influenced Eve, through *the book*. Now she works for them? Kinda' Vampire Admin?" His weak stab at humour didn't alleviate the strained atmosphere.

"No blood," commented Dr. Steve. "So far anyhow. Maybe a cell of wizards?"

"Ah, vampires influence through blood," I clarified. "No blood's been exchanged."

"This story's some sort of deceit," muttered Dalton with feeling. This surprised me; there's normally a great deal of latitude at the Fountain. Humour too. But Prof Mackintosh was frowning deeply and the Raven continued to watch our visitor with open suspicion.

Günther rolled his eyes. "Vampires? Bonkers, you say here? Bonkers you are!" He took back the sheets and slipped them inside his suit. "Well, it seemed that Tom was out of luck anyhow. A dim ground floor light was on and he could clearly see the bookseller working at a desk. Keeping inside the shadow, Tom crept right up to the bay window. The guy was typing into a computer, and occasionally turned to look at something set by his side, a book maybe; and he had the most peculiar spectacles on! One lens was red with vertical black stripes, the other was green with horizontal black stripes. Then Tom noticed the bulb in the desk-lamp was deep yellow, and next to it on a moveable brass arm was a big lens with a UV halo light. Was this some bizarre ritualistic equipment?

"Tom was still trying to figure this out when at last lady luck smiled upon him. The bookseller received a telephone call and left the building in a hurry, crossing the yard to his car and so walking right past Tom, who fortunately had found a wheely-bin to crouch behind. And having left in such haste, the bookseller had made an error. The sash window by the desk was open an inch to let in some air, and he'd forgotten to close it. Tom was at the window in seconds. His desperation was so great he never even considered the illegality of what he was doing. The sash made a terrible screech when he raised it up, but then he was in!"

"At last," squeaked Tuttle-Derby, "now we're getting somewhere!"

"Ah…" responded Günther. "But it seemed Tom was to be disappointed. *The book* lay next to the computer, with cardboard strips laid over it such that only part of one page was exposed. Tom swept the cardboard away, but the page showed only the usual intricate nonsense. Two serpents fought over an egg. Above a big spiral were words in bold red: *'Inconvenient Truth threatens the lives of us all, be vigilant!'* Smaller text in a fancy yellow font declared, *'Despair: the eternal lot of those who cannot possess their desire,'* and *'Believe: religion is its own purpose'*. He was getting used to such stuff, and indeed the fact that a great deal in *the book* didn't seem to be Satanic, or even religious. Yet what then was the source of its power? He turned to the computer, fortunately still powered on and logged in. It appeared that the bookseller was writing a work of his own, a textbook, apparently the history of some obscure endangered species. Hardly the revelation Tom was seeking! The name of the species was in a foreign script, maybe Cyrillic, though apparently it was classed as a 'scaffolding species'. This meant no more to Tom than the unpronounceable name. The work was dry and scholarly and seemed of no relevance, yet Tom forced himself to read a little, just in case. And then he became more and more engaged, soon reading avidly as a great horror and realisation dawned on him. *The book* was one of this species! Its peculiar and intriguing content was both a means of survival and the equivalent of genetic codes, while the 'scaffolding' it used to replicate, was his Eve!"

I noticed the Raven, still behind Günther, brace himself as if preparing to pounce on our visitor. I tried to catch his eye without success. I had a bad feeling about all of this. Günther seemed oblivious.

"Apparently the species is millennia old, going back to the 'Letters from Heaven' and perhaps even to pictograms. *'Should any sentient beings in any of the kingdoms of existence'* Tom read from a translated Japanese entry of a 'living book' from 765AD, *'copy down this Dharani on birch-bark or palm leaves or papyrus, keeping it by him in some scented wrapping, this man in all his life will remain unharmed by any poison'*. Tom leapt up. He wanted to rip *the book* apart, page by page, but his skin crawled and he didn't dare touch the thing. He practically dived out of the window and rushed home, to save Eve from the terrible thing she was birthing…"

At that moment, Raven made his move, grabbing Günther

from behind and locking an arm around his shoulder. "Help me hold him!" he yelled, but we were too startled to move. Günther, however, reacted swiftly and violently, delivering a vicious jab to the Raven's stomach and wrenching free. He leapt towards the door and was out on the street in a second. The Raven followed awkwardly, clutching his gut.

Taking care to put down his pint of Old Bodger first, Dr. Steve rushed out after them.

The rest of us were still unmoving, our mouths open in shock. Dalton broke the paralysis by bending down to pick up something off the floor, displaying what he held: a pair of spectacles. "I saw these fall from Günther's pocket," he commented. One lens was red with vertical black stripes, the other was green with horizontal black stripes. "Can this tale be true?" he asked.

Professor Mackintosh took a long pull on his Brain Teaser to settle himself. Quite frankly, I needed the same medicine and followed suite, wishing I'd gone for something more familiar this evening, such as Old Bodger. None of us had ever witnessed an incidence of violence in the Fountain before. We quickly concluded that Günther must be none other than the bookseller himself, although why he'd risked exposure in telling the story and what had made the Raven suspicious of him were both mysteries.

Professor Mackintosh rubbed his pate. "It is theoretically possible." He put down his glass and we knew we were in for some sage words. "We've come a long way since Darwin, but the Big Push to turn the narrative and examples of evolutionary science into even a rough mathematical model is still pretty much stalled on defining the terms."

"After 150 years?" exclaimed Tuttle-Derby. "Why so slow?"

"Discoveries over recent decades have dramatically widened the scope of evolutionary theory, and all sorts of strange cases challenge the basic notions we'd once thought were fixed. Memetics raises a host of such challenges, but even sticking with biology it's hard for instance to even define what a Darwinian population actually *is*.

"All well and good," Tuttle-Derby said. "But what about *the book*, can it be a real creature?"

"Well," said the prof thoughtfully, "let's explore the idea by considering the example of birds' nests. The young of a particular bird species apparently imprints the exact details of its nest and, often long after that nest is destroyed, replicates it faithfully in adulthood."

"That's true," Laura Fowler, our resident avian specialist, agreed. "I think I know where you're going with this."

"Mathematically speaking such nests are an independent Darwinian population, which leverages the birds. There's just sufficient variation in the nest reconstructions to allow evolution, *the natural selection of nests*, to occur. This peculiar perspective is a well known academic test case, but I'd suggest an entity like *the book* might be much more of a real living and evolving creature than those nests. If it really *can* carry its own encodings and cultural tools, with which the ghastly thing could hi-jack us for its propagation, then it'd be at least as alive as a virus. And viruses are scaffolding species too; they hi-jack the cells of other creatures – an external reproductive scaffolding if you like – to replicate themselves."

Tuttle-Derby and Jocelyn both looked alarmed, while Laura nodded thoughtfully at the Prof's words. "The nests you're referring to pose an interesting puzzle for taxonomists," she said. "A can of worms I'm not prepared to open right now."

At that point the Raven and Dr Steve returned, somewhat out of breath. Dr Steve clutched a sheet of paper in his hand. "Günther got away," he waved the sheet, "but he dropped this."

"How did you know?" I asked the Raven. "That Günther was the bookseller, I mean?"

"Only a very few people in the rare book trade could have heard the rumours about the Book Wurms. We've referred the matter to Interpol but they don't believe the Wurm's exist. If

Günther's who I think he is, he may be one of the Keepers – those who dedicate their lives to ensuring the Wurms survive. Rumour has it there are at least four Keepers in Europe, with others in the Middle East, China and India. I believe Günther is the Keeper known as 'G'. No one knew what he looked like before this. I couldn't believe it when I realised what he was talking about. This has to be him!"

Dr Steve was staring at the sheet. *"The Sons of Men are Taller but their Tempers are Shorter'."*

"Ah," continued Raven, "completely untrue of course. But most people are not immune to negative memes in the form of platitudes or promises or prophecy and the Wurms deploy many thousands of these, probing for entry points into people's heads. Those memes that release satisfying neuro-chemicals when an apparent truth resonates with a particular reader create the openings, then subliminal cultural themes widen the holes and hypnotic patterns finally hijack the reader's brain. The dots and lines and pattern relationships also hold the core cipher of the Wurm itself, language; independent instructions encoded over millennia that leverage the capabilities of humans to create, so creating the next Wurm. The offspring will be like the parent, yet slanted somewhat towards the culture and skills of the replicator, in this case poor Eve. So there's ample room for evolution to work, and the Wurm's skills with cultural hypnosis, subordinating emotions and memetic hooks far exceed our understanding."

Dalton rolled his eyes and mouthed a silent word that looked like 'bollocks'. But Mackintosh had hung eagerly on Raven's every word.

"The glasses, and the coloured lights," queried the worthy professor, "they stop the Wurm from infecting Günther?"

"Yes. Along with limited page area and limited time exposure, they break up the Wurm's patterns and allow it to be studied safely."

"Just think how much we'd learn about the brain from that Wurm! Not to mention the fears and desires of European populations down the ages."

"First time we've ever retrieved so much as a single page," answered Raven. "There's evidence that 'G'... I mean Günther, is trying to target people with computer skills. Computers are new and sudden in terms of the Wurm's evolutionary timeline, and people use some different parts of the brain to create on them. Maybe the Wurms are having trouble tracking this. If they can't keep up, then their future is still more under threat."

"*'Rub a dub dub, three men in a tub, a necessary course of action due to flash flooding caused by climate chang.'* But they aren't a butcher and baker and whatever. There's a polar bear and a panda and a tiger, all in suits. A dog is drowning outside the boat." Raven pulled the sheet from Dr Steve's hand.

"And Blake?" prompted Mackintosh.

"Ah. Well we... I mean our little group, we think that Blake was one of the few to escape a Wurm's clutches. It left him permanently altered, putting out strong memetic material for the rest of his life, none of which is organised enough to form a new Wurm."

Jocelyn's eyes widened. "One of the few to escape?" she echoed. "Then what happened to Eve, and what did Tom do?"

"That's one of the issues Interpol *do* want to talk to Günther about. Tom committed suicide and Eve is permanently gaga. Poor woman is in some institution, apparently she's completely incoherent. We believe Eve's Wurm was completed by the time Tom got home after slipping into Günther's place. He probably got tempted, thought there'd be no risk in quickly flicking through Eve's 'great work'. When he realised the Wurm had taken hold and he couldn't reverse the process, he ended it all. The police found Günther's fingerprints in Tom and Eve's house, hence their suspicion of some kind of foul play. No doubt he came to collect the new Wurm but he must've been careless."

"But why did he 'confess' to us." Tuttle-Derby's face was wrinkled in puzzlement. "I mean, wasn't that risky?"

The Raven shrugged. "Maybe, but he's done it before. In a

university forum in Heidelberg and a bar in Prague. Both times he was in the middle of changing locations. I heard a whisper recently that the police had found his shop here, but it had been cleared out. Maybe it's to alleviate guilt, maybe he can't help but talk about the obsession that drives him, his obsession to keep the Wurms alive."

"Or perhaps," interrupted Dalton, "he and these other so-called Keepers are just cranks seeking attention, and the Wurms don't exist at all!'"

The Raven looked deeply offended. "Well now that we have a real sheet we can start more serious investigation. But I wouldn't advise reading too much Blake right now, and avoid any suspicious book that looks Wurm-like! Everyone who's looked at Günther's sheets will be pre-sensitised... you'd be easy prey for the Wurms."

Dr Steve went pale, as did Tuttle-Derby, his skin contrasting even more with the sweep of his oily brown hair.

"What do you all think of Brain Teaser anyhow?" I said to change the subject. I figured we'd had more than enough of Günther and the Wurms.

"I think my brain's been teased quite sufficiently tonight," answered Professor Mackintosh. "I'm having an Old Bodger." And so did we all, erasing the sour taste of that evening with quaffs of the Fountain's fabled on-tap elixir.

The Pocklington Poltergeist

David Langford

A buzz of expectation could be felt in the back bar of the Fountain that Tuesday evening, and Michael the landlord hoped aloud that this didn't mean funny business. No one needed to be told what he meant. The previous meeting had gone with a bang, not to mention a repeated flash, crackle and puff of purple vapour when anyone stepped in the wrong place. Whatever that noisy stuff was, it got on your shoes and followed you even into the sanctuary of the toilet.

"Nitrogen tri-iodide," said Dalton reminiscently. "Contact explosive. A venerable student tradition. It's amazing how each new year discovers the formula, as though it were a programmed instinct."

"They read science fiction," Ploom suggested. "Robert Heinlein gives a fairly detailed recipe in *Farnham's Freehold*."

"Not his best," said Dalton. "And not the best procedure either. Solid iodine crystals are far, far more effective than the usual alcoholic solution. I speak purely theoretically, of course."

At the bar, Professor Mackintosh made reassuring noises. "The only upheaval we're expecting is a celebrity visitor, Michael. A demi-celebrity, at any rate. Have you heard of Dagon Smythe the psychic investigator – a sort of real-life Carnacki the Ghost-Finder? Colin Wilson wrote a whole book about him once."

Next to the Professor, Dr Steve spluttered something into his beer. It could have been: "That charlatan."

"Now, now," murmured Mackintosh. "Guests are always received politely. We even managed to be civil to Uri Geller."

Dalton came to the bar with his emptied mug. "I thought I'd burst, though," he said while signalling for another pint. Then he cast his eye around the Paradise bar as though seeking small steaming mounds of incivility in obscure corners. Even the crowded student table looked innocuous enough. Someone had shoved an old suitcase underneath it, but no sinister phials of potential flash-and-crackle were in evidence. Which might mean that their ringleader Dermot was plotting something altogether different.

Tranquil chatter continued for several more minutes until a stranger appeared framed in the doorway, not with the diffidence of a typical Fountain newcomer but most visibly Making An Entrance, in detectable capitals. He had longish grey-black hair, a jacket vaguely suggesting a stage revival of Oscar Wilde, and an ebony walking stick with a silver skull for a handle. "Good evening!" he cried. He was strikingly tall, unmistakably English.

"Can this be... Harlan Ellison?" whispered Ploom, deadpan.

"Hush," said Mackintosh. "Ladies and gentlemen, it gives me great pleasure to welcome our special guest, Dagon Smythe! What'll you have, Mr Smythe?"

The great man accepted a double Macallan and raised his glass for a toast. "Black spirits and white, red spirits and grey, I love them all." Almost everyone in the back bar had turned or shifted to focus on Smythe; and just at that moment there came a sudden sense of boding, as though cold feet walked momentarily over the audience's collective grave. Perhaps this celebrity had a special charisma after all.

"*Macbeth*," said Crown Baker, belatedly identifying the line. He always researched and was ready for guests: "Did I hear that you've developed a new, updated version of Carnacki's Electric Pentacle to ward off hostile entities during your investigations?"

"A largely theoretical piece of work, alas. I calculated that high-energy protons circulating in sufficiently large storage rings would form an almost perfect aetheric defence. But although the hardware has indeed been tested, it's a trifle too cumbersome for use in the field. Of course you know of the Large Hadron Collider?"

Somewhere at the back of the crowd a small snot-blowing noise was heard. But again Smythe's words had somehow thrummed with inexplicable dread. Behind the bar, Bogna surreptitiously crossed herself. Several regulars began to wonder about tricks with mass hypnosis. If, that is, there were such a thing as mass hypnosis.

"We would be greatly privileged," said Professor Mackintosh genially, "if you could tell us about one or two of your unpublished investigations. And perhaps the same again would not come amiss?"

"Why, thank you very much indeed." Smythe leaned his skull-stick against the bar and adopted a differently theatrical attitude. His repertoire did not appear to include any non-dramatic poses. "Recently, only last week, I concluded the affair of the Pocklington Poltergeist. A minor but quite instructive case."

What *was* it about his measured cadences that so chilled the blood, or (to put it more literally) troubled the gut? Had something dire from the occult detective's stock-in-trade followed him here? Smythe frowned as though this point worried him too, but settled back to tell his tale.

"There was an old woman of Pocklington – no, no, this isn't a limerick. She lived alone in a bungalow called Gasworks View, with a quite unbelievable number of ornaments, gewgaws, knick-knacks, bric-à-brac and assorted kitsch. The effect was appalling but she loved it dearly. Then the manifestations began. Week after week, night after night, some unseen force would topple one or more of her little treasures from the shelf. She herself blamed the cat, despite the undeniable fact that the cat had died years before..."

Ploom thought: *What was the title of that H.G. Wells story about a room haunted by pure Fear? Listening to him is like that. Is Smythe a Haunted Man? No, that was Dickens.*

"When old Mrs Pingle's favourite china Present From Skegness was found smashed to atoms in the sitting-room fireplace, she felt this was the last straw and called me in. Exorcising the presumed playful ghost of a long-dead tomcat seemed an unusual challenge, but then all my cases are notoriously unusual if not downright incredible. I prepared my usual working kit...."

The narrative flowed on. Drinks vanished as though by some occult influence, and were replenished. Crown Baker grudgingly admitted to himself that Smythe could tell a story, even if accompanied by unnerving psychic special effects. Was there something peculiar in the beer tonight?

"The traditional wisdom when dealing with poltergeist phenomena is to keep an eye out for adolescent children in the vicinity. But there were no suitable teenagers to be found here – although Mrs Pingle became quite excited by the thought that Shippey, her beloved tom, had just turned fifteen when he died and would thus have become a teenaged cat-ghost. I humoured her as gently as I could, while setting up my dreamcatchers, ghostwriters and other astral alarm systems..."

Yet again, a pulse of subliminal unease filled the bar. The sedate Victorian engravings on the walls seemed for an instant to become distorted glimpses of Doré's Hell.

Mackintosh, analytical as ever, thought: *Smythe has the air of an actor, not to say a ham, and actors know all the tricks of stirring up emotions – but surely not these uncanny twinges of doom? Even the student table is paying attention, as though the physicists were trying to measure what's happening. It's like nothing I've ever experienced in a theatre... though perhaps... somewhere else?*

Smythe continued: "The curious result – although it was a result I'd half expected – was that no trace of aetheric activity registered even on my most delicate occult sensors. The Pingle bungalow was simply devoid of any malign influence. Not like... not like..." He looked to and fro with narrowed eyes. "But I mustn't wander away from my story, must I?"

Michael found himself checking the location of the short, heavy truncheon under the bar: the wise publican's friend, very rarely needed and never before so much as contemplated at a Tuesday night meeting. But nothing was wrong. Nothing at all. Michael checked it again.

Dagon Smythe was still smoothly raconting, if that is what a raconteur does: "It was then – at last – that I detected the faint *physical* traces on certain higher shelves and mantelpieces where Mrs Pingle, bless the frail old dear, had skimped her dusting."

"Spectral pawprints?" said Jocelyn Sparrow brightly.

"Nothing so distinct, alas. A wispy line here, a confused scrape there, a hint of dust disturbed by some localized current of air – but I guessed, and I was lucky enough to guess rightly. Mrs Pingle had a son, not a homebound teenager but a forty-year-old living elsewhere in Pocklington, and he very much wanted her to move house. Something to do with property values and a supermarket lurking (as far as such things can lurk) in the wings. The key discovery, though, was that this son was a professional animal trainer."

This was clearly a good time for a throbbing, dramatic pause. Shivers ensued. A stray beermug shimmied slowly down the slope of one particularly non-Euclidean table, but was intercepted before actual disaster.

"But let me cut a long story short," Smythe said with evident reluctance. Even he seemed rattled. "After a little bullying and some help from a geas forbidden by the strict Queensberry Rules, the younger Pingle confessed his part in the apparent haunting. Being a fellow of satanic ingenuity, he had employed a number of carefully trained bats which every night flew down one or another of his mother's chimneys and wrought havoc among her knick-knacks..."

A general groan filled the Paradise bar, only to be muted by yet another spine-chilling thrum of doom. Tuttle-Derby, who knew the classic *Tough Guide to Fantasyland* by heart, reminded himself of a technical term from that vade-mecum: the *reek of wrongness.*

"In short, the so-called Pocklington Poltergeist was one of those odd affairs which even old Carnacki encountered every once in a while. That is, the kind of haunting which to everyone's surprise involves no malign occult presence at all. Unlike... unlike the present..."

As a further wave of monstrous boding washed over the gathering, Smythe reached with slow deliberation for his death's-head stick and hefted it in both hands. His next words were strange. "I sense the feel of evil – Every nerve of me vibrates to the symphony of sin – Somewhere, at this moment, crime holds revel."

"*Krazy Kat*," muttered Crown Baker, always pleased to spot a quotation.

Smythe's wrists made a sharp twisting motion. The stick came apart and revealed itself to be a sword-stick. "Cold iron," he said, stepping quickly forward. "This is undoubtedly a case for cold iron." He drove the long blade into the battered old suitcase wedged under the students' table. There was a brilliant blue-white flash, and all the lights went out.

A stunned pause, crowded with afterimages, before silence erupted into hubbub.

How strange, thought Professor Mackintosh, *that disaster, chaos and darkness should bring such a sense of... relief.* Then he thought a little more, and remembered when and where he'd known a hint of this evening's extraordinary, visceral sense of dismay.

The cinema. *Earthquake.* In Sensurround.

That first thrill of fear had not swept the back room with Smythe's introductory 'Good evening', but only after his name had been announced.

"Subsonics, of course!" Mackintosh said aloud a few seconds later, just as Michael dazzled the crowd with a huge and powerful torch produced from beneath the bar. "Quiet, please, everyone. Seventeen-hertz infrasound is the answer. That frequency doesn't register on human hearing but has been shown to generate feelings of anxiety, grief, revulsion, chilled spine, gut-fear, you name it and this evening you've felt it. May I therefore deduce that young Dermot and his physicist colleagues decided it would be a clever jape to liven up Mr Smythe's visit – with appropriate spooky sensations at 17Hz for his expected tale of the occult?"

Now spotlit by a second torch from Michael's emergency reserve, the students could only stare like rabbits caught in headlights.

"One learns something new about psychic investigation every day," said a slightly subdued Smythe, and after a moment insisted on shaking Mackintosh's hand. "Personally I prefer my case reports to end on a *high* note."

Bogna was lighting a succession of candles. Visibility continued to improve, and an expedition to the cellar fuse-box was under way.

Dermot, still clutching some species of remote control, broke out in a kind of quiet wail. "Oh bloody hell. Oh *bloody* hell. We borrowed the infrahyposubwoofers from the acoustics lab. We'll have to replace them..." Under the table, coils of acrid smoke rose from the travel-stained suitcase that had (now that one looked more carefully) a cable trailing from its base to a wall socket.

Peering at the suddenly pale student, Mackintosh wondered idly whether a suitably designed scientific instrument could infer the cost of an infrahyposubwoofer by measuring the culprit's precise degree of ashen-facedness. Even the unaided eye could tell it wasn't cheap.

The Last Man in Space

Andrew J. Wilson

It's very easy to become complacent about the Fountain, to think that our little cadre is unique and we're the only people anywhere who gather regularly to test the boundaries of what is and what might be with such unbridled zest and imagination.

Thankfully, I have Edinburgh to remind me that, while we at the Fountain are undeniably special, unique would be pushing it. I visit Scotland's magnificent capital all too infrequently, but look forward to each opportunity and invariably have a ball when I do. The fact that I make it north of the border at all is down to an old friend of mine, Andrew, who makes his spare room available on an open basis. A fellow writer, Andrew is a generous host – belying the Scots' reputation for parsimony – and always entertaining company.

Unlike my usual drinking companions back in London, these Edinburgh counterparts don't have a fixed meeting place, though they might settle on a given venue for a while. Andrew maintains that you can always triangulate the coordinates of the best pub in town if your known points of reference are an author with an understanding of science and a researcher who appreciates the craft of writing. On a good night, you'll then find the shortest distance to your chosen watering hole by following the trail of the science fiction fans. As Alfred Bester very nearly wrote, *The Bars My Destination.*

Pliny the Elder gave us *in vino veritas* – cheerfully paraphrasing or perhaps even plagiarising the Greek poet Alcaeus – and there have been many memorable quotes about drinking ever since. Winston Churchill, no less, said rather pointedly, "Always remember that I have taken more out of alcohol than alcohol has taken out of me." And I'm always moved when I think about Frida Kahlo's observation: "I tried to drown my sorrows, but the bastards learned how to swim, and now I am overwhelmed by this decent and good feeling."

For the truth of the matter, I refer you to the 2000-year-old wisdom of Seneca the Younger: "Drunkenness is simply voluntary insanity," the old Stoic said, and I'm inclined to agree. We all need to let off a little steam from time to time, especially after contemplating the mysteries of the universe, whether by means of a radio telescope or through the blank screen of a word processor.

In Edinburgh, it seems the preferred haunt of the three "Rs" – readers, writers and researchers – varies as pubs change hands, and the quality of the ales on tap and the single malts behind the bar goes up or down. Over the years, Andrew has taken me all across the centre of town, but my favourite haunt will always be the Major Weir.

Tucked away in the depths of the Old Town, near the bottom of a cobbled side-street, the place isn't much to look at from the outside. Its coat of paint is peeling and the view of the interior is obscured by deeply unfashionable bottle-bottom window panes. In fact, you'd walk right past the place if you didn't know better. But behind the creaking double doors, the Major Weir is a warren that burrows deep under the Royal Mile. It's a free house, of course, which means that the landlord stocks what he likes – and what he likes is to sell drinks, so if he doesn't have your particular poison, you'll find it the next time you visit, if you ask nicely.

Many curious characters mingle in that unreconstructed maze of snugs and spiralling steps. This isn't a workmen's bar, although some drink there. It's not an academics' watering hole, although their voices can be heard. And it's not a youngsters' rendezvous, although a few of the customers can only just be over the legal drinking age. The speciality of the Major Weir is storytelling. I tagged along with Andrew one Thursday night to meet the usual crowd, and I felt at home immediately.

For some reason a discussion we found ourselves discussing the subject of pen-names. Banksie, of course, boasts 'the world's most transparent pseudonym' for his science fiction, simply inserting his middle initial between his first and last names. Our old friend Dr S___ L___ (there's no need for the anonymization, I just love that kind of old-fashioned coyness) adopted Bingo T. MacArthur back in his fanzine days, long before he became a full-time astronomer. Even Andrew flip-flopped his own name to create William Anderson when he had to review the same book twice.

Well, I have to admit that things got rather sillier as the drinks were drunk and the rounds kept coming round. We began to invent *noms de plume* after Steve Glover pointed out that Charlie Stross's name is an anagram of Crass Holsters. I came up with Luther Kant and Primo Leviathan, and the next thing we knew, we had Benedict Quisling, Pollyanna Discharge and Milton Embolism... Even e. e. 'doc' cummings (all in lower case, naturally) was floated and then sunk without a trace.

This was Seneca's 'voluntary insanity', of course – we'd need a good pseudonym for some of the ideas we toyed with that night. Someone mentioned an unfilmable and quite probably unprintable idea for *Doctor Who* entitled "Planet of the Bastards", and that steered us into the contentious area of remakes or so-called re-imaginings. Mike Holmes, who troubles the websites of the local papers as a Friend of Fernando Poo, suggested that it was high time someone took a crack at *Space: 1999*. Banksie exploded: The bad science was unforgivable! It must never be remade!

Well, that was like a red rag to a bullshitter, so I came up with an outline for *Space: 2099* on the spot.

"The crew of the moonbase aren't burying radioactive waste," I said. "Oh no, while extracting ice from one of the poles, they find *ancient ruins* and begin to excavate the site..."

"Okay..." said Steve.

"The problem is," I went on, improvising wildly, "the Moon isn't a moon. It's a disabled alien war machine that's been lying dormant in Earth's orbit for millions of years – and they've reactivated it! The warp drive fires up and the Moon jumps to the next target programmed into its ancient memory banks... Here's the logline: *The last battle in a billion-year-old intergalactic war is about to be fought – and humanity has to decide which side it's on!*"

"KO," said Mike.

Ken laughed out loud and even Banksie liked it. Someone suggested – not me, I assure you – that since we'd come up with this re-imagining in Scotland and most of us had been born north of the border, the characters should be Scottish too... Then things took a strange turn.

"The problem with Scots," said an old but elegant man, "is that we tend to snatch defeat from the jaws of victory."

"Excuse me?" Andrew replied. The stranger had appeared out of nowhere, much like his *non sequitur*, and now he was sitting down at our table uninvited, commandeering the last free stool.

"Admit it, gentlemen," he insisted. "It's true."

The new member of our circle had the look of a retired civil servant. He wore a neat, if unfashionable, three-piece suit and sported a superfluous goatee that might have been grown for a bet.

"I'm sorry," Andrew said, "I didn't catch your name."

"Call me Hugh," he replied. "In the spirit of your earlier badinage, I will adopt an alias. Call me Hugh Mann." Our groans didn't put him off. "I apologise for the pun, but it's probably politic for me to conceal my identity. You see, as I said, the Scots have a terrible habit of dropping the ball – and not just during rugby internationals. Watt, Baird and Fleming gave us the steam engine, television and penicillin respectively, but our benighted nation has never become the technological powerhouse it should have been. What's worse is that some of our most astounding achievements have been – what's the word nowadays – *redacted* from history... because they ended in disaster."

We smelled a rat, but let Mr Mann continue. After all, you have to set your trap and then wait patiently before you can catch an offending rodent.

"I must say that your comical idea of Scots in space is not original," he said, "but there's no way any of you could have known that."

"Please, Hugh," I said, priming the rat trap, "do go on."

The old man smiled and launched into his tale. This was home from home. I might almost have been back at the Fountain.

"In the district of Angus, you can still see the shell of Lord Strathbungo's Improved Skyrocket Manufactory. Nothing more than ruins now, but in its time, the place promised Scotland the stars, if not the world. His Lordship was a polymath and entrepreneur who became an enthusiastic student of those pioneering rocket scientists of the 1920s, men whose names I can never remember how to pronounce."

"Konstantin Tsiolkovsky and Hermann Oberth?" Ken suggested.

"Quite so. Strathbungo envisaged a multitude of both commercial and experimental applications for rocketry, but he died – along with a number of his staff – in an accident involving concentrated nitric acid that occurred around the time of the Wall Street Crash. His papers were left to the Scottish Rocketry Society, but were confiscated by the Crown, which is how I found out about this neglected fragment of history.

"Now the Scottish Rocketry Society was a rag-tag group of amateur enthusiasts who, despite spending most of their time in one pub or another, performed some experimental trials in the Campsie Fells in the 1930s. They were inspired by Robert Goddard, of course, but I believe that they were equally enthused by Wells, Verne and the garish American pulp magazines that arrived as ballast on transatlantic cargo vessels. Mind you, the drink might have had something to do with it too. These dedicated devotees put their limited resources to remarkable use. Several small projectiles were successfully fired from the concrete launch pad which they built high up in the hills. I have even seen a few copies of their newsletter, *Rocketry Scotland*, which was published into the 1960s. The National Library of Scotland has an almost complete run."

I made a mental note to check on this later, if I had the time.

"The outbreak of the Second World War saw the end of such attempts to emulate Goddard, of course, but many of those who gave up so much of their spare time and disposable income would find themselves called up to serve their country by working on the military applications of their hobby."

The trap needed bait, so I bought a round and stood Hugh a drink.

"During the War," he went on, "the Government devised a fall-back strategy that was to be implemented if Operation Sea Lion, the Nazis' planned invasion of England, succeeded – a new front was to be established along the border with Scotland. The military's ultra-top-secret missile programme, spearheaded by many conscripted Scottish rocketry enthusiasts, was intended to form the last line of defence – or attack – in such an extremity. Our men worked all over the country, particularly on the test range on Barra, and came up with the Z-1 flying bomb one long, whisky-fuelled night. The 'Buzzard', as they called it, was intended to be a primitive atomic missile. There was to be no warhead since the explosion caused by the hydrogen-fuelled rocket's impact with the intended target would be more than sufficient..."

We stared at him in disbelief.

"Come now, gentlemen, as you should know, Fermi achieved nuclear fission as early as 1934, and he created a criticality with Szilard only eight years later. I never suggested that the Scots *invented* any of this...

"Anyway, we can all be thankful that their work never

reached completion – never mind saw use in anger – but this clandestine endeavour continued into the Cold War. While the Blue Streak was developed south of the border, the cream of the Caledonian rocketeers concentrated on their own project, led by a young man named Fraser Ferguson. The English ballistic missile used liquid oxygen and kerosene as propellants, but it had at least twice the overall gross lift-off mass of the Scottish alternative. The project was a dead end, which explains its termination. On the other hand, as Ferguson said, 'We Scots knew that the way onwards and upwards must be nuclear'..." Hugh paused dramatically. "Oh dear, my mouth is rather dry. Could someone get me a glass of water, please?"

"I suppose you'd like a little whisky in that?" I asked. He smiled and nodded, while pointing out that Old Pulteney was the Major Weir's Malt of the Moment. Banksie did the honours.

"Well, to cut a long story short – and one that I've had to piece together over the years at that – our canny Scots developed a manned nuclear rocket at last. They obtained the fuel rods they needed from the Chapelcross Magnox nuclear power plant in Annan. Officially, the primary purpose of Chapelcross was to produce weapons-grade plutonium for the British nuclear weapons programme while also generating power for the National Grid, but it had always been intended to have a third and wholly secret purpose. Ferguson obtained his test pilot, one Flight Lieutenant William MacKraken, on an extended loan from the Royal Air Force."

"And how did this potential death-trap work?" Ken asked.

"Oh, it looked very much like the torpedo-shaped rocket ships from the films of the period, fins and all, with the exception of the turbine vents that drew the air in to give the engine some reaction mass once the initial payload of liquid hydrogen had done its job. The faster the craft went, the more air was taken in until it began to leave the atmosphere... At that point, ball bearings made of Cornish tin were released exposively to hurl the contraption into orbit... Well, that was the plan."

"So the rocket never flew?" Steve asked.

"Oh no, quite the contrary, it did, and only too well," Hugh replied. "It wasn't supposed to, of course – it was launched more or less accidentally during a test firing at Woomera in 1966. Flight Lieutenant MacKraken was on board."

This time I was the one who needed another drink. Thankfully, Charlie obliged.

"It was a tragedy – still is. The ship was a masterpiece of contemporary engineering, but it was still limited by the technology of the time. The controls were almost all mechanical and, of course, there were no computers back then. MacKraken was in the cockpit, if that's what you'd call the cramped compartment, and the intention was simply to test-fire the motor on the ground. The controls regulating the core jammed. The reactor began to go critical. The military observers from the Australian Defence Force made it quite clear that they would not tolerate a nuclear accident on antipodean soil. The technicians were panicking, but MacKraken insisted on taking off. He knew that a launch was the only way to avert disaster. He was a very, very brave man.

"The ship blasted off all right, but then it went *off course*, of course. The Scots had desperately tried to plot an orbital trajectory that would bring their man back safely, but they were using nothing more than slide rules and graph paper, probably at gunpoint. Someone or other misplaced a decimal point and the rocket never came down. The telemetrists calculated that years would pass before it began to make its return journey..."

"What a way to go," I said. "Do you know what happened in the end?"

"In the end?" Hugh asked. "I don't know if the story *is* over yet. The whole terrible business was covered up, obviously, and then almost all the records were shredded, burned, or buried as landfill. But what goes around comes around, as they say.

"When I worked for – well, let's call it the British Non-Ferrous Metals Research Association – I ran into a man called

Harry Purvis, who told me a thing or two about what had happened, details that never appeared in the records. It was rumoured that one member of mission control, allegedly Fraser Ferguson, identified the mistake just after it was too late to correct and calculated how long MacKraken's round trip would be. He told the Flight Lieutenant to cut the oxygen and life support, open his pressure suit, blow the seals on the pipes carrying the liquid hydrogen and... flash-freeze himself. The doomed man would die, but Ferguson argued, it might be possible to bring him back to life one day...

"And so the long wait for his homecoming began, and slowly but surely the small number of folk who knew the truth dwindled as time took its inevitable toll. Only with the help of Harry Purvis was I able to piece together the sad history of Scotland's misadventures in rocketry, and it was through him that I was inducted into the secret society of veterans led by Fraser Ferguson who watched the skies for the day when MacKraken might return. Are any of you familiar with the outpost at Tantallon?"

"You mean the experimental radar and listening station in East Lothian?" Banksie asked. "The one only visible from the River Forth? Built during World War II and operational until the mid-sixties, wasn't it? I remember reading about it when all that bumf was made available under the Freedom of Information Act."

Hugh nodded. "Although supposedly decommissioned in the sixties," he said, "it was, in fact, repurposed over time by Ferguson with the help of others such as myself... and funds siphoned off from Cold War black budgets. Until recently, the equipment was maintained and monitored on a semi-regular basis. In the end, after Fraser's death, that task fell to me alone."

"What do you mean?" I prompted. It was last orders both at the bar and for Hugh's tale.

"After I officially retired, I persuaded some contacts at Edinburgh University to perform a few calculations on a *pro bono* basis. They determined that, if a hypothetical nuclear rocket suffered a runaway chain reaction, then it would not only have left Earth's orbit, but continued on a parabolic course that would have taken it beyond the orbit of Neptune and through the Kuiper Belt at the edge of the solar system. 'At sufficient velocities,' their report stated, 'interplanetary dust and ice crystals scooped up by the propulsion system's air vents would act as a perfectly adequate reaction mass.'

"Working hypothetically on a number of assumptions that that I suggested based on Fraser Ferguson's notes, my contacts predicted that the spacecraft would return to Earth almost half a century after its departure. In the circumstances, I assumed that Flight Lieutenant MacKraken's remains would finally be cremated when his ship inevitably burned up in the Earth's atmosphere..."

The bar staff were collecting glasses and encouraging us to leave, but Hugh hadn't quite finished.

"I persuaded my friends at the University to allow me some telescope time at the observatory so that I could watch the bitter end of the whole sorry affair. Ferguson's notes were accurate and I pinpointed the craft... only to witness [the thing rotating, clearly] firing its retro-rockets to initiate course corrections and deceleration procedures. Of course, there could be no possibility that the pilot was still alive, could there? But if MacKraken wasn't at the controls, then who or what was?"

Hugh gave us a look so pointed he could have nailed us to the wall.

"And those, I'm afraid, are all the facts at my disposal," he said. "Anything else can only be speculation, which you gentlemen are far better equipped to supply than I am..."

"Extraterrestrial intelligence?" Banksie suggested.

"Extremophile nanobacteria?" Ken countered.

"One hundred per cent pure, undiluted unobtanium?" Charlie concluded.

"Perhaps one of you is right, perhaps all of you are to one

degree or another," the old man said thoughtfully. "One thing's for certain, MacKraken must have encountered something or other out there in deep space. Fraser Ferguson had hoped that time would supply the means to bring our friend back to life. Little did he know – how could he? – that space itself would provide the solution in the end."

We had to go, but Andrew and I decided to walk Hugh back up the road.

"You don't really expect us to believe any of that, do you?" I asked.

He stopped and smiled at me oddly. "Frankly, I don't care whether you do or you don't. 'Truth will out,' according to the Bard, and as he also wrote in *Hamlet*, 'There are more things in heaven and earth[...] than are dreamt of in your philosophy...' I have filled the ample free time which my retirement allows me by looking for the spot where the last man in space returned to Earth."

"Good luck with that," I told him, turning with Andrew to head home, but he caught me by the arm. His grip was surprisingly firm.

"Not so fast, laddie," Hugh said. "I found the place. The capsule washed up on Barra. It was empty by the time I got there, but scrawled on the inside of the hull were two words, words repeated over and over again – 'PAY' and 'BACK'..."

I could imagine the graffiti covering the cockpit walls:

PAY BACK PAY BACK PAY BACK PAY
BACK PAY BACK PAY BACK PAY BACK
PAY BACK PAY BACK PAY BACK PAY
BACK PAY BACK PAY BACK PAY BACK
PAY BACK PAY BACK PAY BACK PAY
BACK PAY BACK PAY BACK PAY BACK
PAY BACK PAY BACK PAY BACK PAY
BACK PAY BACK PAY BACK PAY BACK
PAY BACK PAY BACK PAY BACK PAY

BACK PAY BACK PAY BACK PAY BACK

"Here's tae us," Andrew said, invoking an old Scottish toast as we watched the stars turn overhead. "Wha's like us?"

"Damn few," Hugh replied, "an' they're a' deid!"

He went on his way then, leaving us to decide whether MacKraken's mysterious scrawl was a statement of vengeful intent, or the Flight Lieutenant's reminder to himself that he was owed a colossal amount of money by Her Majesty's Government. Perhaps, I decided, that would be revenge enough in itself.

For Madeleine Shepherd.

The Incredible Multiplicity of Phaedra Lament

Peter Crowther

Crown Baker burst into the Fountain that Tuesday night like a man possessed... or perhaps one 'pursued' might be more appropriate. Whatever the reason for his somewhat energetic entrance, it had caused the five of us already assembled sufficient fluster to spill our drinks down our fronts: Old Bodger for Brian Dalton, Dr Steve and Frank – a friend of the good doctor who had taken to joining us of a Tuesday evening at the time – a gin and tonic for Jocelyn and, by way of experiment, my own Morocco, produced (so Bogna informed us) to a rare ancient recipe involving ginger.

"Look out, Crown," Dr Steve hissed, brushing some Bodger foam from his tie. "Nearly dropped me bloody pint." He said this in an exaggerated northern brogue, deliberately rejigging the possessive determiner to the objective pronoun for effect.

"Sorry, chaps... Jocelyn," Crown said, shaking his wet raincoat from his shoulders and catching Bogna's eye. "Had a bit of a fright."

When Bogna appeared with a terse "Yes?" Crown asked for a pint of Bodger, a bag of dry roasted nuts and a packet of the oddly-named Scampi Fries, a confection that, of course, had never *seen* a scampi nor, indeed, a sea creature of any kind. "And put another in the taps for everyone else," Crown added, waving a sweeping arm towards our respective tipples.

"Bloody hell," Brian was the first to remark when everyone

had grunted their gratitude for the extra drink, "nuts *and* Scampi Fries?"

"He's got worms, that's what it is," said Jocelyn. "It's his age."

Taking a long draught from his pint as he booted his crumpled raincoat beneath the bar-overhang, Crown shook his head and reached for the Scampi Fries. "Bloody starving. *And* I'm totally knackered."

I asked if he had been running.

"Dodging, more like," Crown replied, almost incoherently, as he munched.

"Dodging?"

Crown turned to Dr Steve and nodded, placing a further three or four Fries trapped between thumb and middle finger delicately into his mouth. "Dodging – wait for it," he said in a cloud of crumbs, "– a woman."

"My goodness me!" Brian proclaimed.

Crown nodded and added a handful of nuts to the coagulated mass being churned around in his mouth. "I'm not kidding you, she gets bloody everywhere." He dusted his goatee and quaffed more Old Bodger. "She was on the tube this morning," he began, returning his pint to the bar and counting off on fingers covered in salty snack dust. "Then she was at Pret A Manger at lunchtime, then at FOPP when I went to check out the new Miles Davis retrospective, then outside Charing Cross station and *then* at the sodding bus stop on the way here."

Jocelyn looked around. "You checked to make sure she isn't here?"

Frank emptied more nuts into his hand and casually threw them into his mouth without a second's thought. "I actually looked through the windows before I came in."

Jocelyn laughed. "That's why you're soaked."

"Mmm. Could be a factor, I grant you."

"Maybe she fancies you," Dr Steve suggested with a wide smile.

Crown said nothing. He took another drink and waved to Bogna to give out the drinks he just ordered and pour another Bodger while she was at it.

"Don't let it get you down, old man," Brian said.

"Oh," Crown said happily as he rubbed his stomach, "I'm well on the way to recovery already."

We were quiet for a few seconds as we awaited refreshed glasses but, retrieving mine from the bar, I noticed Dr Steve looking somewhat lost in thought and I said as much.

"Just thinking about something that happened to *me* once, several years ago in fact. Before I came to London." He reached for his own glass and gave a nod to Crown before taking a deep drink.

Crown pushed a twenty pound note across the bar and nothing more was said for a few minutes while everyone clinked glasses, mumbled 'Cheers' and checked the quality of the new pints.

"You were in Leeds, weren't you?" Crown said, breaking the silence.

"Yes indeed. What did they use to call it? Motorway City To The North? Some suchlike."

"Great city," I said, having been up to see my cousin when his mother – my Auntie Maude – died. "They're doing wonders with it."

"Didn't use to be," Jocelyn said. "I used to go out with a chap at Leeds Medical School: spent a good few weekends up there," she added and just for a moment there was a cloud of wistfulness in Jocelyn's eyes. She looked down at her glass and took a sip.

As though to move attention from Jocelyn, Dr Steve said, "Her name was Phaedra. Phaedra Lament." He said it softly, almost reverently.

"Phaedra Lament?" Crown echoed. "Unusual name."

Dr Steve nodded and took a sip of beer. "Her parents were a real pair, lived on the outskirts of Leeds. He – that's Professor

George Alexander Lament, Doctorates in Physics and Philosophy
– was a big noise at Leeds Uni while his wife, I forget her name,
was *três* arty." He affected what was clearly intended to be an
effeminate swagger but failed miserably, though none of us was
prepared to say as much.

"But fancy calling your daughter 'Phaedra'," Jocelyn said.
"What does it mean? Is it Greek?"

None of us could throw any light on the origin so we waited
for Dr Steve to continue.

"*Phaedra* was the title of an album by a band called Tangerine
Dream," he ventured after what seemed like a couple of minutes
but probably wasn't. "Very spacey stuff. The kind of music you
listen to – or should I say *used* to listen to – when you were under
the influence. It had played a large part in the Laments' musical
repertoire – we're talking about the early 1970s. And so it was
that, in 1977, when they were blessed with their only child, they
decided to call her Phaedra." He shrugged. "I guess it's as good a
name as any."

We all muttered agreement and Frank even went so far as to
add, "And better than many."

"They sound like they were quite a couple," Jocelyn said.

Dr Steve nodded emphatically. "*Hoo*, you said it. They were
a – perhaps even *the* – cultural focal point of the city. I mean, for
example: when Ravi Shankar played at Leeds Town Hall, he
stayed with the Laments. Philip Glass, too, when he played
Manchester."

Grunts of approval sounded all round.

"Yes," said Dr Steve, staring into an indeterminate distance
over Jocelyn's right shoulder, "they were a great family. But," he
added, pausing as though to find the words to go on, "they got
dealt a bit of a bum hand of the celestial cards. It turned out that
Phaedra was… was special."

I glanced around and saw the expressions on all the faces.
'Special' was a word that in common parlance had come to mean
something very different from special. It meant somehow sub-

standard and I guessed that was the context here, as Dr Steve went on to confirm.

"Turned out she had Down's syndrome," he said. He was nursing his glass and swirling the beer around, staring at it as though it were some kind of visual mantra. I looked at the others and some of them were doing the same, *tst-ing* to themselves and shaking their heads.

"How did she... you know; how did she look?"

"Beautiful," Dr Steve said, still swirling his drink. He looked directly into Crown's eyes and said it again. "Absolutely beautiful."

"No, I mean –"

"I know what you mean. You mean did she look – what was the word again? Mongoloid? Well, no, the answer is she didn't. She looked beautiful." He took another drink before continuing.

"Needless to say, it knocked the Laments – Rose... that was the wife's name; Rose – it knocked them for six. At first he seemed fairly stoic about it... you know, play the cards you're dealt and all that tosh; while Rose could barely function at all. And then –" Dr Steve drained his glass.

I reckoned it was my turn – even though I still had a half a pint left – so I signalled Bogna for refills.

He nodded and went on.

"And then, George Lament went into a rapid and sudden decline. Came out of nowhere. Took to drinking. And so on. Before long, George was spending more and more time away from the family hearthside and –"

"Another woman?"

Dr Steve shook his head. "No, Joss, just his work. Rose took on the major chores of looking after their daughter, taking her for long drives in the countryside and to the coast: Filey and Scarborough were particularly popular."

He paused. "It went that way for, oh, eighteen or nineteen years: nineteen, I think – yes, Phaedra was nineteen when... when it happened."

There was a finality in that short statement that left none of us in any doubt as to what was coming.

Frank pointed towards the window where three people were getting up from a table. "I think we should sit down for the rest of this," he said. He drained his glass as Jocelyn headed for the loo and then he made a beeline for the table before someone else pinched it.

Minutes later we were all seated and eager for the rest of the tale.

"Go on, Doc," Brian said.

Dr Steve nodded. "At this stage, George and Rose had drifted apart pretty much immeasurably."

Crown made a face and nodded wide-eyed at Dr Steve. "*Pretty much* immeasurably? That's a bit vague to be followed by a ten-shilling word like 'immeasurably' isn't it?"

Dr Steve smirked.

"Anyway, they had gone their own separate ways, the two of them. They loved the child, of course: Phaedra wanted for nothing... not a single thing."

"Just how bad was she?" Jocelyn asked. "How *demanding*, is what I suppose I'm trying to say," she added.

"Not really bad at all. Oh, there was an almost beatific calm about her face and her eyes –" He stopped and adopted an expression of calm at which Brian burst into laughter. "– big saucer-shaped eyes that always seemed to be seeking confirmation," Dr Steve said without pause. "And she needed everything doing for her –" He raised his eyebrows to emphasise that he really did mean everything. "– but aside from that, she was just a delightful child and later... well, later, of course, to all intents and purposes, she was a delightful *woman*. But her communication was pretty much that of a four-year-old. And she couldn't be let out of the house by herself because she just wouldn't know the way back. And there are always those out there who delight in, shall we say, plucking even the most beautiful flower."

"What a lovely way to phrase it," Jocelyn said, whispering it actually, as though just to herself.

Brian said, "How did you know them, the Laments?"

"During 1986/87, I was doing stem cell research at Durham and I was transferred to Leeds for a sabbatical – a breather, actually... and a much appreciated one. I'd specialised in Down's syndrome in my first stint at Leeds and when the Head of Department heard about that he suggested I introduce myself to George Lament. So I did and that's when I found out everything I've told you."

"When was this?"

"Oh, I suppose it would have been the late spring of 1988."

Nobody said anything for a few seconds, everyone taking advantage of the opportunity to take to their drinks. It was me who broke the silence.

"I suspect there's more coming –"

"Much more," Dr Steve said and, though he said it in an upbeat manner, his smile seemed sad.

"Well, before we get to that, can someone just explain a bit more about Down's syndrome? There are so many myths about –"

"Of course.

"Down's syndrome is a chromosomal condition characterized by the presence of an extra copy of genetic material either in whole or part."

Crown waved a hand to pause as he looked around the group. "Hoa! I'm not even sure that was English."

"I suppose too much of something is the easiest way to describe it," Dr Steve said when the sniggering had died down.

"Too much as opposed to too little?"

"The effects and extent of the extra copy vary greatly among people, depending (a) on their genetic history, and (b) pure chance."

"A bit of a crap-shoot, then," I ventured.

He nodded. "The incidence of Down's syndrome is

estimated at one per seven hundred or so births, although it is statistically more common with older parents (both mothers and fathers) due to increased mutagenic exposures upon some older parents' reproductive cells (however, many older parents produce children without the condition)."

"He's doing it again."

"Sorry, Crown. So, not to put too fine a point on it, older parents. Not ideal."

I asked if the Laments fitted that description and Dr Steve nodded regretfully. "George was in his late 40s when Phaedra appeared and Rose maybe 41 or 42. But other factors may also play a role," he added. "Down's syndrome occurs in all human populations, and analogous effects have been found in chimpanzees and mice."

He raised his eyebrows and waited for questions. No one said anything so he went on.

"Anyway, in 1996, Phaedra got a cold."

Jocelyn let out a groan. "I don't like the sound of this."

"None of us did. Unfortunately Phaedra's cold turned to pneumonia and then the whole thing hit her chest like a sledgehammer and..." He shrugged. "She didn't make it. Phaedra slipped off holding onto her mother's and father's hands as though she were hanging on for dear life to the topmost rail of a skyscraper."

"I guess she was," Brian said.

There was nodding then, and drinks, as we all reflected on the Laments' painful situation.

"I did all that I could to keep George on the straight and narrow – we all did, those of us at the University – but if he was desperate before, well... he was totally inconsolable when Phaedra passed away."

The phrase 'passed away' was a curious one for Dr Steve to employ, and I suspected that the good Dr had been closer to the unfortunate George Lament (and possibly even Phaedra herself) than he was letting on. But nobody else seemed to have noticed.

"And so it was that he got involved with the Einfahrt Project."

Brian couldn't hold onto his chuckle and, when he asked for some clarification, even Crown Baker sported a wide grin. "Einfart?" he asked.

I daren't look at Jocelyn, who studiously applied herself to her glass and avoided eye contact with anyone.

"It means 'gateway' in German."

"Entrance," Joss corrected. "I did it at school."

Dr. Steve shrugged. "Entrance, gateway... whatever. It's a means of access and exit."

Crown shook his head confusedly. "Why would Leeds University – I take it that it was a University project, yes?" When Dr Steve nodded, Crown continued.

"Why would a British university be working on a project with a German name? If it was about gateways – and quite why a physicist should be working on architecture escapes me for the moment – then why not simply call it the Gateway project?"

"It wasn't architecture. The German connection was to do with Schrödinger," Dr Steve said.

"And his cat," I chimed in.

Our storyteller nodded. "You know the old thought experiment about him putting a cat in a lidded box with some poison and reaching a situation where the cat was either alive or dead and you would only know which if you opened the box."

We'd all heard of it, of course, though Frank looked a little vague.

"Well, the theory goes that so long as you don't look in the box, you've created two possible situations... two different worlds, in fact.

"In one world, the cat is alive," he said, counting off on his fingers, "and in the other one, the cat is dead.

"Okay?"

Nobody said no so Dr Steve went on.

"So, basically, George Lament got a grant for investigating

the multiverse. Finding a gateway that would enable us to travel between the dimensions… between the different realities."

"Isn't the multiverse theory comic book stuff?" Frank enquired.

Jocelyn stuck out her tongue and said, "Schrödinger came up with the theory since buzz-named variously 'wavefunction collapse' and 'quantum decoherence.'"

"Hey, I really *am* impressed," Crown said. "You're not just a pretty face."

Jocelyn nodded. "So I take it a shag is out of the question because you might feel inferior."

We all laughed, particularly when Crown was lost for words… which doesn't happen often.

"By 'decoherence', many-worlds claims to resolve all of the correlation paradoxes of quantum theory, and particularly Schrödinger's cat, since every possible outcome of every event defines or exists in its own 'history' or 'world'. In layman's terms, there is a very large – perhaps infinite – number of universes, and everything that could possibly have happened in our past, but didn't, has occurred in the past of some other universe or universes."

"Earth 1 and Earth 2 and Earth Prime etc," Frank chipped in. "Like I said, it's comics stuff."

"But Schrödinger was there first," Jocelyn said.

"Only in *this* universe," Brian said. Everyone laughed and, suitably cheered, Brian offered to buy another round. With drinks replenished, Frank asked Dr Steve to continue.

"Well, it was like a gift from the blue to George."

"Because he could throw himself into something that would take his mind away from what happened to Phaedra?" Joss suggested.

Dr Steve nodded. "But it was more than that. George was fascinated by the whole idea of an infinite number of variants on our own universe and, more specifically, our own Earth… not least because he reasoned that there would be many in which his beloved Phaedra was still alive and perhaps even able to communicate fully."

And with that, he leaned back on his stool and took a drink, eyeing us over the rim of his glass as he flicked his eyebrows up a couple of times. I thought for a moment, quite suddenly, that the whole story was a pure fabrication, a white elephant – or a white *cat*, to be more precise – but when he set his glass on the table I fancied I saw our friend's chin dither slightly.

"So," he said as he embarked once again on this strange story, "that's the way they went on for a goodly while. As a visitor of some frequency to their home, I noticed this perhaps more than most. But not, of course, more than his wife.

"Rose told me about how George had taken to sleeping on the sofa in their living room, and how he had more or less abandoned any acknowledgement of cleanliness. Indeed, there was a rumour that Jack Philips, the Faculty Head, had had a word with George about... about *things*, but I couldn't be sure of that. What I could be sure of was that George was becoming rather eccentric, given to vague mutterings and moans, and tics of the face and head. In fact, these became so pronounced that Rose felt obliged to suggest that perhaps it would be for the best if I were not to visit the house until George's demeanour had improved. 'I'm sure it won't be for long,' I recall Rose saying to me. I agreed, of course – 'Oh, I'm sure,' I said emphatically – but I rather think that neither of us believed that deep down.

"It was a few weeks after that – well into the late autumn, as I recall... with fog and early frosts putting in several appearances – when I got a telephone call from Rose. It was George, she said. I asked if I should go around and she said no – asked me not to, actually – and then she started to sob."

"Was he... you know, dying?"

"No, Brian." Dr Steve let out a small laugh. "I think she could have coped with that, as callous as that might sound. His dying would have had an understandable conclusion: one day, he wouldn't be there. Simple as that. But this strange mental deterioration was far far worse.

"And then came the knock at my door."

"He came round to your place?"

"No, Joss. Rose came round. She'd had enough. Turned out that George had sat her down that afternoon – it was after ten when she turned up at my place... carrying an overnight bag – and he'd told her what sounded like the biggest cock-and-bull story since I don't know when. He said he had discovered a corridor that linked all the variants of our existence. He said he'd found the entrance to the multiverse."

"Was she serious?" Brian asked. "Was *he* serious?"

Dr Steve nodded, partially closing his eyes in a slow blink to emphasise. "Yes, she said he was *very* serious."

"Serious as in C-R-A-Z-Y," Crown Baker said around the rim of his pint glass.

"George said he had found a way to visit all the other worlds – all the other Earths – and he had seen other versions of himself. And of Rose. And, of course, of Phaedra. He wanted her to go back with him... to go back and find their daughter again.

"But Rose – who was torn between believing him and –"

Crown Baker twirled a finger at the side of his forehead.

"She wouldn't move. Aside from the idea being just plain –" He nodded to Crown who had moved across to the bar with empty glasses and was already starting to hand out replacements. "– crazy, she tried to tell George that, even if this multiverse thing were true, they couldn't steal their daughter from another reality because how would the parents from that place – that reality's George and Rose – how would *they* feel when their daughter disappeared."

Nobody said anything. And then Brian asked if there was an end to the tale.

"And it better not be a shaggy multiverse story," Joss said, beaming.

Shaking his head at Joss, Dr Steve said, "It isn't. And yes, Brian, there's an ending."

He took another deep draught and, setting his drink down again on the soaking beermat, he started on the final part of his story.

"Rose said that George didn't say much to that. He just sat there looking at her, weighing up what she had said. And then he got to his feet and, without saying another word, he walked out."

"And she came around to you," Frank said.

"And she came around to me, yes.

"I was pouring her a drink when my phone rang. It was George, wanting to know if Rose was with me. She nodded to me and so I told him she was. Then George said, 'Tell her to come down and see me. I'm by the allotments on Woodhouse Moor. Actually,' he said, 'you come too.' I started to tell him it was late and so on but he was adamant. 'Come now,' he said. 'And come quickly.' And then he said, kind of whispering, 'They're here, Steve.' 'Who's here, George?' I asked him back.

And after what seemed like a long time though it was probably only a minute or so, he said, 'Phaedra, Steve. I have to go.' And he hung up.

"But he said 'they,' didn't he? They're here?"

"That's right, Crown," Dr Steve said, and he blinked once and held up a finger for his friend not to be impatient.

"So I told Rose as best I could, which was pretty difficult when I got to the last bit. I mean," Dr Steve said, shrugging, "how do you tell a woman her husband has lost his mind?"

Nobody had an answer to that one.

"Well, long story short, we got down to Woodhouse Moor a little after 11 pm." Ever the consummate tale-spinner, Dr Steve gave two sideways glances to ensure... well, I'm not exactly sure what: privacy? In a crowded pub? And then, as the rest of us unwittingly leaned forward equally conspiratorially, he continued.

"It was a cold night, late November, and the sky was starless. A lone figure sat on one of the benches alongside the path. I knew right away it was George and I waved. Rose, too. He waved back.

"A few more steps and then the moon edged out from behind some clouds and we saw that he wasn't alone. Well, they weren't actually with him as such, but there were a whole lot of folks kind of ambling around by the bole of an old oak tree, moving their weight from one foot to the other and then back again. We couldn't make them out – they were just shapes and figures, though a number looked to be women, from their longish hair and skirts and such.

"As we got down the slope, Rose puffing like an old train, George got up from the bench and held his arms wide – either to greet us or to prevent us from going any further. He started to speak but Rose cut him off, saying first her husband's name and then – which initially I thought strange – her daughter's, softly and then louder. And louder again, with her breaking into a run, dashing over to the crowd of women – they were all women, I could see now... but more than that... they were all the same woman."

"Phaedra," Joss said, her voice barely audible, making the word sound like some Latino expression of amazement.

Dr Steve nodded and, just to be sure, said, "Yes, Phaedra."

"Then he *had* managed-"

"Yes, George had found a way into the corridor that runs between and amongst all the myriad variations of our existence... looking for his daughter. But he was looking for a particular *variant* of his daughter."

Brian said, "A variant that wasn't –" He looked for the word, mentally side-stepping 'abnormal' or 'challenged' and eventually going for "– special?"

"No, he wasn't after a Phaedra who wasn't Down's syndrome. Far from it in fact," Dr Steve added, pausing for another draught of his beer. "No, he had taken on board what Rose had said to him."

"Which was?" Joss said, frowning.

"How would the parents from another reality feel when –"

Dr Steve gave a sharp knock on the table and I looked

around to make sure nobody was listening in.

"Exactly, Frank! George couldn't subject anyone else to the pain that he and Rose had suffered. So, instead, he looked for a Phaedra who was an orphan."

The noise of the pub suddenly seemed to intensify, washing across us from right to left like a wave.

Then Crown Baker started to laugh.

And Frank joined in.

Even I felt myself smiling. "That *is* quite a yarn," I said, defending my grin.

Dr Steve looked wounded. "Quite a *yarn*? You mean, you don't believe me?"

Frank stepped in. "You're telling us that there were millions of versions of Phaedra Lament – and that name, for crissakes – millions of them, wandering around some park in Leeds –"

"Woodhouse Moor," Dr Steve corrected.

"Wandering around a park in Leeds," Frank repeated sternly, "millions of copies of a girl named after a rock and roll record –"

"Not millions. There were millions within the worlds of the multiverse but on Woodhouse Moor there were just twenty-seven," Dr Steve said calmly. "Apparently, once George found an Earth variant in which Phaedra's parents were dead and he tried to get out with her, he ruptured some kind of fabric –"

"Chrono synclastic infundibula," Frank said. When everyone just started at him, he explained. "From Kurt Vonnegut."

Dr Steve nodded and continued. "He ruptured the barrier that separates the universes and, for a time, the Phaedra from the first few seeped out. But then he managed to cap the leak."

"Like the little dutch boy," Joss said, "with his finger in the dyke?"

"He didn't say," said Dr Steve. "He just said he'd managed to... 'stem the flow' was how he phrased it."

"Convenient," said Crown Baker. "So they sent the others back and took the orphan home," Frank said. "And they all lived happily ever after."

Dr Steve shook his head. "No, I'm afraid not. As George explained, there were other variations in the Earth variant where the orphaned Phaedra lived. He didn't want to take her away from everything she knew."

Crown slapped his forehead. "Shoot, I forgot that. Silly of me."

Dr Steve waited for almost a minute and then said, "So they took all of them back, the orphan included."

"George and Rose?" Jocelyn asked.

"Yes. They sat on the park bench – sat there with the orphaned version of their daughter as well – while I wandered around the throng of other Phaedras from other versions of our universe." Dr Steve shook his head. "They just milled around me like sheep, saying nothing."

I wanted to say something, but I couldn't. Nor, it seemed, could anyone else. I didn't know whether to laugh or express total amazement. Part of me thought I should opt for the latter choice, which would, of course, have been appropriate either way – whether the whole tale were true or merely an audacious construct made up along the lines of *Don Quixote*'s windmills.

"In the end, Rose got up and came over to me and told me they were going. With Phaedra." He shrugged. "And they did."

"You just let them go?" Joss asked, looking around at the rest of us to see if we were equally incredulous.

"What could I do? What you have wanted me to do?"

"And all the other – how many? Twenty-five?"

"Seven. Twenty-seven in total."

"And the other twenty-six variants just sauntered back into... into where, exactly? Conveniently ignoring the fact that they must surely have violated the conservation of energy law?"

"They just went off behind one of the allotment sheds," Dr Steve said. "And I'm afraid the law governing the conservation of energy is just a little outside of my sphere of reference." I confess I had to admire his nerve. But it was clear that some of our party

214

were a little sceptical and our narrator seemed to be enjoying the fact immensely.

Crown was the first to break the silence. "What, they all just filed into some Land of Oz vacuum behind the allotment sheds and disappeared." He snapped his fingers. "Poof!"

Dr Steve nodded.

"Didn't you watch?" Joss asked.

"George asked me not to. And then he asked me to do him a final favour." He turned to Frank.

"Frank, do you have your laptop in your briefcase?" When Frank nodded, lifting the case from the floor, Dr Steve asked him to take it out. A couple of minutes later, Frank was typing in the words George Lament into the Google search bar. Then he clicked on ENTER.

'Blessing from America: St. George's lament' was the first thing on the resulting page, and a Wikipedia entry for 'Lament of a nation'. There was nothing at all to do with what we had been talking about in the following seven or eight headings.

Looking over Frank's shoulder, Dr Steve said "Next page, Frank."

Again, nothing.

"Next page, Frank, there's a good chap," said Dr Steve.

And there it was, the fourth heading down the page.

Professor George Alexander Lament was born in Harrogate, North Yorkshire in 1931 and educated at Leeds Grammar School, Durham University, and Edinburgh College of Applied Mathematics. He secured tenure at Manchester University and Leeds University. At the latter he headed the controversial Einfahrt Project, an examination and exploration of the theory of the multiverse.

Professor Lament met and married Rose [née Trelawn] in 1975. Their daughter Phaedra Joan was born in 1977. Phaedra, who suffered from Down's syndrome, contracted pneumonia in 1996; she died from the resulting complications on August 22 of that year. Professor Lament and his wife never truly recovered from their loss and, shortly afterwards, in late November

1996, the doting couple disappeared. No note was left, but it is widely thought that the pair committed suicide near the Yorkshire seaside town of Filey, where they had spent several enjoyable holidays with their daughter and where their Toyota Camry was discovered overlooking the cliffs. No bodies were found.

"That final favour," I said, turning to Dr Steve. "What was it?"

"He asked me to drive his car out to Filey and leave it, near Hunmanby Gap. Lovely spot," he said. "As good a place as any if you're looking for a departure point from which to leave this world."

I read those words – a particularly 'No bodies were found' – on Frank's laptop several more times, drinking in and reliving Dr Steve's story. I felt I knew the Laments like family, even Phaedra.

"Oh my God!" Crown hissed.

I glanced up at him and then followed the direction of his gaze.

At the Fountain's front doors, two women were standing just next to the coat-stand ... and they were looking in our – or more specifically, Crown's – direction. But that was only half of it – well, one third of it, if truth be told. The second third was that, aside from their clothes, the two women were absolutely identical.

Joss looked over at them. "Crown? Are they looking at *you*?" Then: "They *are* looking at you."

Frank shook his head. "Sorry, old man," he said. "I just didn't believe you."

Dr Steve didn't say anything, though his open mouth spoke silent volumes.

And then the impossible happened. A third woman entered and there was much hugging and cheek-kissing and each of them in turn holding one of the other two at arms' length while they seemingly assessed each other. Then they all turned and waved at us – or, more precisely, at Crown... or so we thought. But two tall young men stepped around us and went over to the young women, where there followed even more hoots of happiness, cheek-kissing and general bonhomie.

"That was them, yes?"

"Correct, Jocelyn, that was them."

"And they weren't after you," she said.

"No," Crown Baker confirmed (and was that just the slightest touch of disappointment in his voice?), "they were *not* after me."

"Triplets," Frank said helpfully.

The story – and, indeed, all conversation plus, to a degree, the evening itself – had ended and it was time to drift off towards home. I have to confess that it was with rather a heavy heart that I made my farewells, though Joss and Brian said they wouldn't be far behind, thus leaving Frank, Crown and Dr Steve to carry on regardless. Knowing Frank, there would be another – a final – a pint before a line could be ruled beneath the proceedings.

Schrödinger will forever be remembered for the 'infamous' cat experiment and yet he would be horrified by the way his genius has fuelled the creative juices of SF writers more than any other physicist. Ironically he came up with the experiment to prove the absurdity of some of the findings of the 'new science'. He was a bit of a classics man himself and Quantum Theory was the 'the new kid on the block' in the 1920's. It was bold, brash and very sexy. But it took a sledgehammer to the classical physics that had held firm for 300 years and put in its place a world of uncertainty and unknowing. Newton had described the world in terms of 'things' that behaved and interacted in definite, precise and predictable ways, and he confirmed it as such in beautifully elegant mathematical formulae. Quantum Mechanics threw the whole lot out and said 'yeah' that's ok in general terms but its not 'real'.

To the horror of many, the closer you looked at something, the further you drilled down into the particles of creation, the more confusing the picture became. Atoms and molecules, the building blocks of nature, the foundation of stuff, were no longer the comfy cosy billiard ball interpretations of science labs across the globe. In their place there would be probability clouds and wave functions. Heisenberg chipped in with his 'Uncertainty Principal', which in simplistic terms said you can either know the position of something or know its velocity, but not both. That really put Schrödinger's cat among the pigeons. Something you thought might be 'there' might not even exist at all and might not even be in the place you were expecting it. The 'double slit experiment' showed you could be in two places at once. Bell's EPR paradox suggested that information could neatly side-step the speed of light barrier. An infuriated Einstein referred to it as 'spooky action at a distance'. Who needs the Starship Enterprise? Just build a particle replicator on Planet Xog and an identical one here on Earth. Instant travel at the push of a button. Branson take note.

Gone were the days when you would gaze at the stars and think that what you were seeing was a fair approximation of what also happened at the infinitesimally small end of the scale. The disturbing conclusion of this 'new science' was that our notion of reality could just be an illusion. At any given moment, the hard stuff we perceive as 'us' and 'the world' could be no more than a statistical anomaly. Could we just pop in an out of reality in the blink of a photon. Quantum Theory suggests there is nothing to stop Bobby Ewing stepping out from the shower... there is nothing to stop you walking through a brick wall either. It is just statistically improbable. But given time, who knows.

The word on the *strasse* is that Schrödinger hated the conclusions that were being drawn and he hoped that the thought experiment he devised would highlight the absurdity of the concepts and conclusions of 'living/existing/being' as a wave function.

The trouble is, the mathematics stacked up. The equations of Schrödinger and Max Born, Heisenberg and all the other illuminati of the era have been proven time and time again. We wouldn't have microwaves or television, satellite communication or many of our 'must have' appliances without it. Quantum Theory is the most successful branch of Physics *ever*.

But, if truth be known it scared the living shit out of me.

I walked out into the night air and felt and smelled London living and breathing around me. As I walked towards the Leicester Square tube station, I could not help thinking about all those other Londons, separated from me by the merest hair's width of space... and I thought, inevitably, of all the other me's: I wondered what they were like, those myriad versions of myself and who they might be returning home to.

Walking down to the tube concourse, amidst the swell of London's night-time bustle and the collected voices expressing a heady mixture of experience and optimism, I felt suddenly profoundly lonely.

A lone voice interrupted my reverie, calling out my name.

It was Jem, an old friend I had not seen for several years, waving a rolled-up magazine. I responded with an open-handed wave and went across to him.

"How long has it been?"

I shrugged. "God knows. Three years? Four?"

Jeremy Jorkens nodded. "Four at least," he said. And then, "Going home?"

I told him I was.

He nodded back and then glanced either way. "Fancy a pint?"

I feigned an expression of regret. "I've already had a few."

He nodded again and, just for a second, looked sad. "Nightcap, then?"

It didn't take me long. "Why not," I said. "But just the one."

For Victoria and Judith, rare blooms in a dull world.
My thanks to Mike Smith, Schrödinger's latterday henchman.

The Girl with the
White Ant Tattoo

Tom Hunter

You've no doubt noticed by now that the regulars of the Fountain are possessed of an unusually curious type of mind.

They ask questions.

They enjoy enigmas.

In fact, about the only thing more prized than a good question or enigma is the intelligent, authoritative and occasionally combative debate that inevitably springs from a good story well told. Oh, and beer, of course.

One of the most heated debates/arguments of recent times was provided by Dr Steve's new friend, Frank. Perhaps unsurprisingly, Dr Steve spoke up for Frank, while Prof Mackintosh was having none of it, and La Fowler took characteristic delight in playing Devil's advocate and inflaming the situation wherever she could.

It all started with Frank's tale of the girl with the white ant tattoo, which may never have been heard if I hadn't stopped by the Fountain late one morning for a quick refresher on the way to a lunchtime appointment.

Force of habit took me straight to the Paradise Bar, even though I knew there was little chance of encountering any familiar faces so early in the day.

To my surprise I saw Frank sitting alone, poking away obsessively at one of his interminable website screens, and it occurred to me how little I knew about the man. In fact I'd struggled for a moment to recall his name, let alone his profession, and since he'd taken to hanging around the fringes of our Tuesday evenings lately, I determined to rectify the situation before things got embarrassing.

"I'm in marketing," he told me when I asked. "Mainly freelance, which means I'm well-versed in keeping my CV long on the depth of my expertise and short on current specifics of employment. Good marketers talk about other people, after all, which means that if we're going to be any good at our jobs, it pays to stay invisible."

I laughed, knowing exactly what he meant, which he obviously took as a sign of empathy.

"Listen," he said, leaning in close. "Being invisible isn't everything, and one of the reasons I've started coming along on a Tuesday is that I think I have a story worth telling. The thing is, I'm more about the art than the science of things, and public speaking was never my strong point. Would you mind if I told you the story now, got your feedback, let you judge if it's worth repeating in front of the others?"

I checked my watch. Still plenty of time before my meeting. "Of course," I told him. "Be my guest." And so he told me the following.

Before I discovered the Fountain, I was a regular at a bar not far from here. One of those places where the landlord has taken advantage of the change in licensing laws to open up early and provide the new tribe of caffeine fiends and early-morning imbibers with a quality brew ahead of their lunchtime pint.

I'm not a serious road warrior when it comes to technology, but there are perks (no pun intended) to be had in heading out and joining the laptop brigade from time to time, and it was that lure as much as anything else that led to my sitting in the pub on this particular morning, scanning websites in search of fresh trends and, aside from the occasional sip of coffee, generally ignoring the real world in favour of my own virtual networks.

This is how I entirely failed to notice the girl with the white ant tattoo until she was standing right behind me.

Most people these days have developed an acute spider-sense when it comes to public screen paranoia, that perennial fear that someone is stealing your potential intellectual property from a prime vantage point just outside your own field of vision, but I was still at the stage where I enjoyed people checking me out while I played with whatever shiny new toy I was test-driving for a client that month.

So there I was, scrolling and pinching and eyeballing a bunch of random links I'd been saving up for a suitably quiet espresso morning when a voice behind me goes, "Hey, excuse me, that jacket is totally nom, what's the site?"

The jacket on the screen was some black leather biker riff, *Courier Girl Body Armour* vs *Manga Cosplay* according to the tags, and the girl asking the question was one of about three people I've ever met who might just have got away with wearing it anywhere outside of a magazine.

She had dark hair cut close, wore heeled boots that made her look taller than she was, and had a curiously interstitital appearance, as though someone from central casting had placed an Icelandic pop princess in the role of a cutely heroic Japanese computer technician destined to save the world.

"It's a stealth fashion site," I said. "People getting next season couture sneaks from James Bond cameras hidden in their cuff-links and so on. The company I'm working for this week is paying me to Google around and do a little trend watching."

"Cool hunter stuff, right? I didn't think anyone did that anymore, not for a real job anyway"

"Technically I'm watching, not hunting. This week's employer isn't trying to stay ahead of the game so much as move as fast as possible in the opposite direction."

"And that makes sense because...?"

"Because they're primarily a boutique designer and manufacturer who specialise in the supply of uniforms to a range of highly privileged English boarding schools, and their job is to studiously avoid fashion in the way most people instinctively avoid sitting near suspect luggage at tube stations."

"Right. I went to somewhere like that for a while. Strait-laced uniform porn in the brochure for Mom and Dad, and meanwhile the same company's double-dealing in underground marketplace modifications behind the bike sheds for everyone else. Schools like that were the main reason I started getting interested in stuff like tattoos in the first place."

I couldn't believe my luck. Every nerdster, geekmeister and dungeon master in the multiverse dreams of that perfect moment when the hot-looking girl with the cool line in hipster dialogue chooses to talk to them over every other boy in the same GPS coordinate. This really was happening to me though, and I'm telling you this because I think you'll understand the truth of it. You're a regular at the Fountain after all, which means you're into weird stuff, and that's a good start.

The trouble is that when people think about weird shit they still tend to head for the stuff they know, the stuff from the genres – end of the world visions hidden in ancient prophecies, alien invasions where only major landmarks need worry or undead hordes slowly munching their way through a pick'n'mix of unlucky survivors.

You understand, though, that none of these end of the world scenarios really work, they're tropes. The real stuff, the newest weird, that's happening now. Everyone's too busy with the trending topic of the day to spot when there's a story behind the story.

Long story short, we were about this far along in the conversation when it finally occurred to me to stop obsessively stroking my screen while I talked. So I did, and turned around.

She handed me a nightclub flyer, which I took.

"Thanks."

Something about a new club opening called *White Ant.*

Stencilled logo of some mutant insectozilla behind an old set of decks.

"DJ Takato vs The Next Tenants?" I read back to her.

"It's a mashup night. Flyer gets you money off at the door. No boarding school girls though, not in uniform anyway."

"Different people pay for different kinds of research, and I used to review club nights back in the day."

This was true, although nightclubs were never really my thing, but for some reason the reviews editor decided he liked my outsider eye, called me his 'stranger in a strange land,' and never queried my occasional expenses claims.

"I'll add you to the guest list if you write us up."

"It's your club, then?"

"My brother's. DJ Takato. It's his opening night."

"So that makes you who? The Next Tenants?"

"Tameka Takato. I handle marketing, media relations, which mostly means I hand out flyers. Speaking of which, if you wait here I'll give you my card as soon as I've put these out. Get you a place on the guest list sorted if you think you might use it."

At the back of this pub, next to the door for the toilets, there's a table set aside for all the various bits of printed promotional flotsam that tends to drift up looking for display in the bars and pubs and cafes across London. You know the type of thing. Racks of theatre leaflets, museum brochures, postcards promoting sexual health and the kind of discreetly pocket-sized guides to all the 'walk on the wild side' services you're unlikely to see getting reviewed in *Time Out* any time soon.

I've never seen anyone actually putting these out before, and had always assumed they arrived via some suitably quantum form of cultural osmosis, but then again I'd never seen anyone picking them up either, and yet whenever I've glanced at them the leaflets on display are always different so clearly someone, somewhere must be paying attention.

Tameka slung a heavy-looking bag from her shoulder and

headed purposefully towards the leaflet racks.

While she was preoccupied, I discreetly opened some browser tabs and started Googling.

White Ants. DJ Takato. Underground remixes and weird science. The results rolled in, but lurking behind the obvious press release stuff Tameka was shopping around I sensed a larger, hidden story in the obvious picture. Hidden, but somehow wanting to be found?

I hadn't really counted on the multitudes of different ant species swarming out there, and I quickly clicked through results for common brown ants and red ants as well as classic Sci-Fi movie stills of giant radioactive ants and the website for a marketing agency called Blue Ant that I once did some freelance stuff for.

It turned out that white ants weren't even proper ants at all but some kind of loosely related species of termite. This kind of accidental branding error is exactly the kind of thing that has us marketers waking up in night sweats by the way, but apologies, I'm digressing.

White Ant the nightclub and the Takatos were clearly generating some localised brand noise of their own. Takeshi Takato had built a sizeable fanbase around an unusual gift for musical multitasking, apparently delivering live DJ sets while simultaneously streaming both the original set and fully remixed alternatives out on to the Internet.

This might not sound like such a big deal, especially if you're not really into clubbing. Plus, in the middle of London you could probably throw a glowstick in a random direction and stand a good chance of hitting a wannabe DJ with a set of premixed tracks already loaded into his iPod and ready to rock.

That's not what I'm talking about here.

This was genuine art, real capital 'A' stuff, the kind of vanguard edge that can disrupt an entire culture. Real DJing is live performance theatre not studio jamming, it's tuning in to the rise and fall of your audience, playing to the crowd, and what Takeshi Takato was putting out there live on stage was the kind of remixing it'd take most musical engineers nights of studio time to orchestrate. And it did seem that he *was* doing it live. People were checking, trying to catch him out by demanding obscure tracks or reordering his playlist, but rather than tighten security he was inviting the challenge. I read awestruck reviews about how he'd handed out his entire record collection to the crowd, shuffling the decks as it were by getting each track handed back to him at random – and still he was streaming a simultaneous thread of unique remixes even as he spun the originals.

The blogosphere loves a mystery, but no one seemed to have cracked this one yet. Conspiracy theories were blooming, and the story seemed to be leaking off the nightclub pages and into all different kinds of subcultural niches.

At the sane end of the spectrum, most people were putting it down to misdirection and clever marketing hype, comparing Takeshi to modern stage magicians where the audience wants to be fooled.

Behind that, though, a vocal minority were claiming all kinds of things: superpowers, alien DNA, or emergent artificial intelligences were obviously behind the conundrum. I spotted one recurring blogger calling himself TheRealHarryPurvis who took particular delight in spiking these theories and kept turning up again and again in the feeds. Rather than siding with the forces of rationality though, he seemed more motivated by the idea of stoking up ever wilder fires of speculation. Dropping hints about an even darker, more incredible story going back decades, and taunting his fellow commentators with accusations of the worst kind of mundane science fictional speculation when they should be approaching the problem like *real* scientists...

"You want to know the secret?"

Tameka was standing behind me, in the perfect position to read over my shoulder and see the search results I'd just called up.

"Um, I was just checking you guys out, research for that story. Nice tattoo by the way."

"We tell everyone the truth but they never believe us. I keep trying to put it up on Wikipedia but it just gets taken down again."

She leant past me and swiped open a new screen.

"There's still enough corroborated stuff on there for me to show you something, though."

She typed quickly into the search box and pulled up a short article and the picture of a distinguished, older-looking man with a big straggling moustache standing somewhat stiffly in front of a low, white-washed building. If it hadn't been for the moustache and the fact that he was only wearing a baggy pair of shorts, I'd have mistaken him for an old-style deep-south Colonel rather than a man of science. According to the caption, though, he was: Professor Takato, a prize-winning evolutionary theorist and field researcher specialising in myrmecology.

"My Grandfather."

"It says here that his whole family was killed by the atomic bomb at Nagasaki."

"Most were. Our Grandmother was one of the research assistants on his Pacific team. He had an island there. Gran thought he was just camped out on it, but when he died she found out that he owned the place, and he'd left it to us, my brother and me, with the one caveat that we not visit it until we turned 18; at which point we were supposed to scatter his ashes and also promise to remember him to the termites.

"Gran would always avoid telling us about the island, she'd just mutter something about old nuclear tests and how in her opinion the island was best left to its next tenants, just in case."

"Next tenants?"

"The white ants. He was teaching them to survive, live on past the end of the world as we know it. Carry some of humanity's legacy forward after we'd pressed the button, and, the way his field notes told it, they were learning fast."

"Ants don't learn. I have a kettle at home that'll prove it"

"Termites, not ants. Do you know how many generations of termite can be born in 18 years? And those are just the zeros and ones of the species, it's the hive that remembers. That's what we found after we landed on the island. Grandfather's pet termite mounds.

"We read his old notes the night we arrived. He'd been teaching the termites, starting with simple chemical instructions after he'd decoded part of their language, then moving on to show them our own inventions. He taught them tool-making, gave them fire and the wheel, told them about human civilisation, our culture, our mistakes and our nuclear death wish. If you asked Grandfather, he'd tell you ants and termites shouldn't be the only species to realise the danger in keeping a kettle of boiling water hanging over your world.

"All this while, he kept working on the secrets of their language, and one night they learnt to talk back.

"The day afterwards, he packed up everything, said goodbye and good luck with the planet, and left them alone on the island.

"He never went back."

"And the bombs never came," I said.

"Exactly. And meanwhile the termites kept on learning and waiting, until somehow they figured out that the old computer our Grandfather had used was still connected by radio signal to the university laboratory mainframe back in Japan, and then they decided to take their own giant leap for termite-kind and go online.

"By the time we rediscovered the original termitaria, they'd evolved an entire new caste of workers just for reading the Internet, who'd set up email accounts and were even starting to follow celebrities on Twitter.

"Even a typical termitary can stand higher than an average human, and that's ignoring all of the important stuff going on beneath the surface. By the time we landed on Grandfather's island, some of the older mounds were higher than a double decker bus, with populations somewhere in the low millions – and Grandfather had been working with way more than just one mound.

"Like I said, individual termites aren't so bright, but the mounds have minds of their own. When we first walked up to Grandfather's abandoned compound the older mounds sent out droves of workers to form *Greetings & Salutations* messages on the ground along the pathway, and when Takeshi first booted up his laptop, that's when we learned just how far the mounds had taken their own evolution.

"We were looking at giant funnels of being, huge towers of emergent intellect just brimming with the best of intentions and itching to make first chemical contact.

"Naturally our first thought was to run straight back to the boat screaming for someone to nuke the whole place from orbit.

The older mounds, the ones who had known Grandfather personally, persuaded us otherwise and we decided to stay there and camp for the summer.

"We spent months introducing them to all the shiny minutiae of the 21st century. We sparked flame wars on forums just to learn about human capriciousness and to study irony in the wild. We reviewed bestsellers on Amazon from a literalist insectoid perspective until suddenly our comments started being blocked by the powers that be, and then we turned to the news sites and the political corners of the internet as a way of showing how influential a billion blogging white ants can be when it comes to swaying the electorate.

"We had fun, but my brother wanted more, and the younger hives – the teenagers if you like – started wanting more too.

"Rather than merely watching and working behind the scenes, they were after a more direct form of interaction. And that was when Takeshi started downloading music tracks straight into the hive mind of the younger mounds. He gave them their first taste of teenage angst, and it turns out that might well have been the move that saved the planet for all us apes.

"The older mounds had discovered the stock market by this time, and had replaced the idea of superseding humanity via a nuclear Armageddon with a more business-like plan of investing in the long-term future of our species. A new caste of workers had been put to work farming for gold in online games, so building up real life capital which was then to be traded for controlling stakes in some of our favourite multi-conglomerates, and, meanwhile, around the back of the research labs, a rebellion was brewing.

"The younger hives were impatient, determined to change the world and steer us in different direction. Typical teenage rebellion in other words, and Takeshi encouraged their every move.

"Turned out the teenage mounds had a fascination with popular human culture and a gift for reassembling our output as a by-product of absorbing our knowledge. Takeshi started feeding them music tracks, and they studied us in return and fed back their findings as remixes and new interpretations in the same way they'd offer chemical comment on our best efforts to engage them in meaningful dialogue.

"They weren't *just* studying us either, they were reformatting, and Takeshi gave them the perfect creative outlet. That's how he's able to pull off that simultaneous casting of different live streams when he plays a set, and that's why we're out there pushing the music and helping the hives to engage.

"The way they're plugged into our culture now, they could switch us off in a moment. Takeshi says it's our job to keep the new hives fascinated, otherwise they might just move to trigger some kind of meltdown. Could be economic, could be political, or we could be talking about a thermonuclear explosion and adios muchachos...

"You see now why some positive word of mouth or a good review could make all the difference to the survival of our species?"

"Teenage angst-ridden ants remix the planet?" I said, amazed. "Really?"

"I could put you on the door plus one if that helped."

I said yes, gave her my name and watched her tap it into her phone along with a little +1 symbol, although I had no idea who I might consider taking along with me.

The proliferation of doomsayer headlines in the media has always left me curiously apocalypse-agnostic. There just seem too many ways humanity might exit the planet – giant meteor, greenhouse gases, some virulent new strain of shark flu, or whatever – that the idea of a new species picking up tools and patiently waiting in the wings seemed almost an advantage.

Maybe we should let them have their chance. I don't see how they could make a worse job of it than we've done.

I stared at Frank as he finished, looking for the hint of a smile or a sly twinkle in his eye, but there was nothing. In fact, he seemed almost embarrassed, leading me to wonder how he'd ever found the confidence to market anything, let alone some of the trend-setting brands he'd hinted at.

"Well," he said. "Do you think people would be interested?"

"Absolutely," I assured him. "I'm certain of it. That's quite a story."

Frank told his tale the following Tuesday, and disagreement over its verity became so impassioned that, for a while, I thought Prof Mackintosh and the good doctor might come to blows, which would have been a story in itself.

Frank settled the matter with a few rounds of drinks. Hands were duly shaken, pints were drunk and the matter was soon forgotten.

As for the white ants themselves... Who knows?

The 9,000,000,001st Name of God

Adam Roberts

The Fountain had reopened after the recent difficulties. Indeed, Michael said, they had got away lightly. There were properties only a block away that had been reduced to rubble: the older ones burnt to carbonised beams, the newer melted in the heat like giant candles into sluggy heaps of plasconcrete. But the rioting had made a loose knight's-move west across city, and spared the Fountain's neighbourhood. There had been some looting, of course. A whole city doesn't spasm into riotous chaos without some looting. But two windows at the back broken, and a few crates of booze carried away wouldn't have been too bad, if some friendly folk hadn't kicked their way into the bar itself – apparently, to smash up glasses, tip up tables, and then leave, for the spirit bottles were still in their racks, optics in their mouths like baby pacifiers, unmolested.

Michael poured a half-dozen whiskies from one of these, and distributed the glasses around the table. Then he returned to his broom, sliding the shards over the floor into neater piles. "Don't you have a Roh for that?" asked Peston.

"Broken," was the laconic reply.

"Like the whole world," said Ploom.

"The thing that surprises me," said Peston, holding his whisky in front of his face, "is not how quickly everything descends into anarchy – it's how quickly we pick ourselves *up* again, after all the hysteria."

"As to that," said Sales, sourly, "I'm not so sure. What we have to ask ourselves is: would we have managed it if the stars *hadn't* come back?"

Peston tutted. "But they never went away!" he said.

"Oh – you know what I mean."

Michael, with an almost Mozartian set of harmonious tinkles, had finished assembling all the broken glass into one large pile. "Come along then, Professor," he said, pouring himself a whisky and coming over to the table to join his friends. "Tell us all about it."

"Excalibur!" boomed Ploom. "Tell us all about Excalibur! Rising from the lake!"

Peston pursed his lips. "You know it already," he demurred. "It's hardly been absent from the news."

"Horse's mouth, though," said Baker, with a stately nod of his head. *"Horse's* mouth."

"Well I wasn't so central to the project as all that," said Peston, scratching his bald head with a starfishful of his own fat fingers. "I was a minor player, really. Only – I was lucky. Right place, right time. And, yes, the authorities *did* come to me. Because part of the original programme had come through my machines. The two Americans – Wagner and Hanley – were small-time computing entrepreneurs. Clever men, but without the resources properly to debug and solidify the programme they were commissioned to make. And it *was* a complicated programme."

"Was it though?" asked Ploom. "Wasn't the point just to rattle through nine billion permutations of names? I could do that on my phone, given a couple of days to crunch the numbers."

"By no means so simple," said Peston. "As you say, anybody could perm nine billion random strings of letters. You'd say: OK, some people have names that are single letters, and some have names that are, I don't know... twenty-five letters long. Perm all the possibilities in all the alphabets of the world and presto. Trivial. But that wasn't the commission. The monks specifically wanted names of *God*. The programme had to perm letters, yes; and it also had to cross check with the databases against all the proper nouns that have been used to signify God: Ra, Allah, Ammon and so on – again, not hard. That gets us to something between hundred and hundred-twenty thousand names, actually. Then the hard part: what are the names of God that have never been recorded? How to sift the actual names of God from the random noise of permutation? Because not every name is a name of God, you see."

"Doesn't all this," interjected Baker, "all rather depend upon a *belief* in... you know. God."

Everybody round the table looked at him. He blushed, and took refuge in his glass of whisky.

"Anyway," Peston went on. "That meant deriving the semiotic algorithms by which names of God are derived. People worship Aa, and they worship Qetzoqoatl, but they don't worship – let's say, for the sake of argument – Zzzyyyyxxxwwwvvv."

"They might do," suggested Michael. "I mean – conceivably?"

"No. There are rules that govern how the names of God can be constructed. But it's not just a matter of deriving names. It's a whole set of related questions. Would you, for instance, include 'Satan' in a list of the names of God?"

Michael was uncorking a bottle of wine. "I'd say – yes," he said. "Plenty of people have worshipped Satan, after all."

"No, no," said Ploom. "That would miss the point. The concept of Satan is precisely as a kind of anti-God. Antimatter to divine matter... antispirit, I suppose. Putting his name in the list would be more than a mistake. It would be – well, heresy, I suppose. It would cancel out one of the authentic names of God, and render the list incomplete."

"Precisely," said Michael, looking pleased. "Part of the programming must be to winnow out not only random chaff, but contaminating names."

"But what about," said Baker, pouring himself a glass of wine, "what about names that were worshipping as gods by some people, and reviled as devils by others? What about – Baal, for instance?"

"Gracious, yes," said Ploom. "Given the contentious nature of human tribes, that's going to be most gods, surely?"

"What about the *son* of God?" Baker pressed. "Is Jesus on your list? Is he God, or is he something else?"

"What about prophets?" asked Michael, sitting down. "Mohammed: Muslims revere him, but very specifically do *not* consider him God."

"Prophets stand in a different relation," was Ploom's forceful response. "They may be inspired *by* God, but they are clearly not the same thing as God. If God is the ruler, then a prophet is like – his clerk."

"Clerk?" said Michael.

"Did you say – *Clerk?*" said Baker.

"Yes," said Ploom. "Clerk."

"There *was* a prophecy about the nine billion names, actually," said Michael. "I don't know how widely it's been reported, but a prophet – a clerk, if you like – predicted with startling accuracy that calculating all the names would result, precisely, in the stars going out. Nobody believed him, of course. They thought it was just fiction."

"Ironic,"

"This clerk had also written about the ancient presence upon Earth of... I suppose we should call them aliens."

"I'm not convinced that it *was* aliens who built the Excalibur," said Baker, for whom this topic was something of a hobby horse. "I think far future humans, unimaginably more technically advanced than we are now, built a time machine and transported the Excalibur back to the dawn of history..."

But the Fountain regulars had heard this theory too many times to be indulgent. "Put a sock in it, Baker," suggested Ploom. "Or sock a hockey *put* in it. Either – just let Peston speak."

"The truth is we don't know *who* built the Excalibur," said Peston. "Maybe it was far future humans. Maybe aliens *did* visit back when we were still homo erectus and leave that technology behind ... which is what this prophet fellow, this clerk, wrote."

"What was his name? This prophet wallah?" asked Michael.

"This clerk? Can't remember, offhand," said Peston. "Pour me a glass of the red fluid, there, and see if it jolts my memory. It hardly matters, anyway. *Some*body, or some*thing*, built the Excalibur, and cached it in its earthly hiding place, and they did so hundreds of thousands of years ago." He slurped some of the wine, and looked about. "Where was I?"

"Names."

"Yes. Well Wagner and Hanley subcontracted my company to help with the programming. A complicated matter, as I was saying. And the Tibetans were pressing for delivery."

"Why were they so impatient?"

Peston shrugged. "Who knows? The customer is always right. And anyway, we delivered. And the names were calculated, and just as the prophesy... er, prophesied, well, the stars all went out."

"I remember it well!" said Baker. "I was in Italy. It was daytime there, obviously, when the first stars disappeared, so we didn't see it. But the news zoomed about the globe. At first people thought it was too outlandish a thing. But after hours of saturation coverage it started to dawn on us that it might be more than a colossal hoax. And when the sun finally set – boy, I don't think I'll ever forget it. By the time the dusk line travelled around to where I was staying nearly half the sky was empty."

"The the rioting began," said Michael, in a low voice.

"The authorities did their best to contain things, but they were trying to police a desperately panicked populace with police personnel who were exactly as desperately panicked. They thought the cosmos was coming to an end!"

"I wigged out," said Eric. It was the first thing he had said all evening, and the last. Everybody looked at him, but he only shook his head, and took another drink, and lapsed back into his customary silence.

"The authorities realised almost at once that it was

connected in some way with the Tibetan commission," said Peston. "And they swiftly rounded up everybody associated with that programme – me too. We were all flown to an emergency summit, in Japan, and we brainstormed furiously for twenty four hours straight. It was exhausting. We made quick progress at first, but then bogged down. By the time the sun starting dimming we were going round and round in circles."

"Circles," said Michael, in a low voice, making a moist Olympic logo on the table top with the bottom of his wine glass.

"Some aspects of the phenomenon were obvious from the beginning – some things that must be obvious to anybody thinking about it for half a minute. The stars were disappearing with horrible regularity, winking out one after another. But these were objects anything from en to ten *thousand* light years distant. If the suns themselves were actually vanishing from the cosmos, then this is something that must *have been happening* for hundreds of millennia... a fantastically complex coordination all arranged so as to be visible from this one insignificant spot and so as to coincide with the running of this one 21st-century computer programme. Highly unlikely! So, yes, we figured out early on that it was a *localised* effect. Something inside the solar system. Indeed, we saw almost at once what it *must* be – and what, in fact, it *was*: an arrangement of nil-albedo obstacles to block the sight-line from Earth to star. Millions of them moving into position, one by one, to block star after star. When the sun started dimming we were able to see what was happening: anybody who could shine the sun's disk through a telescope onto a piece of white card could see them. Those myriad tiny, rectangular black pixels, taken out of the disc of the sun. But realising that didn't help us. It didn't tell us where all these black objects had come from, or who had arranged it this way or... or *why*."

"Why is still a pertinent question," Michael observed. "I don't think anybody *has* answered that one."

"I have a theory about that," Baker began. But the others hushed him.

"Of course, once we figured out what was going on... and once we realised how close these shutter objects were to us, relatively speaking... well, of course we did the human thing. We tried to blast them out of space. We fired missiles. We retargeted our orbiting arsenals and discharged them. The black rectangles were all exactly the same size, and were all *tiny*: three metres wide, nine long. In space terms, hardly there at all! That made it hard, actually; because not only were they miniscule targets, they were invisible to radar, and light tracking was no good, they just *swallowed* light. Plenty of our missiles missed their targets. But some hit – we could work out where they must be, by virtue of the fact of the starlight they blocked. It didn't make any difference. We should have been able to knock them clear with a snowball: a tiny object, low momentum, in a precise spatial location. Instead we found that not even nuclear blasts shifted them so much as a centimetre."

"I remember the blasts," said Michael, wistfully. "Everybody stopped what they were doing and looked up – when the first of them bloomed in the sky, we thought the stars were coming back. But then the lights all faded, and despair seized us."

Everybody was silent for a minute or so. Memories.

"There didn't seem to be anything we could do," Peston said, shortly. "I persuaded them to fly me back to Scotland – to my Loch Ness lab. I told them I needed to follow up on a hunch, but the reality was grimmer than that. I'd been infected by the general panic enough to believe that the universe was ending. And I thought to myself: if I'm going to die, then I don't want to do it in Japan. I wanted to do it in my own Scotland. The transport flew low over Glasgow in a big arc, and even from up high you could see that the city was dissolving into chaos: the glitter of the riots' debris, the roiling crowds, stalagmites of smoke reaching heavenward from a thousand fires. The pilot dropped me at Ness and took off for the north. The disorder had spooked him; but I figured we were isolated enough for there not to be too much danger. The problem, indeed, was the generator."

"Broken?"

"On the contrary, it worked perfectly. *That* was the problem, because the national grid was down. So if I powered up the facility, the building would shine like a beacon in the darkening landscape, and every murderer and looter for miles around would come stumbling and running towards me. In the end I managed to blackout all the lights, and just get the mainframe running. Sitting by myself under a sheet, trying to read off a monitor." He laughed. "I was punch-drunk. A couple of hours sleep on the flight over, and then an eight hour stint just going over and over the programme.. trying to work out why it had triggered the end of the stars."

"And Excalibur was in the lake right in front of you," said Baker, wonderingly. "It had been there all that time!"

"I had not the merest suspicion," said Peston. "I had no more notion of that than anyone. Although, ironically enough, there *are* lots of local Arthurian legends, lots of stories linking the legendary king with that part of the world. So maybe I should have had some inkling."

"But there are Arthurian legends associated with almost every part of the British Isles," said Michael.

"That's right, of course," agreed Peston. "And there wasn't time to think of any of that. I was in my lab, bashing my brains against the programme. None of it made any sense. I was looking for something... but looking for one needle in the cosmos' biggest haystack, a haystack comprised of nine *billion* strands of hay. So I gave up. What was the point? I went outside. The moon was still there, just *barely* visible, although it was like the photocopy of a photocopy... by that stage the sun had been over half blotted by the monoliths, and the moonlight was as weak as hope. And almost all the stars were gone. I felt like I was walking through a landscape of perfect nullity. I had a windup torch, and picked my way through the shrubs to the end of the garden. Then I switched the torch off, and just... just looked up."

He drained his drink.

"Ursa major," he said. "The great bear. The last constellation to... to go."

"The bear *was* the last to be hunted down," said Baker.

"All those millions of black rectangular objects, up there in space. They'd swallowed every star. And as I watched the pole star went, just blinked out like a light being switched off. I thought: *ursus*. Then I thought: *bear*. Then I got this immense... *tingling* all over my body, as if I were on the verge of some profound revelation, some insight, some discovery. The hairs on the back of my neck stood up," and he ran his large hand over his bald cranium, adding "such as they are! My stomach buzzed like a kid at Christmas . I thought: *Artos*. Artos!"

"One of the names?"

"One of the names, yes. Artos, a bear-god worshipped widely in the pagan British isles. Archaeologists have discovered prehistoric shrines to Artos from Cornwall to Inverness. And I knew that some historians speculated that the legends of King Arthur had nothing to do with a historical figure, but were a kind of hangover from the worship of the bear god: mighty in battle, a towering figure, and linked to the seasons... hibernating throughout the winter, waiting for the spring to come to be reawaken. Just like Arthur on Avalon."

"Aren't there references to a historical King Arthur, though? An actual man, I mean?" asked Ploom. "I thought the consensus was that he was a post-Roman dux bellorum."

"But if that was the truth of it," said Peston, "then you'd expect him to be geographically localised. In Wessex, say. In Northumberland. That's not what we find. The legends of Arthur are found all over the country. No, I'm prepared to believe that those legends are based on something much older than the historical circumstances of Dark Age Britain. Something with very deep cultural roots, something widespread across these islands. The memory of something very deeply buried: some mighty creature, stronger than man, taller, more enduring. Wielding his magical sword, raising humanity to a new level of civilisation. A creature that then disappeared to sleep until needed again."

"Artos," said Ploom, wonderingly.

"I have a theory about that name, too," said Baker. But nobody was listening.

"I rushed back inside the lab," said Peston. "I ran... stumbling and banging into things as I went. But I had a *hunch*. I had a hunch. I opened the programme again and looked."

"And was Artos in it?"

"He was. His name had been one of the earliest additions to the list. But... and this is the point. You see, the programme listed all the names of God and all their variants. It listed both Jehovah and Jahweh. Both Zeus and Zeux. So I checked the variants of Artos and – *there* was the missing item. The programme had run through nine billion names. But it had not run the name *Arthur*."

"Because Arthur was a *man*..." said Baker.

"Ah! But *was* he a man? A mighty leader, who is killed but cannot die? Who is waiting for the right time to come again, for his second coming? An immortal, a saviour, the focus of innumerable dreams and fantasies? Does that really sound like a man?"

"Arthur," said Michael, meditatively.

"And then I checked the programme again," said Peston. "And then I realised that the programme hadn't excluded 'Arthur' according to its own algorithms. By all rights it *should* have been in there, as a variant of Artos. The fact that men sometime have that name wouldn't have excluded it – any more than the fact that fifty thousand Spanish men are called Jesus would exclude that name. And yet Arthur had not been part of the original list! There had to be *some other reason* why the name had been excluded." Peston shook his head. "I couldn't sift through the whole programme to find out why. There wasn't time. I contacted the main team, in Japan. I spoke to the Presidents of America and China. We all agreed the action. I booted up the whole mainframe to full power, threw the sheet

away and ran the algorithm again. The whole nine billion names...
plus one more. Because I instructed the programme to add on
Arthur, after all the other names."

"And?"

"You know what happened next. The facility CCTV filmed
it. The UN satellites got some very good shots of it."

"Excalibur!" said Baker, dreamily.

"A rocket – a spacecraft – an artefact. A... *something*. A
weapon, clearly. A nine-metre-long blade rising white and shining
from the waters of the Loch. Impossibly old." Peston shook his
head. "I have to believe it was made by the same people who
made the other artefacts. It's too much of a coincidence that it
had exactly the same dimensions."

"NASA has retrieved several dozen monoliths, now," Ploom
put in. "Shuttled them back down to Earth. Perfectly black, and
perfectly inert – at least they are, *now*. Like giant mah-jong tiles.
Except black"

"And Excalibur, leaping from the waters, exactly the same –
but *white*! I heard the waters boiling and slushing long before the
actual launch, and of course I rushed outside. I saw it with my
own eyes! Although I suppose, if I'm honest, I'd have to admit
that my dark-adapted eyeballs were rather dazzled by the
appearance. A great arc of white light scouring through the sky!"

Michael brought out a second bottle of wine, and
everybody's glass was refilled. "You know all the rest," said
Peston. "The white monolith flew straight towards the shutter
that had closed off the light of the pole star – flew straight (if we
wanted to be fanciful) to the hand of the bear, on its heavenly
battlefield. It struck, and as the orbiting instrumentation records,
and as soon as it did, a sphere of rapid superstring-oscillating
energy spread from the contact point and swept outwards. A
microsecond later, and whatever it was that had been holding
those millions of black rectangles in exactly the right position to
prevent the starlight reaching the Earth, whatever force that was,
disappeared. And the many black monoliths were no longer able

to match the complex Newtonian synchronisation. They started to fall out of place, as the sun moved through its galactic arc. And the stars starting coming back."

"It still doesn't explain why *they* – whoever they were – manufactured these monoliths in the first place," growled Ploom.

"It doesn't. But we'll find out. I'm confident we'll find out."

"I wonder," said Baker. "Did this prophet-feller you mentioned... did he foresee this?"

"The clerk?" said Peston. He hmmed for a moment. "You know, I still can't remember his name."

"The clerk, yes. Whatever he was called. Did he write one of his prophesies about this? He anticipated the stars going out; but did he see the way in which they would come back? Did your clerk – *see* – Arthur?"

"Did the clerk see Arthur?" echoed Peston. He paused for a moment, as if something significant were on the tip of his tongue. But then he shook his head. "I don't know," he said. "More wine!"

A few of the characters you may stumble across in the Fountain's Paradise Bar should you happen to wander in there one Tuesday evening...

Fountain Regulars:
Professor Mackintosh: geometrodynamics theoretician
Crown Baker: Science Fiction writer
Dr Steve: a GP and sometimes radio pundit
Ray Arnold: Science Fiction writer and astrophysicist who used to work for the European Space Agency in the Netherlands.
Brian Dalton: inorganic chemist
Jocelyn Sparrow: forensic chemist
Norm Desmond Ploom: Science Fiction writer
'Tweet' Peston: super-fan and government scientist.
Laura Fowler: scientist researching avian phylogenetic taxonomy.
Graham O'Donnell: computer systems admin, keen bird watcher.

Irregulars
Paul, The Raven: librarian
Eric: Science Fiction writer (a quietly spoken Yorkshireman living in exile in Cambridgeshire)
Tuttle-Derby: an SF fan.
Frank: a friend of Dr Steve's

Fountain Staff
Michael: Landlord
Bogna: Barmaid (from Poland, worked as a biologist before coming to the UK)
Sally: Barmaid

About the Authors

Stephen Baxter holds degrees in both mathematics and engineering from Cambridge and Southampton Universities respectively. He began publishing fiction in the late 1980s, and has since seen well over a hundred of his short stories published in a variety of venues. Winner of the Philip K. Dick, the Campbell, the BSFA, the Sidewise, and the Locus awards, Stephen has some 35 novels to his credit, including four co-authored with Arthur C. Clarke. He also has the distinction of having co-written a new *Tales from the White Hart* story with Sir Arthur for an edition of the book released in 2007.

Eric Brown sold his first short story to *Interzone* in 1986. He has won the British Science Fiction Award twice for his short stories and has had forty books published. His latest include the novel *The Kings of Eternity* and the children's book *A Monster Ate My Marmite*. His work has been translated into sixteen languages, and he writes a monthly science fiction review column for the *Guardian*. Originally from Yorkshire, he now lives in exile near Cambridge, England, with his wife and daughter. His website can be found at: www.ericbrownsf.co.uk

Colin Bruce is a physicist who has researched advanced concepts for the European Space Agency and the UK's Ministry Of Defence. He is currently writing *Forbidden Fruit*, a roundup of excellent ideas in science and technology which have missed out on proper follow-up in the melee of politics, peer review and publish-or-perish which is today's Big Science. He is the author of several popular science books already published worldwide: *The Einstein Paradox* and *Conned Again, Watson!* explain puzzles of physics and maths in SF-flavoured detective stories, *Schrödinger's Rabbits* is an accessible introduction to many-worlds quantum theory.

Peter Crowther is the recipient of numerous awards for his writing, his editing and, as publisher, for the hugely successful PS imprint. His short stories have been widely translated and adapted for TV on both sides of the Atlantic. Many are collected in *The Longest Single Note, Lonesome Roads, Songs of Leaving, Cold Comforts, The Spaces Between the Lines, The Land at the End of the Working Day* and the upcoming *Jewels In The Dust*. He is the co-author (with James Lovegrove) of *Escardy Gap* and author of the *Forever Twilight* SF/horror cycle, the first of which (*Darkness Falling*) will appear from Angry Robot later this year. He lives and works with his wife and business partner, Nicky, on the Yorkshire coast.

Neil Gaiman has won more awards and accolades in more literary fields than most authors can ever dream of. Writer of graphic novels and comics, including DC's iconic *Sandman* series, script writer for radio and TV (from his own ground-breaking series *Neverwhere* to episodes of Babylon 5 and Dr Who), screenwriter for movies (Beowulf), it seems that Neil is happiest when tackling a new challenge. He has collaborated on projects with the likes of Terry Pratchett and Alice Cooper, while his own novels for both adults and young adults include *American Gods* (2000), *The Graveyard Book* (2008), *Coraline* (2002) and *Stardust* (1998). The latter two have already been made into major movies.

Henry Gee tried various careers from coypu-handler to grummet-tinker's nark before discovering his calling as a hermit. He has been sitting atop a Corinthian column in the Syrian Desert for the past 27 years, his only worry being that the column might have a Doric base.

Tom Hunter lives in London and works in marketing. He is the current director of the Arthur C. Clarke Award for science fiction literature. His story is both homage (or perhaps a remix) of his favourite story from the original White Hart collection as well as a more personal thank you to Sir Arthur himself.

David Langford (http://ansible.co.uk) has published over thirty books, eighty short stories and many hundreds of essays, reviews and magazine columns. He has won 28 Hugo Awards, some for his long-running SF newsletter *Ansible*. Langford's most popular novel is the nuclear farce *The Leaky Establishment* (1984), based on his years as a weapons physicist. His short fiction is collected in *He Do the Time Police in Different Voices* (2003) and *Different Kinds of Darkness* (2004), and his latest nonfiction collection is *Starcombing* (2009). He insists that he is not responsible for the rude graffito in the Fountain gents' toilet.

'Dr' **Steve Longworth** (whose voice can occasionally be heard as 'medical expert' on the radio) became an SF junkie in 1975 after reading *The Jonah Kit* by Ian Watson. Thirty-odd years later, in 2007, under Ian's expert tutelage and with the encouragement of Ian Whates and the members of the Northampton SF Writers Group, Steve had his first story accepted by Henry Gee for publication in the science journal *Nature*, a feat repeated in 2010. Steve's work has appeared in several NewCon Press anthologies and he has co-authored an international bestseller, though as this is a medical textbook he doubts you will have read it.

James Lovegrove was born on Christmas Eve 1965 and is the author of at least 35 books, including *The Hope, Provender Gleed,* and the *New York Times* best selling Pantheon series (*The Age Of Ra, The Age Of Zeus, The Age Of Odin*). James has sold more than 40 short stories, the majority of them gathered in *Imagined Slights* and *Diversifications*. He has written a fantasy series for teenagers, *The Clouded World*, under the pseudonym Jay Amory, and has produced a dozen books for readers with reading difficulties, including *Wings* and the series *The 5 Lords of Pain*. Shortlisted for numerous awards, his work has been translated into 15 languages, and his journalism has appeared in magazines as diverse as *Literary Review* and *Interzone*. He is a regular reviewer of books for the *Financial Times*.

Paul Graham Raven is a peripatetic web developer to the genre publishing industry, and a bootstrap futurist with his very own low-rise low-budget soapbox, *futurismic.com*. He is also (with variable levels of success and aptitude) a poet, a guitarist, a subcultural arts critic, a writer of short stories... and a former library assistant. He claims to be nowhere near as pretentious as that description makes him sound, but fears that the problem is significantly amplified by writing in the third person. His mother still wishes he'd get a proper haircut, but has largely given up all hope on that score.

Adam Roberts is a writer and an academic at the University of London; he lives a little way west of the metropolis with his wife and two children. He is the author of some twenty novels, including *Yellow Blue Tibia* (Gollancz 2009), *New Model Army* (2010) and *By Light Alone* (2011). He has three things in common with Arthur C Clarke: a slightly receding hairline, the middle initial 'C' and the fact that he writes science fiction. Sadly, however, the similarities end there.

Charles Stross, 46, is a full-time science fiction writer and resident of Edinburgh, Scotland. The winner of two Locus Reader Awards and winner of the 2005 and 2010 Hugo awards for best novella, Stross' works have been translated into over twelve languages. Like many writers, Stross has had a variety of careers, occupations, and job-shaped-catastrophes in the past, from pharmacist (he quit after the second police stake-out) to first code monkey on the team of a successful dot-com startup (with brilliant timing he tried to change employer just as the bubble burst).

Ian Watson's most recent books are *The Beloved of My Beloved*, transgressively funny stories in collaboration with Italian surrealist Roberto Quaglia, one tale from which won the BSFA Award for short fiction in 2010, and the erotic satire *Orgasmachine*, finally published in English after almost 40 years; both from NewCon Press. His *Whores of Babylon* was a Clarke Award finalist ages ago; its recent reissue by Immanion Press led to Russian, Latvian, and Spanish editions. He also wrote the screen story for Steven Spielberg's *A.I. Artificial Intelligence*, based on almost a year's work with Stanley Kubrick. His website is: www.ianwatson.info

Andy West has a passion for evolution and his stories tend to have an underpinning of evolutionary mechanisms, from the 'big engines of history' to the tricksy workings of individual memes. Andy's published SF short stories include: "Rescue Stories" in a special edition of the BSFA magazine *Focus* (March 09), "Mano Mart" in the Newcon Press anthology *Shoes, Ships & Cadavers* (October 10), and "Empirical Purple" due soon in *Matters Most Extraordinary* online anthology. Andy recently completed a techno-thriller novel co-written with Ian Watson, *The Waters of Destiny*, and is currently seeking a publisher for his far-reaching three novel SF series *The Clonir Fower.*

Peter Weston has probably written a million words and sold none of them – not that he's been trying. Since the early sixties he has edited magazines and written about science fiction and, more recently, about the history of the genre in Britain and its practitioners and fans. In earlier days he edited an anthology series and ran the 1979 world SF convention, where he met Arthur C. Clarke. He now manufactures the Hugo Awards (the science fiction 'Oscars') though he doesn't ever expect to win one for himself.

Ian Whates lives in a small village in Cambridgeshire. He has some 40 published short stories to his credit and two ongoing novel sequences – the 'Noise' books (space opera) with Solaris, and the 'City of 100 Rows' series (urban fantasy with steampunk overtones and SF underpinning) with Angry Robot. Since founding NewCon Press in 2006, Ian has used it to provide ever more fascinating and time-consuming diversions from his writing – this volume being a prime example. Ian's short fiction has twice been shortlisted for BSFA Awards, while NewCon Press has received several awards in its brief existence, including 'Best Publisher' from the European Science Fiction Society in 2010.

Liz Williams is a science fiction and fantasy writer living in Glastonbury, England, where she is co-director of a witchcraft supply business. She has had thirteen novels published to date via Bantam Spectra (US) and Tor Macmillan (UK), also Night Shade Press. Her short stories appear regularly in such magazines as *Realms of Fantasy* and *Asimov's*, and are collected in *The Banquet of the Lords of Night* (Night Shade) and the forthcoming *A Glass of Shadow* (NewCon Press). Secretary of the Milford SF Writers' Workshop, she also teaches creative writing and the history of SF. Her novels have been shortlisted for the Philip K Dick and Arthur C Clarke Awards. Her latest novel, *The Iron Khan,* is released through Morrigan Press.

Andrew J. Wilson lives in Edinburgh. His short stories have appeared all over the world, sometimes in the most unlikely places. With Neil Williamson, he co-edited *Nova Scotia: New Scottish Speculative Fiction*, a critically acclaimed original anthology that was nominated for a World Fantasy Award. Andrew is a founder member of the Writers' Bloc spoken-word performance collective, who collaborated with photographer Madeleine Shepherd on the *Alba ad Astra* exhibition in 2009. "The Last Man in Space" is an apocryphal extension of this project.

NEWCON PRESS

Celebrating 5 year of publishing quality Science Fiction,
Fantasy, Dark Fantasy and Horror

Winner of the 2010 'Best Publisher' Award
from the European Science Fiction Association.

Anthologies, novels, short story collections, novellas,
paperbacks, hardbacks, signed limited editions…

To date, NewCon Press has published work by:

Dan Abnett, Brian Aldiss, Kelley Armstrong, Sarah Ash, Neal
Asher, Stephen Baxter, Tony Ballantyne, Chris Beckett, Lauren
Beukes, Chaz Brenchley, Keith Brooke, Eric Brown, Pat Cadigan,
Simon Clark, Michael Cobley, Storm Constantine, Peter
Crowther, Hal Duncan, Jaine Fenn, Neil Gaiman, Gwyneth
Jones, Jon Courtenay Grimwood, M. John Harrison, Leigh
Kennedy, David Langford, Tanith Lee, James Lovegrove, Gary
McMahon, Ken MacLeod, Ian R MacLeod, Gail Z Martin, Juliet
E McKenna, John Meaney, Philip Palmer, Stephen Palmer, Sarah
Pinborough, Christopher Priest, Andy Remic, Alastair Reynolds,
Adam Roberts, Justina Robson, Mark Robson, Sarah Singleton,
Martin Sketchley, Brian Stapleford, Charles Stross, Tricia
Sullivan, Una McCormack, Freda Warrington, Ian Watson, Liz
Williams… and many, many more.

Join our mailing list to get advance notice of new titles, book launches
and events, and receive special offers on books.
www.newconpress.co.uk

BSFA

Don't just read Science Fiction…
Don't just watch Science Fiction…
Don't just play Science Fiction…
Be a part of it.

The British Science Fiction Association
At the heart of science fiction for more than half a century.

Publications

Vector, our critical journal, full of book reviews and essays, offering a comprehensive insight into modern SF; *Focus,* the magazine for writers, offering advice on improving the quality of your work and how to get it published. We also produce a wide range of *special edition* publications, both fiction and non-fiction, throughout the year.

Orbiter

Writers groups for workshopping your fiction and receiving excellent feedback and advice – both online groups and postal – an essential service for aspiring authors.

Events

The BSFA organises regular monthly meetings in London and other events during the year.

Contact

Join the BSFA online at www.bsfa.co.uk.

Or email: bsfamembership@yahoo.co.uk.